Dreaming Spires

If André hadn't been so quintessentially masculine he might even have seemed vulnerable, standing there with his eyes shut waiting for her to touch him. As she drew closer her breathing stirred the dark hairs on his thighs and he shivered, the way a horse shivers when a fly lands on its skin. He smelt of aroused male – of mud and sweat and soap. Just smelling him was an erotic experience. He wouldn't be a man to touch lightly, or to tickle. He needed to be treated like a strong animal, simply, straightforwardly, with a strength to match his own.

She ran her tongue around her lips, moistening them so that when she took the head of his cock into her mouth it would slide in smoothly. She wanted him to remember this. She recalled his words: 'I haven't had it for months.'

Dreaming Spires

JULIET HASTINGS

Black Lace novels contain sexual fantasies.
In real life, make sure you practise safe sex.

First published in 2001 by
Black Lace
Thames Wharf Studios,
Rainville Road, London W6 9HA

Typeset by SetSystems Ltd, Saffron Walden, Essex
Printed and bound by Mackays of Chatham PLC

ISBN 0 352 33584 X

Prologue

Dearest James,
You'll never guess where I have been today.

Catherine pushed herself back from the computer and stared into mid-air. James thought it charming, but odd, that she wrote emails as if they were letters. His replies were always sprinkled with peculiar abbreviations and symbols, so that they read more like a code than English. All very well for him, the always-urgent journalist, but she loved words and couldn't bear shortening them and mauling them. Besides, telling him her thoughts in literate language was great practice for writing them again some other time.

Or maybe you will guess. No surprise, really: I'm still working on Catullus, so that means that my mind is in Ancient Rome.
  When people think of Rome they think of palaces and jewels and orgies and slaves, don't they? But that's not the Rome I was in today. I was working on one of the bitter poems, one of the ones he wrote when she was sleeping with other men. Just take two lines for example:

Nunc in quadriviis et angiportis
Glubit magnanimi Remi nepotes.

The best I've got to so far is:
Now at the crossroads and in alleyways
She sucks off Remus' sons and strips their threads.

It's got a nice raunchy sound to it, but it doesn't really convey the Latin. Translations never do, I don't know why I bother sometimes. *Glubit* means 'she strips the bark from a tree'. You can just imagine it, can't you? Lesbia, the heartless aristocratic beauty, stripping the bark from lover after strapping lover, leaving them gasping in the shadows with their cocks skinny and limp as dishrags.

Had she ever left James's cock a limp skinny dishrag? Well, maybe once or twice. She would have liked to have him there now, with her in the room, eyes glinting, distracting her from her work with a slow sweep of his hand from her nape to the hollow of her spine.

But he was thousands of miles away, somewhere in Asia hunting for war, and it was a long-standing part of their agreement that they didn't say that they missed each other. Yearning and regret were banned from their e-correspondence. Better get back to the bit they would both enjoy.

I worked hard at that translation, and it filled up my mind with images. Do you remember that incredible church in Rome, where underneath the pillars of the nave and that squat dark crypt you could squeeze down and round a corner and find yourself in a Roman alley? A real Roman alleyway, preserved for thousands of years, dark and damp and narrow? Imagine an alleyway like that on a hot June night, under the heavy black Rome sky, the stars glowing like candle flames guttering in the strong hot wind. Here's our Roman lady, rustling in layers of diaphanous silk, lolling in her litter as the matched team of blond slaves carry her down the street. She's fucked all four of them, by the way, but that's not what she wants tonight.

There's a young man on the street, alone, armed, up to no good, no doubt. Painted eyes flicker up and down, gauging his potential. He passes beneath a torch, guttering on some great man's doorstep, and the gleam of the torchlight on the muscles of his arm makes up her mind.

The litter stops, the curtains part, just a little. Intrigued, like a cat, the young man approaches. He is wearing a gold torc, a prize of war in some barbaric land. Has he been a soldier? He hardly looks old enough. His clothes mark him as an aristocrat, but that does not mean that he will be safe.

Good. She does not relish safety.

Half a dozen soft words, and he meets her shadowed eyes with a look of hunger. His brown hand lies on her white wrist, below the sleeve of her gown, and he pushes the silk back, revealing the tender crook of her elbow, blue vessels pulsing beneath the translucent skin. He leans forward with his lips open and touches his tongue to the spot, a flicker of movement, like a snake. She draws in a deep breath and her fist clenches, shell-pink nails biting into her soft palm, rings of pearl and lapis gleaming in the light of the torches.

He looks up. The rims of his nostrils are pale. 'Now.'

She does not answer him, but her breathing quickens. Her eyes are dark with lust, the familiar shape of lust curls in her throat and her belly. She leans forward, stretching out her arms to him, and he catches her by her shoulders and pulls her from the litter to stand her on the stones. They stare at each other and slowly, deliberately, he reaches out and scratches his nail against her nipple where it protrudes through her embroidered stole. She sets her teeth and clenches the muscles between her legs hard. The slaves stare straight ahead, but one of them cannot conceal the erection that lifts his uniform tunic.

Without another word they back into the shadows of the alley. At the front of the street is a perfume shop, and the alley is giddy with the reek of shit and sandal-wood, roses and refuse, jasmine and urine. He

A knock at the door. Catherine cursed and enabled her screensaver, then swung round on her chair. David's head appeared, tousled and amiable. 'Sorry, am I inter-rupting?' he said, pointlessly.

'No, no,' she lied, because she always felt that being truthful with him would be like hitting him.

'I brought the post,' he said.

'Just stick it on the shelf, would you?'

Despite herself, her tone betrayed her irritation. 'Oops,' said David, pulling a face. 'Sorry, sorry.' He put down the post and withdrew.

Now should she explain to James what had happened to interrupt her flow, or just carry on regardless? Carry-ing on seemed like the best option. Why would he be interested in the peccadilloes of her landlord? She closed her eyes for a moment, then reread the last few para-graphs and took a deep breath.

He holds her shoulders and presses her against the wall. She tilts back her jewelled head to watch him, exposing her white throat. His fingers push back the heavy stole, then move deftly among the brooches that hold her robe closed. Suddenly the fabric is loose. It falls open, revealing her to the waist. Her breasts gleam in the faint torchlight with a sheen of sweat and scented oil, and her taut nipples are like another pair of eyes.

Catherine shifted uneasily, conscious of the fact that she was already wet. She closed her eyes for a moment against the frustration.

Frustration! Jesus, James, you know what happens next. You know that they don't even kiss, that he grabs her robe and lifts it and she opens her legs and wraps them

4

around his waist and he thrusts his cock right inside her and then he fucks her, her back against the rough wall, her heels drumming on his buttocks, her nails digging into the back of his neck, he fucks her until she cries like an animal and sinks her teeth into his shoulder, he fucks her with fierce jerks of his hips until he snarls and comes and I wish you were here with me now, James, fucking me.

If you were with me I'd suck your cock. You know how I love to have you in my mouth. Perhaps I wouldn't let you fuck me at all, perhaps I'd just suck you until you came in my mouth. You know how it makes you shout. Or perhaps

It was no good. Sometimes there was real relief in writing to James, but today was not one of those days. Today virtual sex was no substitute for the real thing. She didn't even want to masturbate today, and she'd be resorting to David before the night was out, she could see it coming. Poor old David, it wasn't as if he was bad in bed or even bad looking, but he knew he was just some sort of default option and you could see that it didn't do his ego any good.

David had brought the post. Post! Perhaps there would be some distraction there, a letter from her publisher or a new catalogue to browse. Not another bill, God forbid.

She picked up the letters and stared at the first one. It had a Cambridge postmark. She looked at the college crest on the back of the envelope and swallowed hard, then opened it and scanned the letter in one rush.

James, do you know who is writing to you today? The new writer in residence at St Henry's College, Cambridge, that's who. I start there in October for one term! At last, a chance to get this damn translation finished and get started on the novel. A whole three months without bills to pay or anything to worry about. Except getting laid, of course, James dear. You know they say that Oxford is the city of dreaming spires, and Cambridge the city of perspiring dreams? Let's hope some perspiring dreams come my way!

Oh, James, I can't wait. Beautiful environment, everything sorted out for me, new people to meet, intelligent people . . . I'll be telling you about them. The men particularly, James. Rely on it.

You'll enjoy that, won't you?

Chapter One

Henry's Parade was Maggie's favourite part of Cambridge.

The colleges were beautiful, but they were removed from the real world. She liked Henry's Parade because it linked the colleges, and St Henry's in particular, with the world of work and shops and cars that other people lived in. And also, of course, because it was beautiful too. On one side was St Mary's church and the higgledy-piggledy row of old houses, half-timbered and Georgian, with shops in the bottom and college accommodation above, which she was lucky enough to live in this year. On the other was the Senate House and its smooth square lawn, then the rearing, etiolated towers and windows of the Chapel, and then the glorious screen of pierced and fretted stone which separated St Henry's from the town, and in the centre of the screen the pretty pale Gothic gatehouse. Unlike most colleges, which hid themselves from the world, you could always see into Henry's through the screen, and the fine green lawn looked welcoming and cheerful.

The street was busy, as it always was, with bikes and people hurrying to and fro. She stopped at number sixteen, unashamedly thrilled to be living at such a splendid address. Number sixteen was a dress shop on the ground floor and a crooked, black-and-white, half-timbered house above. She unlocked the door and sidled through with her shopping bags.

Beyond was a warren of stairways, kitchenettes, loos and doors to rooms where people lived. Maggie smiled again, because she really still couldn't believe her luck, and started up the narrow, leaning staircase towards the top floor.

Someone was coming down, and she stood to one side on the first-floor landing to let whoever it was squeeze past. It was her neighbour, this term's writer in residence. Maggie said, 'Hello,' and gave her a bright smile.

'Hello,' said the writer in residence, returning the smile rather wanly. She was an attractive woman, with thick, silvery brown hair pushed back from her long oval face, pale skin and huge dark eyes. She didn't look happy. In fact she looked anxious and lonely.

'How are you?' Maggie said, prolonging their encounter.

'Oh,' said the woman, as if she was startled to be asked, 'fine. Thanks.' She hesitated slightly, then added, 'I'm Catherine, by the way.'

'I'm Maggie. Your neighbour.' What amazing eyes those were, big enough to drown in. And a heavy, sensual mouth, too. She looked like someone it might be rewarding to get to know. How old was she? Middle thirties, probably. Hard to say anything more. And what looked like an interesting body, currently hidden beneath jersey trousers and a Peruvian knitted tunic. Definitely interesting altogether.

For a moment Maggie thought of asking her in for a cup of tea and seeing what developed. But that would mean missing Ash, and she had rather got herself ready for seeing Ash. The flesh between her legs tightened at the thought. So she just said, 'We ought to have a cup of tea some time.'

The sad eyes brightened. God, she must be lonely, if

8

the offer of a cup of tea cheered her up that much! 'That would be very nice,' said the writer in residence.

'Right.' Ask her in now? Try to cheer her up more thoroughly? Tempting, tempting. No, Ash would be on his way. 'See you, then.'

Maggie climbed the rest of the stairs and put down the bags in front of her door. As she opened it she drew in a deep breath, preparing to be amazed again.

Her room was awe-inspiring, astonishing, a great and mighty wonder. She was so brilliant that she had to wrap her arms around herself and squeeze hard in sheer delight.

'Damn, I'm good,' she said, taking in the full majesty of the view.

The room was *huge*. It was enormous. Not high ceilinged and posh, more cottagey and quaint, with odd diagonal corners where the roof-beams crossed: but all the same, it was huge. The little poxy shoebox she had occupied in her first year would have fitted into one corner; thank God she was almost a postgrad. And it was a room with a view, too: the wide window, filled with panes of warping, old glass, opened on to a magnificent vista of the college, all the way over the court and through the arch of the McLean building down to the river.

How clever had she been to get this room and this view? Bloody clever. All it needed now was someone to show it to, someone to impress. And because she was so brilliant, Ash would be there any minute. She put the kettle on to boil and got a packet of chocolate Hob-Nobs out of the shopping bag, because they were his favourite and this was cause for celebration.

It was just as well she hadn't asked the writer in residence up this time. Part of the point was to show off the room, and a person in their mid-thirties wouldn't be impressed by it in the way Ash would. Also, she wanted to fuck Ash. Sex with women was great, but sometimes she wanted to feel a cock, and today that's what she wanted. Ash would fit the bill just fine. Of all her many

9

sexual partners he was the one she preferred for everyday consumption, and she had not seen him for three whole months. Not that she'd been entirely celibate, of course, but she was still pleased to be back at Cambridge and its multiplicity of delights. Her breasts were already tight with anticipation.

She also intended to tease Ash for as long as she could keep it up. Let him think that she wasn't interested. It would be fun to keep him in suspense.

A knock at the door! She dashed across to it and said, 'Helloooo?' in her best silly voice.

'It's me, you plonker,' said Ash.

'Prepare – to be – amazed!' Maggie opened the door slowly, with a flourish, and watched his face change.

'Fuck a duck and die a cripple,' Ash said, walking slowly into the room and looking around him. 'God Almighty, Maggie, there is no fucking justice. How the hell did you swing this?' He moved to and fro, lean brown hands touching things as he named them. 'Room three acres big. Sofa, a bloody three-seater sofa, big fat armchair, desk and chair and a fucking *telephone*, for Christ's sake, table and six chairs so you can hold a dinner party any time you want to, and Gordon Bennett,' he stopped in front of the *pièce de résistance* and shook his head, 'a double bed. I don't believe it, Maggie. A *double bed*.' He grinned. 'It was nice of you to invite me to see it now, before the whole thing becomes submerged beneath a foot-thick stratum of dirty underwear.'

'How dare you impugn my housekeeping skills,' Maggie huffed, unable to disagree.

'Never mind. It's so big, it'll probably absorb more underwear than your other haunts. It might even absorb your inexhaustible supply.' Ash smiled slowly and walked towards her, tapping his fingernail thoughtfully against his straight, white teeth. 'Maggie, it's magnificent. And you know what? I would like to fuck you on or over every single piece of furniture in this magnificent room.'

She grinned. It was good to know that his intentions matched hers. But she wasn't going to say what she wanted to say, which was: Right! Let's get stuck in! Instead she folded her arms, turning slightly away from him, and said lightly, 'That's what I like about you, Ash. Your Hindu sensibilities make every word you utter as delicately erotic as the Kama Sutra.'

'Don't tell me you asked me here just for a cup of tea and a chocolate Hob-Nob.' He sounded more irritated than anxious. More work was needed.

'Tell me,' she asked rhetorically, moving towards the window with its glorious view of Henry's Parade and the rearing spires of the Chapel, 'which cliché of student life do you prefer? That they engage in existential debate, dressed in battered corduroys, fuelled by incessant cups of tea and chocolate Hob-Nobs, or that they are sexually insatiable layabouts who squander the taxpayers' money on cheap booze, Lycra clothing, clubbing and easy lays?'

'I'd go with version two,' Ash said, 'except that I don't believe the bit about the taxpayers' money. Have you seen my overdraft?'

'Mine too, sweetie, mine too.' She jerked her head towards the window. 'Look, Ash, you can see right into the Court. Old King Henry on his pedestal could look right into this window and see us.'

'He wouldn't like that,' Ash said, as he moved to stand behind her and look out at the view. 'Once upon a time some women danced at a party where he was and their breasts were bare, and –'

'And he said, "Fie fie, for shame, forsooth ye are much to blame." Old story, Ash.' Maggie tossed her head and turned. Ash was standing behind her, so that she found herself in his arms, but she didn't react. She kept her face as calm and imperturbable as she could. 'You know why I asked you here?' A tiny pause, and his pupils dilated as his lips quirked with expectation. 'I wanted to show off my new room to you.'

For a moment his face was shadowed. Had she

11

convinced him? Did he really believe that that was all she wanted? Could he? She only had to look at him and she wanted him: smooth, *café-au-lait* skin, sloe eyes, thin lips, long limbs . . .

He laid the palms of his hands against her temples, pushing her hair back so that he could look directly into her eyes. For a moment he held her gaze, and she tried not to quiver. But then his sombre face relaxed into a slow grin. 'Wind-up merchant,' he said, accusingly. He jerked his chin down at her T-shirt. 'Look how hard your nipples are.'

She made a rueful face. 'The erectile tissue never lies, eh?'

'Never,' he said, nudging closer to her. Through her thin skirt and his jeans she felt his cock swelling, hot for her. Her smile faded and she pressed her lips together against the sudden dryness.

'I've missed fucking you,' he said in a whisper, and she closed her eyes and let herself relax into his hands, leaning back, letting him support her weight on one circling arm, arching her neck away from him. All of her consciousness slipped into the tension of her skin – pale throat down to the hard bone between her breasts, taut ribcage dilated with her deep breathing, stomach flat and eager – one smooth tight curve all the way from her chin to her pubis. The curve of her spine rested against his supporting hand. She kept her eyes closed, waiting for him, because there was no hurry now.

His lips brushed her neck. She sighed with anticipation and he stirred her skin with his tongue, then bit softly, sucking. With his free hand he pushed up her T-shirt. The air kissed her naked breasts and edged her tight nipples.

'Suck my breasts,' she whimpered, not because she thought that he wouldn't but because she loved to hear herself begging. 'Suck my nipples hard, Ash, please. Bite them. Please, Ash, please.'

She kept her eyes closed. Daylight, and they were standing in front of her window. Could someone in the

12

street look up and see them? Perhaps, and that made it all the better, that little extra frisson of danger. Ash's teeth nibbled on her left nipple and she groaned aloud with the sheer pleasure of it. She was giddy with leaning backwards, her head was spinning, and he sucked and tugged at her breasts as if he wanted to bruise them, and her whole body was drunk with lust.

Ash took his mouth from her breasts and pulled her upright. 'On the sofa,' he hissed. 'I've never had you on a sofa. No, not on it. *Over* it.' He pushed her away from him, held her at arm's length, comparing. 'God, why are you so short? Get a pair of high heels. Really high.'

She nodded and walked to the wardrobe, resisting the urge to pull down her T-shirt. The mirror on the door showed her herself: little, slight, T-shirt under her arms, her exposed breasts shallow as saucers, the nipples long and dark and hard against the pale skin. She yanked the door open and kicked off her loafers, pulled out a pair of Charles Jourdain shoes, a ridiculous extravagance, crystal acrylic mules with thick transparent soles and ten-centimetre heels and rainbow plastic straps, crazy, kinky shoes that made her legs look long. She slipped her feet into them and turned back swiftly, so that her little skirt flipped and swirled.

Ash stopped unbuttoning his shirt and stared at her. 'That's better,' he said. 'God, you look like –' Words appeared to fail him and for a moment he chewed his lip. Then he said, 'Take off your T-shirt.'

She crossed her arms, trying to move gracefully, and obeyed.

'Now the skirt.'

She hesitated, because she had imagined that he might have fucked her while she was still wearing it. But he looked as if he knew what he wanted, so she obeyed this time, too. Underneath was an M&S thong, plain white, not too tatty, considering.

'Turn around,' said Ash.

Now that didn't surprise her. One thing that Ash

13

loved was a rear view. She turned, and when he saw the string of her thong he let out a breath of delight.

'Now,' he said, 'go and bend over the back of the sofa.'

The sofa was old and battered, but its back was strong and straight. It was just the right height, so that when she bent over her belly rested on it and the upper half of her body dangled towards the seat. She closed her eyes again, imagining the white moon of her arse split by the white string of her thong, imagining Ash's eyes on it.

His footsteps came up behind her and she heard a rustle. Probably his shirt. For a moment she was sorry that she couldn't see him, because his body was so beautiful, but then she decided she didn't care, because this was new and different.

'What a beautiful arse,' Ash whispered. 'God, Maggie, I love that little tight arse of yours. It's like a ripe, juicy apricot. I'd like to sink my teeth into it.'

A moment of silence, and she waited, expecting his teeth. But then she jumped and drew in a quick breath, because what she felt was his tongue, wet and cool on the back of her ankle. He drew a line of saliva up the back of her leg, up to the hollow of her knee, tracing on to the inside of her thigh. She couldn't keep in a little moan of pleasure and expectation.

'So gorgeous,' he whispered, and she heard the clunk of his jeans buckle and then the whine of the zip. 'There's the string of your thong, and then this little white pouch with soft hair escaping either side of it, and it looks so plump and sweet.' His tongue touched her again, this time on the inner curve of her buttock, slipping up towards her crack. She shuddered with the perennial delicious agony of wondering if she was clean there, if it mattered, if he wouldn't like it anyway. And then his tongue was working under and around the string of her thong, delving right into her crack, exploring the soft entrance to her arse, and she would have fallen over if the sofa hadn't been holding her up. He

14

squeezed his tongue inside her and she moaned and put her hands to her breasts, pulling at her nipples, and whimpered, 'Oh God, Ash, please fuck me, please, please.'

'Now,' he whispered, and he eased her thong off her hips and down her legs. 'Ah, that's it. Look at that lovely little hole just waiting for me. Is it wet, do you think?'

'It's fucking soaking, Ash, what do you think?' She could feel the moisture at this moment, oozing out of her and making the whole of her labia slippery with wanting him. 'Ash, please –'

'Patience is a virtue,' Ash said sententiously. 'Keep your feet together, Maggie. Nice and modest. And –' He dipped a finger in her juice and slipped it down to touch her clit. She groaned and stuck her arse out further, trying to rub herself harder against his finger, but now he was dipping and slicking the juice backwards, around her arsehole.

He leant forward, and she felt his body against hers, jeans rough against her calves and thighs, his smooth chest against her lower back, and against her backside the hot harsh crispness of his pubic hair and the hot smooth rigidity of his cock. She heard the rustle of a condom wrapper and the little slick sound as he smoothed the rubber on. Into her ear he whispered hoarsely, 'I'm going to fuck you up the arse.'

She swallowed hard, readying herself. Half of her wanted to scream that arse-fucking was more fun for him than for her, and what about her? But this was Ash, and she knew that he would take care of her pleasure as well as his. Then Ash hissed again, 'I'm going to fuck you up the arse over your fucking sofa.'

So do it, do it now! she screamed silently. And then she felt it, the head of his cock pressing up against her anus, squeezing its way inside. For a moment he was stuck, and she gasped and tensed, and then his fingers were there, loaded with her juice, easing the passage. He wriggled one finger around inside her and, as he withdrew it, pushed and pushed until the head of his cock was inside, and then sliding the rest into her was as easy as breathing and she was full, full of his gorgeous cock.

'God,' he gasped, 'it's so tight, I'll come if I move.'

'No,' she whimpered, desperate not to be cheated now.

'Ssh.' He reached around her narrow hips and slipped his finger between her tightly closed legs, touched her clit, began to rub it, so gently that she wanted to scream. His other hand reached over and found one breast, scraped against her hard nipple. She writhed, impaled on his immobile cock, and he slid his finger to and fro, still very, very gently.

'Oh,' she cried, 'oh, oh, please do it harder.' But he wouldn't, and it was like climbing to orgasm up a long, long flight of very shallow steps, unable to take more than one step at a time, when what she wanted to do was bound up them in huge greedy leaps. Her moans were desperate and her upper body writhed as if she was trying to escape, when all she really wanted was for the cock that penetrated her to move and move and move until she split in two.

'Are you coming?' he demanded, circling her aching nipple with his nail. 'You have to tell me when you're coming.'

'I – ah –' she gasped, clutching desperately at his cock with the muscles of her sphincter. 'Oh God, Jesus, I'm nearly there, Ash, please, please fuck me now, now, now, I'm coming now.'

He heard her, and suddenly his cock was moving, plunging into her arse with such strength that she almost screamed, and his finger rubbed hard at her aching clit and the orgasm burst in her, like fireworks in her head, so strong that she didn't know whether he had come or not until the waves receded and she lifted her head and heard his rasping breathing.

'Ah,' he whispered, 'I'm going to pull out, before you squeeze my cock off.'

He withdrew and after a couple of deep breaths she straightened and turned to see him wrapping his wet cock in one tissue, the used condom in another. That was one thing she didn't particularly like about Ash: his care not to get any fluids anywhere. Wasn't the whole point of fluids that they were messy? But he was always very tidy.

'Tea,' she said with a sigh. 'Hob-Nobs.'

'Just as nice as a fag, and better for you,' he agreed.

She curled up on the sofa in her dressing gown and he zipped up his jeans and sat on the chair, because they were friends and sex partners, not lovers. Maggie didn't have lovers, only mates that she shagged. Romantic slush made her laugh.

'So how the fuck did you get this room?' he demanded.

'It's really for graduates and visiting Fellows,' she said smugly, 'but I have a friend working in the college office, and he tipped me off that the Fellow who was supposed to get this room might not turn up this year. Apparently she's got incipient depression. Anyway, she didn't come, and her loss was my gain. I, so to speak, failed to find any digs outside college, and come the week before term I threw myself on the mercy of the college office, and it all paid off beautifully.'

'Jammy cow,' he snarled. 'I'm stuck in some godforsaken hole up Mill Road over a curry house. Don't say a word: if I hear one more "the smell must remind you of home" I'll kill someone. My mother's cooking never once smelt like the bloody crap they serve up underneath my flat.'

'Well, at least you have an interesting job in the summer. Mine was Dullsville yet again.'

'Were you back at the refinery?' he asked. 'I would have thought it suited you, all those big blokes wandering about and hardly any women. Isn't that why you did chemical engineering in the first place?'

'Yeah.' She dunked her biscuit in her tea, making a

17

wry face. 'But I tell you, Ash, once I'm out of Cambridge I come over all modest.'

'Modest is hardly a word I would associate with you.'

'I know. But I worry about what people at the plant think of me. All the other engineers are wimps, and the blokes I fancy are the mechanics and the other work-men, but they don't even seem to realise that I'm female. I think they've all been stuffed up tight with PC non-sense and they're scared of appreciating me in case I sue, and I just don't have the bottle to grab one of them by the nuts and drag him behind a distillation column.'

'Alas,' said Ash ruefully.

'I tell you what, though,' Maggie said, leaning eagerly forward, 'this year is going to be a riot. All I have to do is manage enough work to scrape through my Postgrad-uate Cert and my 2:1 is assured. I should be able to cover that in a couple of hours a day, and the rest – you won't see me for dust!'

'I hope some plans involve me?' Ash arched a perfect, dark brow. 'Subject to my studies, of course.'

'Absolutely. You, and the woman next door.'

'Who she?'

'She the new writer in residence. Early thirties, kind of Roman-looking, big brown eyes, silvery brown hair. She looks sad and lonely and shockable. You know how much I love to shock people.' She knew this was bra-vado, because what had really attracted her to the writer in residence was the yearning in those big dark eyes. But she wanted to keep up a bold face in front of Ash.

'Might I be of assistance?' Ash enquired, archly.

'Well, you might,' she admitted. Yes, he might. But she wanted to seduce those lovely eyes herself, not enlist a man to help her. 'But not straight away,' she said, after a moment. 'I'd like to break her in gently.'

Ash put his mug down and licked his lips. 'By all means. After we've broken in another piece of furniture.'

Chapter Two

Well, I thought I would try to wait you out, but I've run out of patience first. Where are you, James? What's going on? Not a squeak from you for two weeks. God, I hope you're OK. I don't see the TV much these days, but what I see in the newspaper makes me worry about you. It looks as if SE Asia might start coming to bits yet again.

No more of this, though. I know you like to be in hot spots. What have I been up to for two weeks?

To be honest, James, I've been lonely and miserable. I didn't realise when I accepted that I was a sort of experiment. It's the first time that the college has appointed a professional jobbing writer – a hack, if you like – as writer in residence. The idea was that I would be able to work, of course, but also advise students on how they might make their livings at writing if they wanted to. Sounds sensible, doesn't it? But I don't think the rest of the college has understood. When I went to the beginning-of-the-year cocktail party in the Senior Common Room, most of the Fellows treated me as if I was some sort of alien. Had I not written scholarly books, or at the very least impenetrable poetry, or the sort of novel that academics review? I had not? Well, no interest in me, then.

And the students are just as bad. They all seem to think that they are Proust reincarnated. They scorn the idea of actually making a living from writing. At least, the ones I have met so far do.

And worst of all, James, no bloody men! Not one, not one in two weeks. If I don't find someone to have sex with soon I will explode! I did meet one rather hunky bloke at the SCR do. In fact he was very hunky, tall and built like the proverbial, and about my age, too. Some sort of mature student, I think, not sure what in. But I only really caught his name, which is Mike, before some ancient Fellow buttonholed him and that was my chance gone. At the time I thought that he was giving me the eye, but if he did notice me he hasn't gone to the trouble of seeking me out. I've seen him around college once or twice, too. He would have had the chance to talk to me, if he fancied me. Bollocks.

Oh, my rooms are really gorgeous, in the top of a seventeenth century building overlooking the college. But I don't enjoy them as much as I expected because I have a female student for a neighbour who seems to do nothing all day and all night but have sex. I've met her, and she seems a nice enough girl, but she's very single-minded. It does remind me a bit of what I'm missing. So today I'm going to go over to the University Library and try to get a bit of peace and quiet there.

James, drop me an email and let me know what's going on with you? Please?

It was one of those October weeks when it seems as if summer is coming back. The sun was warm in a blue, freckled sky, and the leaves on the big horse chestnuts were just beginning to turn. The rims of gold and paler green on the edges of their leaves made it look as if they were new, fresh spring leaves, when in fact they were ready to drop.

Catherine stood on the bridge that carried the path from St Henry's over the Cam to the Backs. Tourists and students splashed beneath her in punts, enjoying the extraordinary weather, and the little herd of cows which lived on the field opposite the college were galloping about, tails in the air, like mad things.

She was worried about James, but that was normal. It would be good not to worry about him for a while, only she'd never succeeded. Abnormally, though, she was worried about herself too. Had she been trying to fool herself when she came here? Was she trying to behave like a new spring leaf, when in fact she was ready to drop? She was 36. Whatever had she been doing surrounding herself with students, guaranteed to make anyone feel old?

Like that girl in the next room. Maggie was her name. A little bundle of energy, small and slight, with a mop of blonde curls that looked as if it belonged on a three-year-old, and a manic laugh which could be clearly heard through the wall. Along with the rest of the noises she made: moans and gasps and sighs. Not just noises, either: Maggie was very sure about what she wanted. Last night something had made the sounds come through the wall as clear as a bell, and before she gave up and went to the bar Catherine had heard Maggie say, 'Oh, that's so good. Oh please, don't stop. Put your fingers up my cunt. Further, further . . . oh, yes . . .'

Perhaps all Maggie did was laugh and shag. Lucky her.

Catherine shook herself, slung her bag over her shoulder, and walked on across the Backs and past the Fellows' garden to the huge, ugly bulk of the University Library. In her frustrated condition its stumpy brick tower looked more phallic than ever. In the forbidding entrance hall she swiped her entry pass and headed past the busy reading room. She eschewed the temptations of the café – the rock buns would have to wait until later – and went into the north wing, where the books on classical subjects were located and where she could be guaranteed a quiet spot to work.

This early in the term there were few people about in the library. She left the main reading areas and went on into the stacks, the remoter spots where you could spend all day without seeing a soul. There were desks there which looked out of the windows, and on the fifth floor the view encompassed most of Cambridge.

She found a desk she liked, with a good outlook, securely surrounded by the high metal bookshelves that filled this section of the library. The books filled the shelves from one wall to the next, so that the space between each set of shelves was like a little room in itself. There was almost total silence, broken only by birdsong from outside and the occasional sound of the lift, whirring slowly between the floors several shelves away. She spread out her work and opened her note-book, where she had marked the locations of several books that she thought would be helpful. Where would she find the first one?

The page blurred before her eyes. Her mind slipped back to the previous night and Maggie's cries of pleasure. Who had been with her? Catherine had seen a young Asian man at Maggie's door a few times, a very good-looking guy, slender and well made, with flashing dark eyes and a very student-intellectual beard trimmed to the edges of his fine chin. Had he been with Maggie last night, parting her slender legs with his long hands? Had it been his dark, sensitive fingers sliding into her and making her moan and cry out?

She didn't think so. Not last night. Last night she was quite sure that Maggie had been with another girl. She'd seen the visitor arrive, tall and statuesque, dressed in a rather earth-motherly skirt, long copper hair hanging in waves on her shoulders.

Another girl! Her mind wrestled with the concept. Until now lesbianism had been for her something that got put into dirty films and books because two girls together looked pretty and turned the blokes on. She knew, of course, that some women genuinely liked it, whether or not they were all-out lesbians. She just hadn't ever lived next door to one.

But then it was erotic, it really was. It was so easy to

see the two girls together. Who was the, how would you put it, the dominant one? It was easier to imagine the copper-haired girl, because she was big while Maggie was small. And Maggie's cries had proved that, at least at that point, Maggie had been the one enjoying what the other girl was doing to her.

So it had been the copper-haired girl who had opened Maggie's clothes, baring her little breasts, peeled down her knickers, parted her thighs. Maggie looked like a natural blonde: perhaps her fleece was as fair and curly as her hair. So easy to imagine the other girl's tongue worming its way through those pale curls, seeking out the little fleck of Maggie's clit, flickering against it until Maggie moaned and moaned. And then the fingers, long fingers with long painted nails, slipping between the fleshy lips, finding the spot, sliding up and in, making Maggie beg to have those fingers further, further up her thirsty –

'Hello,' said a male voice behind her.

Catherine gave a huge start and turned, breathing quickly, blushing at the idea that someone had come up behind her while she was thinking about –

The man standing there smiled at her. It was Mike, the man from the SCR party. Her heart continued to pound, not from embarrassment now, but with excitement. She said in what she hoped was a steady voice, 'What a coincidence! Mike, isn't it? Are you reading classics, then?'

He shook his head. 'No,' was all he said.

She hadn't exaggerated to James. This man was very attractive. The first impression was of his size; he must have been a couple of inches over six foot and his shoulders were broad. Then you noticed his amazing, extraordinary eyes, huge dark eyes with long, long lashes and a slight almond tilt that any queen of Sheba would have been proud of. Then you saw the rest of him: good bones, a wide mouth, receding hair cropped very short. A few other things, too. He was wearing jeans and a plain white T-shirt, and below the left sleeve a snake tattoo curled around the deeply carved muscle of his bicep. He had an earring, and there was a stud in his right eyebrow, plain gold, gleaming at the edge of the dark eyesocket. His hands were big and long-fingered, with patches of dirt and dark moons beneath strong fingernails, as if he had been doing manual work.

Good-looking, certainly. But rough, too.

He appeared to be completely relaxed as she looked him over. He was unashamedly doing the same to her, and suddenly she felt very self-conscious. Why had she not thought that she might meet someone, and dressed better? She was wearing a scoop-neck ribbed top and a long skirt with flat loafers, and would have felt more confident if her shoes had had heels.

Was that all he was going to say to her: 'No'? She shook back her hair and suggested, 'You like working here, then.'

'No.' This time there was a smile. He looked as if he knew that he had her on the run.

'So?' she demanded, wishing that she wasn't sitting down. He towered over her.

'I followed you here,' he said, still smiling. Then, as if he had seen the moment of apprehension in her eyes, 'I didn't want to talk to you in the college bar, surrounded by all and sundry. Everybody watches your every move in there. This,' he gestured around at the silent miles of bookcases, 'is much better.'

'Yes,' she said, smiling too, with relief at the prosaic explanation. It would have been a drag to pick up a stalker after only two weeks.

He took a step closer, bringing himself within arm's length. 'So,' he said, lifting one big hand, gesturing very shallowly towards her collar bone. 'What were you thinking about, sitting there?'

She knew without even looking down that the skin over her breastbone must be flushed, the unfakeable testimony of arousal. His question brought back her fantasy, two lovely young girls coupling, lips on nipples, lips exchanging lingering kisses, lips sucking,

24

tongues probing. For a moment she couldn't meet his eyes. Then she controlled herself, swallowed, looked up and said lightly, 'Just a daydream.'

'I like that kind of daydream,' he said. He didn't move, and she became aware that he was standing too close, in her personal space. She couldn't get away from him, either, because to get up from her desk and go she would have to push past him. His big dark eyes were running up and down her body. As if his hands were running up and down her, too, her vagina clenched.

Trying to ignore the symptoms of her arousal, she said, 'I would have liked to talk to you at the SCR, but –'

'Why would you have liked to talk to me there? With all those ancient monuments around?' He didn't move, but his eyes held her still. 'And who wants to talk, anyway?'

Catherine found that her mouth was slightly open and her lips were dry. She felt as if she was being manoeuvred, but she didn't want it to stop. In fact, she realised, she wanted it to go on. She wanted him to say, 'Come home with me now,' and take her back to his place so that they could not talk, just have sex. Yes, that was what she wanted. She wanted to have sex with this big, dangerous-looking man with beautiful eyes.

The beautiful eyes darkened slightly. He rested his right elbow on his left hand. The tightening of his left bicep made the tattooed snake move, strangely. He cupped his chin in his right hand, watching her appraisingly. Then he said, 'What sort of bra are you wearing?'

Her breath exhaled in a sudden, small gasp of shock. 'What?'

'It gives your breasts a very good shape,' he explained, without any hesitation or apparent concern. 'What sort is it?'

Well, he seemed to have the right intentions, so she decided not to block him straight away. She glanced left and right, making sure there was nobody else around.

'It's,' she said, hardly able to believe it, 'it's, er, French. I bought it in Paris.'

'Matching panties?' he enquired, as if this were routine.

'As it happens, yes.'

He nodded approvingly, then lowered his hand, straightened and looked directly at her. There was a long silence. Her heart was pounding, beating as fast and as hard as if she had just achieved orgasm. She knew she couldn't speak first.

At last he said, quite quietly, 'I want you, Catherine.'

Now she ought to protest, say things were moving too fast, back off. But she didn't want to. He sounded so certain that she felt a strange, unplaceable confidence. She looked up at him in silence, waiting for him to tell her what they should do.

He took another step towards her, so that he was standing directly in front of her, her face only a couple of feet from his flat abdomen. He lifted one hand and traced his finger down her cheek, and she closed her eyes and licked her dry lips.

Then he stepped back. 'Take off your top,' he said. 'Let me see your French bra.'

She glanced instinctively aside, then stared at him. 'Here?' she exclaimed, her voice high with shock. 'No!'

He didn't smile or reassure her. 'I said I wanted you. That means here. Now.'

'But anyone could come!' she protested.

'So?'

She shook her head. Okay, she wanted him, but sex here, in the stacks? He had to be mad.

He frowned, his head tilting very slightly. The dark brows drew together, and light caught the gold stud. 'What?'

She swallowed hard. 'No.'

Now he lifted his brows, a supercilious gesture, like a teacher who cannot be bothered to rebuke an unruly child. Without another word he turned and began to walk slowly away.

This was ridiculous. What sort of game was he play-ing, walking off and leaving her? 'Mike!' she called, ready to make a joke of it. 'Where are you going? I –'

He turned quickly and his voice cut across hers. He was not laughing. 'Here and now,' he said. 'Here and now, Catherine, or not at all.'

She searched his face for any indication of humour, any lightness, and could see none. Christ, did he mean it? Was he really serious?

How could she do what he was asking?

His eyes held hers. 'Take off your top,' he repeated, slowly, softly.

She got up from the chair, pushed it aside, and sat instead on the edge of the desk. As if they moved against her will, her hands slowly reached down and grasped the bottom of her top. She pulled it up a little, hesitated, and then quickly dragged it over her head, crumpled it into a ball and sat holding it in both hands, hideously conscious of sitting in the University Library dressed in a skirt and a Parisian bra.

He smiled. 'That's really beautiful, Catherine,' he said. He walked slowly towards her, still holding her eyes, like a hypnotist. 'Beautiful.'

She could hardly swallow. 'Mike,' she began.

He lifted his hand, cutting her off. With a shake of the head he said, 'Don't talk. I'll do the talking. Just do what I say.'

Do what he said? What was this, Simon Says? Her fantasy had been of Maggie, demanding exactly what she wanted, and now she wasn't even going to be allowed to talk? She opened her mouth to protest and with a few quick steps he was in front of her, his finger laid across her lips. 'Ssh,' he said.

Despite herself, she fell silent. His finger was warm and dry and carried a slight smell of machinery. Sud-denly she knew what to do, and instead of saying anything she let her tongue press between her parted lips to touch the underside of his finger, slipping over the hard skin until it rested in the hollow of his knuckle.

27

He smiled down at her, wide lips parting to show strong, even teeth. 'Good,' he whispered. His hands touched her face, cupped her chin, tipped her head back, and he stooped over her and put his mouth on to hers.

So long since her last kiss, and she forgot her undress, forgot where she was, forgot everything except the sheer sensual pleasure of kissing, the excitement of having his tongue in her mouth. She didn't know if she made a sound or not, but her hands dropped her top and pressed instead against the buckle of his jeans belt, feeling the bulk and hardness of his body.

After a few seconds he released her and stood up. 'When you're good,' he said, 'you get a reward.'

She nodded, and he smiled again. 'Now,' he said, 'the bra is lovely, but it has to come off as well.'

Her mouth was dry again. She knew now what he wanted. He wanted to have sex with her right here, on the desk, and she couldn't do it. She said, 'Mike, I can't.'

'Yes, you can.' He sounded reassuring. 'It's easy, Catherine. I want to see your breasts. Take off the bra.'

'Mike, if someone comes and sees us, we could be banned, they could forbid us ever to come in here again!'

'Hmm, yes, they could.' He looked thoughtful. 'And how much would you care?'

Well, he had a point. Right now, she cared a lot less about the prospect of never entering the UL again than she did about the prospect of doing without sex with Mike.

She took a deep breath and reached around behind her. The bra unclipped easily, but she sat for a few seconds with her hands in the small of her back. She could still change her mind. Then the dark brows lifted again, and she closed her eyes and took off the bra.

The air was cool on her breasts, although it was warm and airless in the stacks. She didn't want to sit there huddled like a shrinking violet: if she was going to be an Amazon, going bare-breasted into battle, she didn't have to be ashamed of it. She put back her shoulders and lifted her head, then opened her eyes.

Mike smiled again and nodded. 'Very good,' he said. He came closer, put his hands on her knees, eased them apart. She acceded, and he knelt in front of her, pushing the fabric of her skirt against her body, and regarded her breasts with care.

'Please, Mike,' she whispered, 'please kiss them.'

He looked up at her and shook his head. 'I want doesn't get,' he said, sententiously.

She wanted to tell him how bloody illogical that was when all he had said for the last ten minutes had been 'I want', but she bit her tongue and said only, 'Sorry.'

'Accepted,' he said, and he leant slowly forward and touched the tip of her left breast with his tongue.

The touch went right through her, like a needle of ice. Despite herself she let out a little moan, and her head rolled back. She would have liked to hold his head against her, but she needed her hands to hold her up, and besides, she had a suspicion that he wouldn't like it. Instead she just leant back, giving in to the voluptuous sensation of being naked to the waist, bare-throated, abandoned.

And Mike did not stop. First he lapped at her breast, teasing it with the chill of his saliva until her nipple was a tight, swollen peak. Then he closed his lips on it and sucked, hard, sending piercing shards of sensation into her. She moaned again, arching her back, and he turned his attention to her other breast, caressing it. His hands slid beneath the fabric of her skirt, resting on her bare ankles.

Oh, how she wanted him to slide his hands up her legs, lift her skirt, pull her panties aside and push himself into her. She didn't care any more that someone might see, just wanted to feel his cock inside her. But she didn't say so. She didn't want to do anything that might make him stop.

For a few moments he sucked and nibbled at her right nipple while his fingers stroked the bones of her ankles. She felt as if she was liquefying. Then he sat back on his heels, got up, stepped back.

What now? She looked down at her breasts and saw the gleam of wetness on her nipples. They ached, and she lifted her hand to touch them.

'No,' he said.

She looked up at him. If he forbade one thing, perhaps he might suggest another.

He said, 'Lift your skirt. Open your legs.'

A movement caught the corner of her eye and she turned quickly to see someone climbing the stairs, passing through the stack. Christ, would they look? But no, not even a turn of the head. Blinkered academic, intent on learning, ignoring the real world.

Mike hadn't moved, hadn't looked. He nodded at her skirt, and she let out a long breath and reached for the hem.

Over her knees, up her thighs, and now the skirt was draped around her hips. She wondered, when she moved her legs apart, whether he would see a patch of dampness at the crotch of her panties, where she was wet for him. She leant back on her hands and very slowly spread her thighs apart.

He nodded again, slowly. 'Good. Very good.' Did he like what he saw? Was she desirable? He didn't smile or show any sort of reaction, just said, 'Now take off your knickers.'

She braced her feet on the floor, slipped her fingers under the edges of the panties, and edged them downwards. Halfway down her thighs the Lycra released its grip and the panties slipped to the floor, and she lifted her feet out of them.

'Now lean back. Lie on the desk with your thighs wide open.' She opened her mouth to express reluctance, but he said steadily, 'I want to look at you.'

She closed her mind to all the things that were shouting at her to stop, to be sensible. Lying obediently back on the desk, she lifted her hands above her head and spread her thighs wider. The wood beneath her was cold and hard, sunlight sluiced over her body. Every millimetre of her skin was sensitised, waiting for his touch.

Then a moment of horror. Would he have a condom? She didn't have one. How would she tell him to stop now? What would he –

The thoughts vanished as she felt him step closer, in between her spread legs. He took hold of her ankles and pushed them towards her, so that her knees bent and parted even further. His dark eyes looked into hers, lit with a mischievous gleam.

'So,' he said, pressing his body against her until she ached. 'What were you daydreaming about, Catherine? Don't try lying to me, I'll know.'

She licked her lips. If her nipples ached any more, they would burst. The words came out in a rush. 'About my neighbour, the girl who lives next door to me in college, I'm sure I heard her making love with another girl last night. Mike, please –'

'What did you hear her say?'

'She said,' Catherine swallowed, 'she said, "Put your fingers up my cunt, further," and she moaned.'

Mike let go of her right ankle and she felt his hand between her legs. 'How many fingers?'

'I don't know –' She saw his face and blurted out hastily, 'Two,' and then gasped, 'Oh God, Mike, God,' because without any warning, without any preliminary, he had pushed two big fingers right up her, sliding them into her wet cunt with brutal force.

'Two,' he whispered, his face close to hers now. 'And now three.' Another finger joined the first two, and he began to move them, sliding them in and out. Her clitoris shrieked to be touched, she squirmed to try to get some contact, but there was nothing, only the fierce fingers fucking her.

'You know what I think?' Mike whispered as the fingers drove in and out. 'I think the girl was giving her a tongue job while she fucked her with her fingers. That's what I think.' And then he dropped down

31

between her legs and rested her thighs on his shoulders and she felt the impossible, the incredible, his soft tongue flickering just where she wanted to feel it most, encircling her clitoris, sending tremors of pleasure shooting through her. She gave a great sigh of delight and let the sensations flood over her, saying nothing, just moaning and gasping with bliss as he lapped and lapped at her clit and pushed his long fingers deeper and deeper into her wet, hungry cunt.

It couldn't last long, and although she tried to take her time it was only moments before orgasm came, starting in her toes, shuddering up her thighs, jerking her hips against his working mouth, stiffening her ripe nipples and tautening her throat. She writhed, pushing herself down on to his hand to draw his fingers as far into her as she could, and clamped her arm across her mouth to stifle her cries of pleasure. He held her there, his mouth enveloping her clit, not touching it, just protecting it against the aftermath.

Then he drew back, sliding his fingers out of her, standing up. She opened her eyes and pushed herself up, panting, looking forward eagerly to the vigorous sex which had to happen now.

He put his fingers against his nose, smelt them luxuriously, licked them. His mouth gleamed with her juice. After savouring her taste, he smiled and said, 'I'll see you soon.'

For God's sake, was he going? She couldn't believe it. 'Mike,' she said, struggling up, catching her skirt across her body. 'Mike, don't you –'

He turned back. 'I will see you soon,' he said, patiently. 'There's plenty of time.'

'But –'

No use. He really was walking away, he was at the stairs, he was descending. He didn't even look at her.

For a moment she sat as if poleaxed. Then she grabbed up her clothes and hastily dragged them on.

What had happened? Had it been real, or had she fallen asleep and dreamed it? No, she knew it was real, her damp swollen pussy and taut nipples proved it. But how could she explain it, what could she say had happened when she wrote to James? That a man had given her a crashing orgasm with his tongue, and then not even bothered to fuck her?

She didn't have a clue whether this was a compliment or an insult. But she hoped that when Mike had said soon, he had meant it.

Chapter Three

James, where are you? Still not a word. I'm worried now, James. Are you sitting in the bush somewhere hot and rancid? Have freedom fighters kidnapped you? Or can you just not get to a reliable telephone link? What has become of your satellite phone?

And you're not the only missing man in my life, either. Can you believe it, since that extraordinary encounter in the UL I haven't seen hide nor hair of Mike. I haven't even seen him in college. What is going on? Is there something amiss with me? I don't even seem to be able to hold your attention, never mind the attention of a man I've only just met.

As if that wasn't enough, I can't get anything done on this bloody novel. Nothing. The translation's coming on fine, nearly finished, in fact, and I've been trying to write a synopsis or the opening page or something, anything, just to get started. But it's like trying to grasp a bar of soap. I think I've got it and it gets away. What's the matter with me? I know this could be a good book. I know it could.

Well, I can't just sit here and tell you how anxious I am. I have a guest coming: my next door neighbour, Maggie. You remember Maggie, the one who does nothing all day but have sex? She's coming to that most collegiate of institutions, tea. I have to tell you, I'm looking forward to it. I really need someone to talk to. I need to ask someone about what was going on with Mike and why I haven't seen him since. Girl talk, that's what I need. Since I can't talk to you.

She sent the email, trying not to wonder too much about whether James would ever receive it, and closed down her computer. The kettle had already boiled, and she opened the packet of crumpets and stuck one experimentally on the end of her improvised toasting fork (really a barbecue prong, but who cared?). It was really too warm to have the gas fire on, but since the room had one, she was determined to use it in time-honoured fashion, for toasting.

A knock on the door, and she hurried over to open it. She didn't like leaving the door open, the way some of the students did. It never really felt safe.

'Hi!' said Maggie, bouncing into the room. 'Hey, it's lovely in here, isn't it? Even nicer than my room.'

From what Catherine had seen through the open door, Maggie's room was lovely too, and would be a lot better if it wasn't strewn with clothes, coffee cups, and biscuit crumbs. But she just said, 'I'm very pleased with it. Especially the desk.'

Maggie walked over to the desk, which was positioned in the window, looking out over the college and the bustle of Henry's Parade. Catherine followed, because she never tired of the view. Right now it was obscured slightly, because there was a large demonstration all along the screen, several hundred undergraduates doing their best to draw attention to student debt. It didn't look as if anyone was taking very much notice, which perhaps wasn't too surprising. People in a town like Cambridge must rapidly develop Student Fatigue.

'Doesn't it put you off,' Maggie said, running her hand along the edge of the desk and stroking the keyboard of Catherine's laptop, 'having all this stuff to look at?'

'No, I like it. It helps me concentrate, to be able to turn my eyes away and look at something else, something attractive. I suppose that's why some writers like to go away to the country or whatever to get their writing done.'

'It would distract the hell out of me. When I was working I always had to go over to the faculty and just bury myself. Anything puts me off. People especially.'

'Would you like some tea and a crumpet?' Catherine asked politely.

'Crumpets? Cool!' Maggie left the window and hurled herself down on the sofa. It hardly made a sound. She was small and very slight, dressed in baggy khaki fatigue pants and a loose sweat top which almost extinguished her, but she flung herself around as if she was much bigger. It was rather endearing. 'I hope there's loads of butter,' she added eagerly.

'You can have as much butter as you like. I shall content myself with a sliver. When you're my shape, you take care with butter.'

'Bollocks. Life's too short,' said Maggie, with the infuriating confidence of someone who is naturally petite. 'Slap it on!'

Catherine held out the toasting fork. 'Toast away.'

'Excellent, I love it.' Maggie jumped off the sofa and sat cross-legged on the woolly rug in front of the fire, toasting with great concentration. Her fine blonde brows were pulled down in a frown and she held the fork at arm's length, as if the whole operation were highly dangerous. She was very attractive. Not pretty exactly, certainly not beautiful; her eyes weren't big enough, and her face was too pointy, and her mouth was too wide. But her mop of blonde curls was so ridiculous, and she brimmed with energy, and she was so young. Catherine turned her head slightly and looked at her own face in the mirror on the wall by the door. Not that she looked old, or that 36 was old, but even so, how could she compare to a student of 21?

Why should she want to? She shook her head slightly and poured the tea.

'So how are you finding it?' Maggie asked, looking over her slender shoulder as she propped up toasted crumpets on the hearth. 'Are you getting lots done?'

Catherine brought the tea and settled down before answering. 'Well,' she said, 'I've certainly got lots of time. And the translation's going well, the academic environment is perfect for that sort of work.' She saw Maggie's blank expression and explained, 'I'm working on two things. One is a translation of a Latin poet, Catullus. The other thing is a novel about him.'

'A novel?' Maggie brightened. 'What sort of novel?'

Catherine shrugged. 'A historical novel. He had a short life and an interesting one, in an interesting time, just the sort of thing to make a good historical. But it's not – well, it's just not coming together.'

'It sounds like bloody hard work, writing books,' Maggie said, lathering butter on to another crumpet.

'Students work too, don't they? What do you do?'

'Nothing,' said Maggie smugly.

That would account for the amount of time she spent having sex, of course, but Catherine was still surprised. 'What about all this stuff I read about students having to work desperately hard to get a job and all that?'

'Ah, well, you see,' Maggie said, gesturing with what was left of the crumpet, 'I got my degree last year. Chemical Engineering. All I have to do this year is complete a project and get my Postgraduate Certificate, and my 2:1 is guaranteed. And the certificate is a doddle. Apart from anything else, I'm working with another student, and he's such an eager beaver he's going to do everything for both of us.'

'Why would he do that?'

'Smitten,' said Maggie, sinking her teeth into her fourth crumpet.

Catherine shook her head and decided to voice her

thoughts. Maggie didn't seem fragile, or likely to be easily disconcerted. 'So that's why you seem to spend your time doing, ah, other things.'

Maggie opened her hazel eyes wide, the picture of innocence. 'Other things?' An impish grin spread over her face, wrecking the innocent look. 'Don't tell me I've been keeping you awake.'

'Hmm.' Catherine wagged her head thoughtfully. 'Well, from time to time I have gone down to the bar rather than sit here and listen.'

'Why not just come and join in?' Maggie suggested, the innocent look back in place.

'Come on,' Catherine laughed. 'You wouldn't want some ancient writer in residence barging in on you.'

'Wouldn't I?' Maggie said. Her eyes were still wide, but now they looked different, liquid somehow, desirous.

No, they couldn't. It was Catherine's vivid imagination at work again. What would a student want with her? 'Well, in that case, you must have very eclectic taste.'

'Oh, I have,' Maggie agreed. 'Haven't you noticed?'

Catherine sipped her tea. Should she change the direction of this conversation? Did she really want to talk about sex? Well, yes, she did. She'd told James so. So she said, 'I had noticed, actually, Maggie. You seem to have a lot of – partners.'

'Didn't you, when you were at college?'

Thinking back to her time at Oxford, Catherine said, 'Not exactly, no.' Would Maggie believe her? 'In fact, Maggie, I was a virgin when I left.'

'What?' Maggie's mouth was wide open. 'What? When were you there?'

'In the early eighties.'

'But that was before Aids!' Maggie exclaimed, as if horror-struck. 'You mean you could have had loads of sex and no condoms and you didn't sleep with *anyone*?'

'Exactly. I was a bit of a goody-goody, I suppose. And in my day, it was sort of the done thing to sleep with boys but not have penetrative sex with them. Anything but, if you know what I mean.' Maggie looked incredulous. Catherine added, 'And I worked a lot.'

Maggie shook her head. 'Good grief. Well, I take a different view, I suppose.' Catherine raised her eyebrows, and Maggie went on, 'I love sex. I really enjoy it. And having sex with loads of different people keeps it interesting. Like playing squash with lots of different partners. Me and my friends probably keep Durex in business.'

'You don't think of sex as something that happens in a relationship, then,' Catherine said, and immediately thought of Mike. There had been no relationship there, had there? And it had felt good, hadn't it?

'I don't need relationships,' Maggie declared boldly. 'All that slushy stuff is just an excuse to get people tied down, as far as I can see.'

She sounded, frankly, a bit cocky. She sounded like someone who had never been hurt, and who might be riding for a fall. 'Ever been in love?'

'No way.' Maggie drank the last of her tea. 'You have been, I suppose.'

Catherine smiled. 'I suppose you could say that.' Michele, in Rome. James, when they first met: and again now, perhaps, if only they were in the same country often enough. Then Steve. Three men in a lifetime? Was that a good score, or was she underachieving?

'Anyone now?' Maggie pried.

That made Catherine hesitate. 'Well –' How could she describe the relationship she had with James? Did she want to talk to this stranger about him?

Yes, she did, definitely. She slipped off the sofa on to the rug to talk more easily. 'Well, there is someone, Maggie. James. We've known each other a long time. We were in love years ago, ten years ago, and then there were other people for both of us, and we met again about four years ago and when he's here, it's really intense. But –'

'When he's here?'

'He's a journalist. He works in Asia, as a war correspondent. He doesn't get back to England that much.' She sipped her tea, then said, 'I'm really worried about him at the moment, to be honest. I haven't heard from him for what seems like weeks. I keep on thinking that he might be dead, or kidnapped, or something.'

Maggie frowned. 'Is he often out of contact for that long?'

Catherine opened her mouth to say no, then thought twice. 'Well,' she said, after some hesitation, 'yes, he has been.' Sometimes for months, and then some breezy excuse about being busy, or communication difficulties. Not that he ever seemed to have trouble getting his copy through to the papers when he wanted to.

'Maybe you're worrying a bit prematurely, then,' Maggie suggested, her head on one side.

Feeling obscurely reassured, Catherine nodded. 'I suppose I do tend to worry about him.'

'Because you're in love with him,' said Maggie evenly.

In love with him? Was she? If she had been, could she have done what she did with Mike in the UL?

As if reading her mind, Maggie asked softly, 'Are you faithful to him, then?'

Catherine shook her head. 'We've got an arrangement. We're free agents unless we're together.'

'I'm glad about that,' Maggie said.

Another hint? Maggie's eyes had that soft, wanton look again, and Catherine began to think that she hadn't been imagining things the first time. But it was hard to believe, and harder still to know what to do. She said, 'Maggie –'

'You didn't sleep with men at college,' Maggie said, her voice softer now. 'How about women?'

Catherine couldn't help but admire Maggie's nerve, even while she registered her own shock and wondered what her reaction should be. Maggie hadn't hesitated, her voice hadn't quivered, she seemed to feel not the

40

least bit of inhibition or shame. What a wonderful, liberated way to be.

Aloud, she said, 'I've only ever slept with men.'

Maggie was smiling now, a warm, exciting smile. 'Did you go to a girls' school?'

'Well, yes.'

'Wasn't it a hotbed of sexual intrigue? I know mine was.'

Thinking back, Catherine remembered that there had been one or two girls who, in retrospect, were probably having affairs with each other. But it had passed her by, the same way that sex had passed her by at Oxford. 'Perhaps, but I think I missed it.'

'So,' said Maggie, squirming a little closer, 'what do you think, would it be too late to start?'

Catherine looked into the bright hazel eyes and found herself lost for words. She was puzzled, confused – and above everything else, flattered. A cute little slip of a girl in her early twenties, who had lovers of her own age coming out of her ears, so to speak, actually wanted to sleep with her. Maggie fancied her. She hadn't felt so encouraged about her own attractiveness in years.

But could she actually do it? Wouldn't it feel like cradle-snatching, uncomfortable, inappropriate, not exciting? Wouldn't it feel wrong?

She was so confused that she didn't even feel aroused. It wasn't the way it had been in the stacks, when she had been fighting down her own vigorous reaction to Mike's approach. 'Maggie,' she began, 'I just don't think I –'

'Don't think,' Maggie whispered, 'whatever you do, don't think.'

She leant forward, still smiling a little, her face full of the confidence of impending pleasure. Catherine watched her draw closer and at last shut her eyes, unable to bear the suspense and the contradiction of her own response.

Then she felt Maggie's lips on hers, and all her indecision vanished. Such a kiss, so soft, like the kiss of

41

a handsome prince in a fairy tale. Mouth on mouth, no tongues, no penetration, just the most delicate of pressures, sweet, faint.

Maggie sat back, and Catherine opened her eyes. Maggie smiled again. 'Promise you won't think?'

Catherine nodded. She didn't trust her voice. Maggie's smile widened and she reached out to push a lock of hair back from Catherine's face. 'I think it's right that you're writing about Roman stuff,' she said thoughtfully. 'You look like a Roman woman, did you know that?'

How did she know that that was how Catherine flattered herself? She didn't reply, and Maggie went on, 'Big dark eyes, and your skin's really pale. You look like the women in those pictures of the dead, you know, they put them on the front of books about Rome. Those big, big eyes. I'm so jealous.'

Jealous? Catherine said dryly, 'Big eyes are all very well, but looking Roman comes with other stuff too. Like big thighs, and big buttocks, and –'

'And big breasts!' Maggie said, with delight. 'A woman shape. Not a boy shape, like me.' She took a quick deep breath and took Catherine's face in her hands. 'Catherine,' she said, 'You're really going to enjoy this. I promise you.'

Suddenly Catherine wanted to be honest, to say everything. She blurted, 'I heard you the other day, I'm sure you were with a girl. And – and I couldn't stand it, so I went down to the bar.'

'Didn't you like it?' Maggie looked discomfited, anxious.

'It wasn't that.'

The anxious look vanished, replaced by a wicked grin. 'You liked it. It turned you on!'

Catherine nodded. Her breasts were tingling now, as if they were more prepared for what was to come than her mind was. She licked her lips and slowly, hesitantly, reached out to stroke her fingers through Maggie's hair. She could hardly believe that she was about to be involved with Maggie's body, about to touch it, caress it, explore it. Another woman's body.

'That's nice,' Maggie said softly, and she leant forward to kiss Catherine again.

This time the kiss was deeper, fuller. Catherine again shut her eyes, not wanting to keep them open and watch herself in this extraordinary situation. With her eyes closed she could simply enjoy the kiss, enjoy the sensation of Maggie's hands on her arms, on her back, enjoy the feeling of Maggie's body coming closer until it was touching hers. Now they were embracing, tight in each other's arms, tongues curling and probing. After a moment Catherine wound up her nerve and thrust her tongue a little into Maggie's mouth and was rewarded with a delicious moan. That was a sound she knew well! Emboldened, she brought one hand to the front of Maggie's body and ran it down the soft baggy sweatshirt, fascinated by the slight, firm swell of the small breasts beneath it. There was no bra and there didn't need to be, there was no weight there, only a supple convexity capped with a dramatic spike of nipple.

'Oh,' Maggie said, and when Catherine moved her palm over the little stiff cone she moaned again. Catherine kissed her harder and was seized with a sudden urgent desire to do to Maggie what in her fantasies people did to her. She caught hold of the bottom of the sweatshirt and pulled it up, up to Maggie's armpits, revealing the small frail body starred with dark areolae. For a moment she stared, understanding for the first time how a man must feel when he looks at a woman's breasts. Then she pressed her mouth on to Maggie's and kissed her hard and as she did so she cupped her little breast in her hand, caught the nipple between her fingers, pressed and pinched.

'Oh, God,' Maggie moaned when Catherine lifted her lips, 'are you sure you haven't done this before?'

Catherine hesitated. She didn't know what came next. Was she supposed to do something to Maggie, then take

43

turns? Or did it happen all at once? None of her erotic reading had supplied this level of detail. She hesitated, then succumbed to an urge to suckle and dipped her head to Maggie's breast.

The nipple was hard and firm in her mouth, stiffer than a man's nipple, fatter, more sensitive. She flicked her tongue around it, nipped it with her teeth, pressed the tip of her tongue into the tiny cleft at its tip. Maggie groaned and arched her back, then grabbed hold of Catherine's hand and pushed it inside the waistband of her trousers. 'Please,' she whimpered, 'touch me, Catherine.'

Catherine wanted to, but knew that she was a beginner, that she didn't know how. What must it be like for a man the first time he gets to feel up his girlfriend? Terrifying: all those folds of flesh, no simple column to grasp and haul on. She slipped her hand down the flat plain of Maggie's stomach and discovered that as well as no bra, she was wearing no knickers either. Maggie whined and spread her legs wide apart, lifting her hips towards Catherine's hand.

In Catherine's favourite fantasy a young girl was snogged, groped, fingered, and finally fucked on a sofa by her boyfriend and one of his friends. It was a long fantasy, with many permutations, but one thing that never changed was the gradual stripping of the girl, the slow revelation of her breasts, her skirt pulled up her thighs while her boyfriend fingered her. She looked down now at Maggie sprawled on the rug, her sweat-shirt up around her armpits, her trousers pushed down by the pressure of Catherine's groping arm, and the closeness of fantasy and reality made her shudder with delight. She knelt close to Maggie and kissed her, slipping her tongue deep between her slack lips, and she eased her middle finger between the petals of Maggie's cunt, feeling it almost as if she were touching herself.

It was wonderful to feel Maggie's body responding to her, quivering just as she quivered herself when she masturbated. She concentrated on moving her finger very gently, very delicately, gliding the tip around the entrance to Maggie's vagina, feeling the warmth, gathering up the slippery wetness for use elsewhere. Then slowly forward, easing the lips apart, seeking that one certain spot.

She found it. Maggie heaved in her arms, twisting and moaning. Catherine stopped kissing her, because she wanted to look at her body again. She looked so deliciously dirty, lying there with her clothes disarranged, her legs spread wide, Catherine's moving hand visible beneath the loose fabric of her fatigues.

In her fantasy the girl came while her boyfriend was fingering her. Would she be able to make Maggie come? Stooping over her, she swept her tongue over one tight nipple, then the other. Maggie cried out, and Catherine fastened her mouth over one breast, sucking hard, all the time letting the tip of her finger rub gently against Maggie's clit. And there was another thing, something she enjoyed herself very much, when one finger touched the clit and another just probed into her entrance, just reminding her that she had a hole there which might be filled. She touched Maggie now in that way, rubbing and probing, and Maggie's reaction delighted her. Her breaths became deep and shaky, her body tightened. She was about to come, that was clear. Catherine gave her nipple one last suck, then kissed her instead, wondering how her lips would feel as she came, what her tongue would do.

Maggie hardly seemed to know that she was being kissed. Her mouth was slack and her tongue was withdrawn, not responding. But it was thrilling to feel her breath rasping, to feel her throat vibrate with her moans of pleasure. It was like the pleasure that there is in sucking a man to orgasm, and yet somehow more intimate, less foreign.

Now the sounds that Maggie was making were desperate, little helpless squeaks like a trapped animal. She arched her back, pushing her body against Catherine's hand. In response Catherine let herself rub a little harder

45

and Maggie gave a final, tormented cry and collapsed back on to the rug, panting.

Catherine sat back on her heels, looking down at Maggie's dishevelled body. She realised that her fantasy had been lacking in a few little details, like the sheen of heat on the little breasts and the slender belly and the way the hollows of the ribs caught the light. It was lovely, perfect.

Maggie opened her eyes and smiled. 'Mmm, the cat that got the cream. You're a dark horse, Catherine. I was expecting to have to lead the way.'

Catherine smiled, too. 'Now I know what all those writers were going on about.'

Maggie pushed herself up and pulled her sweatshirt off over her head. Naked from the waist up, she looked like a girl tumbler at a Roman party, slender, graceful, and not quite androgynous. 'And all those men,' she added. 'Don't they bore you, going on about how much the thought of women together turns them on?'

'I can't blame them,' Catherine said. 'It turned me on, too.' She was very aroused, eager for her own pleasure, but this was not like the sex she had had before. There seemed to be no rush, and it was – companionable. Friendly. Besides, there was no penis to grow exhausted and rebuke her with its flaccid state. Maggie's hands and lips would never be tired.

'Well,' said Maggie, 'what about men? Have you found any of them yet?' Catherine hesitated, and Maggie crowed, 'You have, you have! I can tell. What happened?'

Perhaps this was the chance to find out. Catherine slipped to a sitting position beside Maggie, her back comfortably propped against the sofa, and said, 'Well, I met him at the SCR cocktail party.'

'The SCR? Dear me.' Maggie looked as disapproving as she could in her half-naked state. 'I hope you aren't thinking of trying it on with any of those awful dons. Trust me, it's not worth it. They're all obsessed with departmental politics and when they're going to publish their next article. Not a decent shag in any of 'em.'

'I'll take your word for it,' Catherine said. 'He isn't a don, anyway, he's a mature student. And I haven't exactly shagged him, either.' Hesitatingly, and with some pauses for embarrassment, she described how Mike had approached her in the stacks and what had happened.

'What I can't understand,' she said at last, 'is why we didn't actually have sex. Why would a man want to do that? I mean, I'm not complaining, I had a wonderful orgasm, but I wanted proper sex too. Why wouldn't he?'

Maggie nodded wisely. 'I think I can explain this one. Though I don't know this bloke, and he sounds worth knowing. Is he at the college, did you say?'

'Well, he must be. But I haven't seen him since, not for days. He doesn't exactly seem to be around very much. Anyway,' Catherine said, as Maggie's possible meaning sank in, 'keep your thieving fingers off!'

Maggie laughed. 'Don't worry, sweetie. If he's the sort of guy I think he is, I wouldn't interest him anyway.'

Catherine looked again at the lovely little body beside her. 'What? Why not?'

'He sounds like a very dominant sort of bloke,' Maggie said. 'They don't like girls like me. I know my own mind too much, and I like to dish it out, as well as take it.'

'Dominant?' Catherine shook her head in confusion. 'But he didn't, well, you know, he didn't want to tie me up or anything.'

'No, no, they don't always want that. But didn't he tell you not to say what you wanted? To let him do the talking? That's what turns them on, being in charge. It's all about power and control. They like to control you, too, and make sure they're giving you all the pleasure you could want. A lot of them don't like it if you want to please them, you know, go down on them

47

or whatever. They have to be the one in charge. The dominant one.'

Catherine frowned. 'That sounds psychologically suspect,' she said. 'Why can't they like someone doing something to them?'

'You never had a man like this, then?'

Reflecting on the men she had slept with, not that there were very many, Catherine said, 'No. My first man, Michele, was very Mediterranean, very macho, but he certainly didn't like being in control all the time. I mean, sometimes he was really lazy, he wanted me to do everything.' And still have an orgasm so that he felt good, too, she could have added. Talk about a crash course in learning to fake it.

Maggie shrugged. 'Well, each to her own. It sounds as if you liked it, anyway.'

'Well –' There was no point in lying. 'Well, yes, I did. Though it was odd. But I did like it.' She frowned. 'But why did he follow me all the way there, and then just disappear? It's been three days, and I haven't seen hide nor hair of him.'

'He'll be playing hard to get,' Maggie shrugged. 'Pretty obvious ploy, I'd say. You know, pretending not to be interested, so that you will be.'

'Oh, God, how depressing. I hate that sort of game-playing.'

'Do you? I don't. Mind you, with me it's me that does the pretending. I'd like to see a bloke try it on me. I'd walk off and laugh at him.'

That bravado again! 'Perhaps someone's trying it already, and you haven't noticed yet.'

'If I haven't noticed, sweetie, it isn't working,' Maggie said, with a brilliant smile. 'But it's just what I'd expect from a dominant type. The whole thing's a big game to them. Mind you, I'd be surprised if it's entirely your bag, given your eagerness just now,' she added sagely. 'But then again . . .' She straightened, and ran one hand up Catherine's arm and on to her breast. 'Then again, I don't know what you prefer until I try doing a little something for you.' She smiled, a sly, satisfied, kitten smile. 'Do you feel like lying back and enjoying yourself?'

Catherine felt anxious for a moment, then realised she didn't have to be. 'That sounds great. But what did you have in mind?'

'Well,' said Maggie, 'the crumpets gave me an idea. It's to do with melted butter.'

Catherine laughed. 'Ever seen *Last Tango*?'

'That's some classic erotic movie, isn't it? No, never have. What's it got to do with butter?'

'Marlon Brando uses butter to lubricate his girlfriend so he can sodomise her,' Catherine explained, feeling old. 'I hope you didn't have that in mind.'

Maggie's eyes opened very wide. 'Sounds lovely. But I don't have any of my toys with me, so if you feel like being sodomised, you'll have to wait for another time and settle for the low tech version for now.'

Toys? Catherine's mind boggled. This slip of a girl seemed to live out in practice the sort of thing she thought people only did in fantasies.

'Now,' Maggie whispered, 'enough talking.' She leant closer and put her fingers very gently against Catherine's lips. 'No more talking, Catherine. Only moaning. I'm going to make you moan now.'

49

Chapter Four

Maggie pulled her bike from the dozens stacked up around the entrance to the college, wondering if Catherine would follow her advice and buy a bike of her own. Bikes weren't exactly a glamorous mode of transport, but in a town as flat as Cambridge they got you from place to place more easily than pretty well anything else, including a car, as the traffic was so awful. They kept the wolf from the door on the fitness front, as well.

It was a beautiful morning, glorious autumn sunshine with a hint of approaching frost in the air, and this early there were not that many people around. The clock on St Mary's church tower chimed the half as she whizzed past it: half-past six and all's well!

She liked this time of day, as long as she hadn't been up too late and boozy the night before. Not a hint of rush-hour traffic, just milkmen and lorries delivering to the town-centre shops. She put the bike into high gear, bounced it vigorously over a kerb, and nipped down a passageway towards the boathouse.

As she passed the King Street fish and chip shop she also passed a bunch of young men in sweatshirts and joggers running in the same direction. Some of them were wearing odd bits of kit in the college colours of purple and white: singlets, shorts, sometimes the broad swathe of a rowing scarf, which was a bit ostentatious given that it wasn't really cold enough yet. She knew most of these from earlier years: the experienced members of the college rowing club. The others, the ones in particularly motley gear, would be the new recruits. Some of them seemed to be struggling.

Being a cox suited Maggie down to the ground. She was naturally small and light, which were the only real physical qualifications for the job. She had a nerveless temperament, which gave her a steady hand on the tiller and the bottle to yell at a six-foot-four rower for some misdemeanour or other. She liked the early mornings and the boatie parties. And in particular she liked the fact that by being a cox she got to meet any number of big, strong young men, none of whom ever seemed to be in such hard training that sex was off the menu. You would never, ever find Maggie coxing the ladies' boat.

She stopped on the road bridge to look down at the river. An eight from St John's was just about to go under the bridge. The sunlight was slanting over the brown water, catching the edges of the blades as they lifted, dripping, flinging reflections against the bridge stanchions. The eight in the boat were very good. John's was a college that had a good reputation for rowing, so people from schools that rowed – public schools, typically – would often go there if they wanted to keep the sport up. Henry's tended to get people who were complete novices, which meant that their boats were not usually the greatest on the river.

The eight slipped under the bridge and on away from the town. She watched them with pleasure. They were well matched, like a team of carriage horses. None of them could have been under six foot and they all looked fit, too. The boat was moving quickly, even though they were rowing easily, and its balance was perfect. It was good to watch, though it would be better in half an hour or so, when they were warmed up and started shedding their sweatshirts. All those well-matched shoulder muscles flexing and pulling in perfect time. Maggie hummed and smiled, half-consciously swaying to match the rhythm of the rowers in the boat.

The runners would catch up with her in a minute. She shook herself and got back on the bike.

When she got to the boathouse there were already a few people there, milling around. Things were always chaotic early in the term, with trials going on and rank beginners learning how to get a boat out, sit in it, row and not fall in. She stood back as a ladies' four came past her with their boat on their shoulders, carrying it towards the river bank to get started. One of them was a lot shorter than the others, and she just ran along under the boat, not carrying any weight at all. Their cox scurried behind them like an anxious hen, calling out instructions.

Maggie propped up her bike and looked around for Richard, this year's boat club captain. He'd asked to see her before the outing. He wasn't visible, and she wandered into the boathouse to see if he was there.

The boats rose up on either side of her, one above the other on their racks. Eights, splendid machines more than eight metres long, including the brand new, very smart racing eight; the shorter fours; slim, elegant pairs and sculls. She'd tried going out in a scull, a single-seater, once. She'd fallen in twice in five minutes and given up.

A tall figure in boatie gear was stooped over one of the sculls. 'Richard?'

The figure straightened, revealing blond hair, not Richard's carrot top. Jesus, it was Ben! Maggie's stomach tightened. She had fancied Ben for two years, ever since he arrived to start his PhD, and she had never succeeded in getting him to notice her. Well, he'd come round once for a cup of tea. But she'd never succeeded in having sex with him, and that was frustrating.

'I think he's in the training room,' Ben said.

Not even a Hello Maggie? Not even a How was your summer? God, how could somebody that gorgeous not be interested in her? 'I'll, er, I'll find him in a minute,' Maggie said. 'How's things with you, Ben?'

'Just going out,' said Ben, heaving the scull off the rack and turning so quickly that she had to sidestep smartly out of the way. 'See you.'

She turned to watch him make his way out of the boathouse, the slender scull balanced elegantly above his head. His loose sweatshirt couldn't disguise the splendid V of his torso, and his legs were long and strong. What a bloody waste! And it was typical, he liked to scull on his own, not row in a boat where she might be able to get her hands on him. Damn, damn.

Richard appeared from the back of the boathouse, scruffy in a thick sweatshirt and a ridiculous beanie hat. He was another one of the boat club that Maggie had never slept with, but this time it was because neither of them wanted to. For a start, Richard had red hair, which she never liked. For a second, he was gay, probably the only gay boat club captain in Cambridge. St Henry's had long had a reputation as a gay-friendly college, and Richard was living proof of it.

'Maggie,' he said, 'need to ask you a favour.'

'Oh, God. What?' She didn't feel like doing anyone a favour after having failed yet again to catch Ben's eye. What was the matter with that man? Was he gay, like Richard? Surely not, she'd have heard.

'I need you to take out the novices.'

'The novices?' Maggie felt insulted. She usually coxed the first boat.

'They need licking into shape. I'm going to coach them from the bank but I want a strong cox. Come on, Maggie.' Richard's pale eyes twinkled. 'There's at least a couple in there I know you'll fancy, you predator.'

She brightened. 'Really? Oh, all right, then.'

'Here's the list.' He passed her a grubby sheet of paper. 'Remember to tell them to leave their mobiles at home, would you? Friend of mine at Jesus says on their first outing yesterday four novices lost their mobiles in the river. Bloody shambles.'

'The communication age,' Maggie said grinning.

The novices were assembled on the bank, trying to keep out of the way. Two or three of them were looking awkward and uncomfortable, most of the rest were laughing and shoving each other and generally being ostentatiously blokish. Maggie eyed them up at a distance, wondering which one to focus on to start with.

Why did she feel oddly as if this was all a bit of a waste of time? God, that little encounter with Ben had really left her in a bad mood. So what if there was one bloke who didn't want to fuck her? There were plenty of others. One or two of the novices were already regarding her with more or less blatant approbation. They were probably mostly freshers, first years, who usually arrived without any commitments and eager to find new friends and bedmates. Well, if they were on the hunt for a girlfriend they were looking in the wrong shop window. But some sex with no strings attached, that was on offer.

In fact, this lot contained a number who were really quite good-looking. One of the blokish ones was grinning at her now, and he was definitely one to catch the eye. Not terribly tall, which was a shame, because Maggie liked her men tall. But a good build, and more than anything else a really roguish, wicked-looking smile beneath a shaggy mop of brown hair. Yes, although there was a fair amount of competition, that one looked likely enough to begin with.

She stepped forward, meeting the winner's eye with a grin. 'You the novices? I'm Maggie, your cox. You're going to do everything I say this term, whether you like it or not.'

'Sounds too good to be true,' said another of the youngsters. He was tasty too and might do for later, but for now Maggie gave him a withering look, because she always believed in making them work for whatever she felt like giving them.

'Right,' she said, ignoring the comment and the chuckles, 'let's get going. Are you all here?' She ran down the names on the list, and when they had all answered screwed it up and put it in her pocket. 'Richard's going to come and coach you but we'll need to get the boat out first. Has he set you up in order?'

They nodded. 'Okay. Line up, stroke to bow, and we'll go and get the boat. And don't embarrass me by making too much of an arse of it. I normally cox the first boat and I like to see standards kept up.'

That put them in their place! They filed into the boathouse under her direction, as meekly as eight six-foot lambs.

They were out on the river without too many cock-ups, and Maggie relaxed into the cox's seat and concentrated on steering. Richard was cycling patiently along beside them on the towpath, and he would be directing the actual rowing. Apart from calling the stroke she wouldn't be likely to have that much to do today, which after all made a pleasant change.

The fanciable bloke was rowing at number 3, so she couldn't easily see him, but because they were beginners they didn't pull particularly straight and every now and again she got a glimpse of his face. Every time this happened he was looking at her, which was excellent. His name, she remembered from the list, was Dave. She kept her face straight and stern, as if as cox she had nothing on her mind other than the performance of the boat.

'All right,' Richard called from the bank, 'we'll try some full pressure. Ready?'

Full pressure meant rowing hard, which with beginners often ended in upset. Maggie shuffled a little lower in her seat and yelled, 'Okay, give me ten. One! Two!'

Eager to impress, the novices gave it all they had. Unfortunately their technique did not match their enthusiasm. Within the first ten strokes one of them caught a crab and slipped half off his seat, and the entire boat came to a juddering, swaying halt amid curses, imprecations and a lot of splashing.

'Oh well,' Richard said from the bank, 'let's try a little more decorously, shall we?'

They proceeded more decorously up the river. Maggie called the stroke, and the rhythmic repetition let her mind drift away. She found herself thinking about Catherine.

She liked Catherine. Not as a lover, but as a person. She liked her, and it bothered her that Catherine seemed to spend so much of her time worrying about this absent lover, this James, rather than looking after herself, getting her novel written, finding herself a nice man to shag, all those other necessary things. That would be fine if James was around and reciprocated, but he patently wasn't. He was on the other side of the world and not even replying to emails.

This felt to Maggie as if Catherine was being taken for granted. She didn't like to suggest it, though. Catherine would probably take it badly. It might upset her, and she didn't seem to be having a very good time at the moment, anyway, without that. No need to add another worry to her burden. The best thing to do would be to take her mind off it by regular bouts of sexual indulgence. Yes indeed. Nobody could feel worried and depressed after a really good orgasm. Next time they could use Maggie's room, and investigate the toy library.

A shout from Richard brought her back to the real world and she shook herself slightly to get back her concentration. The John's eight was ahead of them, and she had nearly steered into it! That wouldn't have bolstered her reputation with these youngsters.

Dave was still looking at her whenever he got the chance, with that slow, roguish grin stitched to his face. He was definitely interested.

Had he heard her reputation already? She knew that the rowers described her as easy. She knew why, too. They used that word to make themselves feel better, because the fact was that she wasn't easy. She was horny, and with the bloke she fancied at the time she would do more or less anything, but that didn't mean that anyone could have her. She'd turned down as many men in the Boat Club as she had had. She didn't set herself slaggish targets, such as fucking all the members of an eight in a single night, or indulging in relay shagging at boatie parties. That bothered them, because they had a polarised view of women: easy lays, or good girls. A girl who simply knew her own mind confused them.

She met Dave's eyes, and didn't exactly smile, just glowed at him. His face brightened. Maggie let the very tip of her tongue slide over her lower lip. All this thinking about sex was making her horny, and when they got back to the boathouse she didn't want to wait.

For a moment she wondered what her life might have been like if she had been born a different shape, very tall perhaps, or fat, or not particularly pretty. She probably wouldn't have been able to whistle for men the way she could. There was something about being small that made them feel safe, however sexually aggressive she was. What would it have been like if she had had to work for their attention, rather than expecting it? Not much fun, she suspected.

Or would the fact that she had to work for them make the whole thing more worth while? No, surely not. That had to be a myth invented by women who found men hard to get.

Her mind slipped back to Catherine, who seemed to find a decent man hard to get, and to Catherine's encounter with that odd bloke Mike. She didn't think that someone like that would be right for Catherine, any more than the absent James was. A journalist ten thousand miles away who ignored her, or a dominant weirdo who wanted to control her every move? Why couldn't she just take a break from relationships and enjoy herself?

The rest of the outing seemed interminable, but at last they were drawing in to the bank by the boathouse. Banking the boat was hard, and the novices made a predictable hash of it, but eventually they were back in with no harm done other than a few bruises caused by crab-catching.

Maggie ordered the rowers to lift the boat and guided them into the boathouse with it. She didn't look at Dave now. Time to make him wonder for a bit, time to make him want her.

'All together: lift!' The boat was old, like most novice boats, and it was clinker-built out of wood. That made it seriously heavy, and the eight grunted and heaved to lift it back on to its shelf. For a moment Maggie was afraid that they would drop it, but then it slid securely into position and back on the rollers and it was all over.

'Okay,' Maggie shouted, 'that's it. Any of you want more coaching in technique today, ask Richard and he'll put you in the shell.' Except for Dave. If Dave wanted more coaching in technique, he had to speak to her. She found his eyes and saw them as bright as buttons. He had obviously got the message.

The others were wandering off, but Dave was still there, still watching her. She pulled off the scrunchie that restrained her cloud of hair and shook it back. It wasn't long enough to touch her shoulders, and it settled around her face. As if this was a signal, Dave took a step towards her.

'Been to the boathouse before?' she asked him, keeping her voice even.

'No.' He shook his head.

'There's some interesting nooks and crannies. Want to see?'

His eyes widened momentarily. Was she going too fast for him? But all he did was grin and say, 'Fascinating.'

She turned and led the way through the gym and past the changing rooms, currently full of steam and shouts from the crews showering. She didn't look behind to see if he was following her: she knew he would. Past the office, and in front of her was the door of the little storeroom – a door with a key in the lock. She turned the key, opened the door and went in.

As she expected, Dave was close behind her. She let him come in, then closed the door and put the key in the lock. She didn't turn it yet, but took a good look at him.

He had put his sweatshirt back on to keep warm, and already traces of sweat were soaking through the thick cotton on his chest and back. He must have been working hard in the boat. His cheeks and throat were still flushed, and the ends of his shaggy brown hair were wet. They hung in flickering points around his face. Occasionally a drop of sweat fell from them and soaked in to his clothes.

He would do, sweaty and hot as he was. He would more than do. She smiled at him and turned the key in the lock.

He smiled back, then glanced around the room, taking in the shelves laden with varnish and paintbrushes, the toolbox, the old padded weight bench and retired rowing machine. 'So,' he said, returning his gaze to hers, 'what goes on in here?'

'Whatever we like,' Maggie replied.

She loved this moment, the moment when he realised that this was not a game, but for real. The moment when he realised that he was going to get fucked now. Her eyes jumped to Dave's crotch, wondering if he would respond in the time-honoured fashion. And as if she had pulled a switch, she saw movement within his joggers as his cock twitched and thickened.

Even though he believed her, he was still almost in shock, not about to take the lead. That didn't bother her, she liked taking the lead. She drew in a deep breath, feeling her nipples harden and her cunt moisten with anticipation. What did she want, right now? What would please her the most?

Yes, no problem, she knew. She said without a smile, 'Dave, do you know what I want to do right now?' He shook his head, his grin widening. 'I want to suck your cock.'

He gave a little jump. His grin vanished and for a moment he looked very young and quite vulnerable. Then he caught back his dignity and managed an almost-shrug. 'Yeah, sure. If you want.'

His attempt to look cool was so transparently put on that she could almost have laughed. But she didn't laugh, of course. It might put him off, and besides, this was too serious.

She walked to the weight bench and sat down. Its padding was old, but it would do, and it was conveniently low to the ground. She made no move to take off her clothes. Not yet, let him wait. 'Come here,' she said.

He came, obedient as a puppy. She caught hold of him by his buttocks and drew him to stand in front of her, looking down. There was no mistaking the size of his erection now. It throbbed visibly beneath the thick fabric, craving release. She looked up at him, and then, holding his eyes, slid her hands underneath his sweatshirt, underneath the damp fabric of his singlet, and rested them on his bare skin just above the waistband of his joggers.

He flinched and sucked in a quick breath. 'Cold hands,' he hissed, 'cold!'

'Wuss,' she scolded, though he felt so warm that her hands must be icy. It was good to feel the heat of his skin. She eased the tips of her fingers beneath the waistband, closing her eyes in concentration. His skin was soft but the body beneath the skin was hard, good hard muscle on his abdomen and obliques. Not much hair, but a line of fur down his belly, crossing the dimple of his belly button. Perfect, just right.

She could have grabbed him greedily, and sometimes she would have done, but today it didn't feel right to hurry. Slowly, gently, she slid her hands downwards, finding the top of his briefs and gradually investigating. They felt like tight cotton trunks; very nice. Her hands pushed inside them, moving downwards, but not towards his groin, just down to the fronts of his thighs. More firm muscle; lovely.

Slowly, her hands pressed to the delicious soft flesh at the join of thigh and hip. She looked up. He was looking down at her, and his expression pleased her, just the right blend of delight and disbelief. He pushed one hand into her hair and his teeth bared themselves as he spoke. 'Go on, then. Go on.'

Did he really think that she would hesitate now? She leant her head back against his hand, putting off for a little longer the moment when she would touch his cock. Then she pulled her hands up and pushed down the front of his joggers, not caring when they fell in an untidy puddle around his feet.

He stood very still. The tight, sweat-soaked trunks outlined the shape of his erect prick. It was a nice one, not spectacular, but nice. And he smelt so good! The sweat was still fresh, and its scent was sharp and strong, like being rubbed with a harsh flannel. Beneath the smell of the sweat was his male sexual odour, a rich, subtle tang. It gave her a premonition of how he would taste, and it was good.

She licked her lips and hooked her fingers into the trunks. Her heart was beating hard and her breath was cold in her throat. Slowly, carefully, she peeled the trunks away.

Flat belly, tanned skin, and that line of hair running down across his navel, just as her fingers had sensed it. She stopped removing the trunks when they were tight across his hip bones, and leant forward to draw in the smell of him even more luxuriously.

The skin was still damp and hot. He had been working hard, for sure. She laid her cheek against his belly and felt even at this distance that his heart was thumping just as hard as hers. With her eyes closed, she turned her face slightly to bring her lips to his flesh. She kissed him just below his navel, and when she let her tongue touch him he gave a soft, smothered moan.

She couldn't wait any longer, much as she would

have liked to tease him. Her fingers caught again in his trunks and pulled them right down and his cock sprang free, bouncing with eagerness. She caught it in her hand and felt its weight and stiffness, then let her hand run up and down its length while she admired the ripe glossy head and the gleam of the shaft.

He didn't have any suntan marks. Where had he been this summer? It was pleasant to think of him disporting himself naked on a beach somewhere. She leant forward, imagining the sea spray flying up between his legs, his cock and balls dangling, sharp with salt. Closing her eyes again, she parted her lips and took him in.

When she closed her mouth around the shaft he moaned and buried his fingers in her hair. She pushed back with her head, just a little, to show him that she didn't like to be controlled while she did this. His hands remained where they were. Was he stubborn, or just inexperienced? She didn't know, and as long as he didn't cramp her style, she didn't care. She flicked her tongue at the base of his glans, the little fragment of skin that seemed to hold the head on to the shaft, and he responded with a whimper and a shudder. She took him in as deeply as she could, swallowing to the very back of her throat, and he gasped and thrust a little with his hips. Gradually, she let her movements settle into a rhythm, a steady, slow up-and-down, coating his cock with her saliva until it slid smoothly between her hungry lips.

She loved to do this. With one hand she steadied the base of his cock and fondled his warm, taut balls, and with the other she touched herself. Not masturbating, she didn't need to masturbate when she was giving head, just touching herself all over like feathers, her breasts, her ankles, her throat, her belly. Her nipples were almost painfully swollen and she knew that she was already wet, soaking, ready to be fucked between her legs as she was even now being fucked between her lips.

It was so good to feel that strong smooth shaft easing

to and fro in her mouth. As she moved she flickered with her tongue, wrapping it around him, teasing the tip, exploring the ridged veins and the glossy edge of the cockhead. Every time she did it he gave a little moan and that turned her on even more. She loved it when men enjoyed themselves, and even more when they cried out. It proved that she was doing a good job.

He was going to come soon. She could sense the pulsing semen coiling in his balls, ready to rise. For a moment she thought of stopping it, squeezing the head and making him wait, but she didn't want to. Responding to his eagerness, she let her lips move faster, sucking now, giving it to him really hard. He whimpered and his fingers clenched in her hair, not holding her, just convulsively reacting to the pleasure she was giving him. She braced herself now with her spare hand and with the other held his cock steady so that she could really fuck him with her mouth, moaning a little as she did so, sucking harder and harder until he cried out, 'Oh, God,' and she felt the explosion surge up his shaft and burst into her throat.

She swallowed quickly with his cock still between her lips and then, very gently, released him. She knew how sensitive penises were immediately after orgasm. He shuddered and sat down beside her on the weight bench, his head in his hands, his breath shaking him.

She was about to ask him if he was all right when someone turned the door handle. Both of them looked up, Maggie startled, Dave apparently horrified.

'Oi,' said Richard's voice outside, 'where's the store key? Hey, has anybody seen the store key?'

Footsteps moved away from the door and Dave leapt to his feet, reaching down to haul up the mess of his joggers and trunks from around his ankles. 'God,' he hissed, 'we have to get out of here.'

'If we walk out of here now everybody'll know exactly what we've been doing.'

'But someone wants to come in. The key –'

'There's a spare. In the porter's lodge.'

Dave met her eyes, gaping, and then relaxed into a grin. The Porter's Lodge was in the college gatehouse, ten minutes away by bike.

'By the time they get back, if they bother, we'll be out of here,' Maggie explained coolly, as if she was an old hand, which of course she was. 'But until then . . .' She smiled at him. 'Can you get it up again?'

He bridled. 'What d'you take me for?'

That touch of competitiveness always did the trick. Maggie nodded with satisfaction, then sat back a little, crossed her arms, and pulled off fleece and T-shirt in one smooth movement. His eyes instantly fastened on her naked breasts.

She cupped her hands under the small swells and lifted them, then closed forefinger and thumb on her nipples and pinched. A delicious jolt of pleasure ran through her. 'Now I want you to do something for me,' she suggested.

He licked his lips. 'Take everything off,' he hissed. 'Everything.'

Maggie pushed her tongue into her cheek as she got up from the weight bench. She was already planning what she wanted to happen next, and she was pretty sure that she was going to be able to make it happen. She pushed off her trainers, then slowly, seductively eased her tight joggers down her legs, pulling off her socks at the same time, leaving her in nothing but a thong.

His eyes stretched. 'Jesus.'

For a moment she wondered what his sexual history was, whether anything like this had ever happened to him before. From the look on his cheeky face, she rather suspected not. So she could make this really special for him, and without that much effort, either. The way he was looking at her showed that she was already the sexiest thing he had ever seen. It wouldn't take much to prove it.

She ran her hands up her body, showing herself to him like a stripper or a model in a men's magazine.

That never failed. The slack length of his softened cock began to perk up and show new interest. Good; but he wasn't going to get his end wet yet. She didn't know him, and that meant that she didn't trust him to last long enough to make her come if she fucked him straight away, even though he had already had one orgasm. First put on a little show, to freshen him up, and then take some easy, unhurried pleasure for herself; a tasty appetiser before the main course.

Slowly she hooked her fingers beneath the top of her thong, suggesting that perhaps she might be about to remove it. He shifted his weight, leaning on one hand, staring. Smiling, a teasing smile, she turned her back on him and flirted her arse at his face, bending a little forward to afford him the view that had so aroused Ash.

'Wow,' he said, his voice hoarse with sincerity, 'nice arse,' and then his hand touched her, just stroking the curve of her cheek.

She whipped around, frowning. 'Look, don't touch until I tell you.'

His hands withdrew into his lap and his eyes widened, like a child chastised. She turned her back again and ran her hands down her body from ribs to thighs, outlining her curves for him. Then she pushed her hand between her legs, front to back, so that he could see her fingers resting on the snug white fabric covering her sex. God, she was hot there, and already the gusset was damp. Why not tell him? 'My panties are soaking,' she announced softly. 'I'm so wet.'

'Come here,' he groaned. He sounded desperate. But he didn't touch her again, and she smiled at his obedience.

'So wet,' she murmured, stroking her fingers along the pouch of the thong. Beneath the cotton her clit swelled with excitement and need. She thrust her bottom further towards her audience and stroked a little, just a little, enough to make her moan slightly. Then she

65

kept her hand still and circled her hips, rubbing herself against her stiff fingers, letting out little uneven sighs.

'Christ,' Dave whispered behind her, 'oh, Christ.'

If she went on touching herself she would come, and that was not her intention. She straightened and turned and saw that Dave was wanking, sitting on the weight bench with his stiff cock in his hand and jerking at it fast and furiously.

What a waste! Did he have no self control at all? 'Don't touch that,' she said, advancing on him. 'It's mine.'

He let go of himself and sat back on the bench, gasping up at her, 'Yes, please.'

'Lie on the bench,' she ordered him. 'Feet on the floor.'

He blinked, but obeyed. The bench was at about knee height, just right. She swung over one leg to stand astride him, her thighs either side of his chest, watching his face. When he had finished adjusting his position she had his full attention. Now it was time really to get going.

She pushed her hand inside her thong and found her clit, engorged and slick with juice. One little touch and she shuddered with need. Pulling her hand free, she moved up the bench until she was astride his shoulders. His mouth was open and his eyes were as big as saucers.

'Can you smell me?' she asked him. He closed his mouth and swallowed hard and nodded. She ran her hands up her body, knowing how she would appear to him now, towering over him, foreshortened like a Michaelangelo painting, nipples thrusting out like arrowheads. She put her hands on her breasts and pinched the tight nipples hard. It felt so good, all it needed to be perfect was his tongue on her clit.

'Lick me,' she whispered, and with one hand she pulled aside the string of her thong. It caught in the cleft of her arse, the string was tight against her, tugging and uncomfortable and dirty.

Dave looked startled, almost as if he wanted to back out. He said, 'I –'

If he'd never licked a girl before, she didn't want to know. She stopped his mouth by sitting on his face.

His mouth was warm and for a moment he didn't move, didn't touch her with his tongue, nothing. She touched her breasts again, squeezed her nipples tight, and circled her hips fractionally against his mouth. That was good in itself, just feeling that wetness and warmth beneath her, and she was so aroused that she thought she would be able to come even if he never did anything and she just humped herself against him.

But she didn't have to. After a moment Dave made a smothered sound, then, very hesitantly, he touched her with his tongue.

Perhaps he didn't have a clue what he was doing, but in that case he was born lucky. His tongue touched her clit so gently, so softly, that she gave a guttural moan and arched backwards, whimpering, 'That's perfect, that's so good.'

She didn't need him to lick hard, she didn't need him to stick his tongue inside her. She'd have his cock inside her soon. The tentative, hesitant movements of his tongue around her engorged clit were just what she needed to pull her onward and upward towards orgasm. It was so deliciously tormenting, never quite hard enough. She groaned and began to push her hips against his face, a slow, reaching movement, and the pleasure built and built in her groin, compounded by the hollow ache of her empty vagina.

'That's so good,' she whimpered, finding her rhythm. She pinched her nipples savagely and cried out as she forced herself against him, grinding her clit into his mouth, searching out another touch of his tongue, and another, and another. Her eyes were shut, she didn't care if she was smothering him, just humped against his face and gasped with the pleasure of it. It was so good that she almost didn't want to come, and when she did she moaned with fulfilment and frustration in almost equal measure.

She stood over him, shuddering, while the tides of her orgasm ebbed. The ache in her sex was unbearable now, it had to be filled. She moved forward, stepping off him, discarded her thong and dived into the pocket of her trackies for a condom. When she turned back he was sitting up on the bench, wiping his face and looking shocked.

'Lie back,' she said with a feral grin. 'I haven't finished with you yet.'

'Jesus H Christ,' he whispered, and slumped back to a prone position.

She stood beside the bench and rolled the condom on to his cock. It flexed under her hand. Then she straddled him, facing away from him. She didn't need to look at his face to enjoy what she was going to do next.

Slowly she lifted his cock until it was vertical. She positioned herself over it and let its sheathed tip rub against her, spreading her juices, titillating her still swollen clit. Any minute now, very soon, she would feel it inside her.

There was no hurry. She let herself enjoy the teasing, the sensation of the ripe firm head nudging against her, begging to be let in. Behind her Dave moaned and cursed softly beneath his breath, but she didn't let him rush her. When she was ready, soaked with the need to be penetrated, she allowed herself to sink slowly down, taking him into her inch by inch until his stiff cock was completely hidden inside her and her blond pubes mingled with his dark ones.

It was so good, to feel him within her. She lifted herself up until he all but slipped out of her, then sank down again, for the sheer pleasure of feeling the hardness part the lips of her cunt, squeeze into the opening, and move up inside her, stretching her, filling her. Her hands returned to her nipples and began to chafe and tease. Already she could feel another orgasm hovering in the base of her belly, waiting to be released.

'Oh, God,' said Dave as she slid up and down on his cock. He said it over and over again, as if the sensations had robbed him of every other word.

Well, he might be without vocabulary, but she wasn't, and there was something else she wanted. She looked over her shoulder at him, squeezed hard with the muscles of her cunt, and said, 'Dave.'

'Uh,' he gasped, and then, 'Yeah?'

She leant forward a little so that he could see the ripeness of her labia surrounding him and the shaft of his cock buried deep inside her. She rose and fell again so that he could watch it gleam as it withdrew from her, pulse as it was swallowed up. 'Dave,' she said, her voice husky, 'finger my arse.'

Dave's only response was another 'uh' as she squeezed him again, but within a few seconds she felt his hand on her backside, moving towards the crease. She leant a little further forward, spreading herself for him. 'Lick your finger,' she urged him. 'Push it up me.'

His cock surged inside her, a twitch that made her quiver. It must turn him on, to touch her arse. She pushed herself even further towards him, and the movement made her stiff clitoris rub against the soft taut pouch of his balls.

There was his finger now, slick and wet with saliva, probing into the tight cranny of her anus. God, it felt so dirty to be touched there, it was wonderful. 'Yes,' she moaned, as he wormed his finger inside her. 'Oh yes, that's good.'

The orgasm was very close now. Every time her clit rubbed against his balls a shiver went through her. What she wanted now was a real fucking. She began to rise and fall on Dave's buried cock with frantic determination. 'That's right,' she gasped, 'yes, yes, fuck my arse with your finger. Oh God, that's good.'

'I'm coming,' Dave whimpered. He sounded panic-stricken. 'Fuck, I'm coming.'

'Push it up me, push, oh yes.' Any minute now she would come, any minute. She fucked him as hard as she could, grinding her clit against the base of his cock, tugging at her nipples and moaning with delight as he thrust his finger deep into her anus. He moaned again and then cried out as he came. His cry turned to a smothered shout as she didn't stop fucking him, just speeded up, banging her clit against his balls until she, too, came with a stifled yell.

She propped herself up on the end of the weight bench, panting. Dave's finger was still in her arse and his cock was buried deep in her spasming cunt. It felt wonderful.

He pulled his finger out of her so quickly that she gasped. 'Jesus,' he whispered, 'I bet someone heard us.'

She stood up, reaching between her legs to hold the rubber on to his cock. He winced as he was unceremoniously released. 'Don't worry,' she said, 'everyone wants breakfast after an outing. They'll all have headed back to college.'

He sat up as she fished in her pockets for a tissue. His face revealed deep apprehension. Now he was going to ask her out. He was bound to, really.

'Would you,' he began, then cleared his throat. 'Would you like to come out for a drink tonight?'

She smiled, quite kindly. 'No, thanks very much.'

He looked angry now. 'What's wrong? Don't you go out with freshers?'

'I don't go out with anyone, really.' That was true, in essence. She was much more likely to spend time with girl friends in the evenings. He was looking puzzled and upset, so she said, 'I didn't say you couldn't fuck me again, though.'

He hesitated while the double negative sunk in. Then his face brightened. 'Cool,' he said. 'When?'

She shrugged. 'Not sure.'

His grin had returned. He looked cheerfully devilish. 'Next time,' he said, as he reached for his joggers, 'next time I'm going to be in charge.'

She smiled sweetly at him. 'How much do you want to bet?'

Chapter Five

James, where the fuck are you?

There really didn't seem to be any point. Catherine stared at the screen for a while, trying to work out whether she was anxious or furious. Furious, probably. Yes, furious, definitely. There had been a piece from James in the *Independent* only yesterday. Bastard! Who did he think he was? Men were all the same. She hadn't seen hide nor hair of Mike, either. He was a bastard, too.

She dropped out of her email programme and returned to the work in progress, the recalcitrant novel, tentatively entitled *Love/Hate* but still determinedly resisting all her attempts to get properly into it. Her hero, Gaius Lucius Catullus, was just as awkward and hard to catch as James. She was in the state of mind when all men are bastards even before the first glass of wine, and right now she heartily disliked Gaius Lucius and every other member of the species.

She wasn't even really sure where to start. A first scene had to grab the imagination, catch the reader by the balls and positively force them to turn the next page. Where should she start with Catullus? Somehow the trials and tribulations of a well-born poet with a country house on Lake Como didn't seem likely to grab a reader by the wrist, never mind the balls.

Perhaps she ought to start with a sex scene, or a row with Lesbia, the aristocratic woman her hero adored and loathed. Perhaps she should start with their final row and tell the rest in retrospect. She thought of the scene, Catullus furious and tearful, Lesbia bored, unexcited. She had worn him out, used him up, and was now consigning him to the waste tip. She imagined Lesbia as small, slight, with a cloud of curly blonde hair and high, tip-tilted breasts.

It didn't seem to work, and she couldn't make progress. In the end she rested her chin on her hands and looked out of the window. The best thing about her big lovely room was this desk, right beside the enormous window, so that she could be distracted without even having to move her chair. The windowsill was low, only a couple of feet from the floor, so that the view from her desk was all-encompassing.

She found she was thinking about buying a bike. Maggie had strongly recommended it, and it would be good to get out and about a bit. Fresh air, blow away the cobwebs, a new approach, crack that damned book. There was a bike shop just along Henry's Parade, no distance, two minutes' walk. Perhaps she should stroll along there and check things out. Not that she was dressed for it. Although it was bright outside it was a chilly day, with a real touch of autumn, and she was wearing a long loose button-through dress in russet brown, a fleece, and a chocolate-coloured pashmina wrapped round her shoulders against the draught that came through the windows and blew over her desk. Change into jeans, perhaps, and then go bike hunting.

The knock on the door made her jump. She looked at her watch and frowned. It wasn't surgery hour, when students could come and pick her brain about writing and make her feel like a fraud, and she knew that Maggie was out, and she hadn't really made any other friends of the type that might just drop round.

As she crossed the room it occurred to her that the visitor might be Mike, and her heart jumped with sudden excitement. Maybe some good dirty sex might break the writer's block. Even if it didn't, it would be fun. What she really should do was tell him to get lost, but she knew that she wouldn't. She actually knew that if she opened the door and it wasn't him she would be badly disappointed. That made it quite hard to put her hand to the lock, but she forced herself.

She needn't have worried. When she opened the door Mike stood there, filling the space. He really was tall, and his shoulders were wide. He had on jeans and a white T-shirt, as before, but this time he was also wearing a battered old brown leather jacket. He wasn't actually smiling, but his wonderful eyes were soft and warm. He said, 'Hello.'

'Mike.' She didn't really know what to say to someone whom she had met twice, exchanged about fifty words with, and had sex with already. In the end she decided that she might as well speak her mind, so she said, 'You've got a damn cheek, ignoring me for a week and then just turning up on my doorstep.'

'May I come in?' he asked, without a word of apology.

If she said no he would go away. She remembered what he was like. He'd just walk away and then there would be no repetition of that strange and wonderful sex. She wasn't as eager for sex as she had been, because after all Maggie was only next door, but when all was said and done there was something about a man which a woman could never imitate. So she said, 'OK,' and held the door open for him.

He walked coolly in and began to give her room the once-over without a word. God, he had more brass neck than anyone she had ever met. 'So what was your strategy?' she asked, not disguising her annoyance. 'Treat 'em mean, keep 'em keen?'

He looked over his shoulder and smiled at her, a slow spreading smile which admitted everything without

73

admitting anything. 'Did it work?' he asked, lifting his eyebrows.

Now if she said no she would be lying, and if she said yes he would know he'd won. 'What do you think?'

Turning fully round, he shrugged off the old jacket and slung it over the chair, then perched on the back of the sofa, extended his long legs, and crossed his arms. His head on one side, he examined her thoroughly. The head of the tattooed snake on his arm also appeared to be watching her. The way he looked at her made her want to blush, but she didn't. At least she didn't think she did. 'Hmm,' he said after a while. 'All in all, I would say that you look pretty keen.'

Was he suggesting that she looked as if she wanted to have sex with him? Now that did make her blush. And it made her angry, too. After that session in the stacks he seemed to think he had some sort of right. 'Mike,' she said, crossing her arms in an angry mirroring of his body language, 'who the hell do you think you are? Did you just walk in here expecting to have sex with me again?'

'Again?' he said, brows lifted. 'I didn't realise we had actually had sex already.'

She frowned. 'You don't think that what we did counts as sex? Anyway, I've met you precisely twice. Don't you think we should, I don't know –'

'Get to know each other?' he suggested, his voice mocking.

'Yes,' she said angrily. 'Yes, that is what I mean.' He was shaking his head, and he looked so damned arrogant that she flushed with anger. 'What the hell do you mean, no? What do you take me for?'

Suddenly his eyes were very serious. 'I take you for an attractive, sensual woman who is here for only a short time, who may have other entanglements about which I know nothing and care less, and who was unorthodox enough to do what I wanted in the UL when she barely knew my name.'

His educated language was strangely at odds with his

rough voice. Catherine couldn't immediately think of a reply. She swallowed hard, trying to fault his logic. She couldn't. She was in Cambridge only for one term, and they had done what they did in the stacks, and then there was James. Yes, she'd wanted to get laid while she was in Cambridge, and she had meant it to be with no strings attached.

Mike pushed himself from the sofa and stood up, still watching her. 'I take you,' he said, 'for someone I want to take. Right here, right now.'

Maggie had described him as dominant, and he was. Catherine hadn't met a man like him before. Literate James liked to talk during sex, but he would ask for things, ask her what she thought, make suggestions, not come out with that kind of verbal demand. Maggie hadn't thought much of dominant men, had she? But then she had more than a touch of dominance herself. And for Catherine to have a man say something like that to her in total seriousness, meaning every word . . . Well, that was new. And it was sexy.

'So,' Mike said, taking a step towards her. He reached forward and down and caught her hand. Not knowing what to expect, filled with excitement, she followed him. He guided her round to the sofa, released her hand, sprawled on the low seat and looked up at her.

'So,' he said again. 'Let's start.'

What was it to be this time? He'd said he wanted to take her, so that must mean sex. But what could he want, what would he demand of her? Where would he begin? There was something very arousing about having no say in what was about to happen. Arousing, and somehow languid, lazy, free of responsibility. She knew that she didn't have to say anything, that he meant to do the talking and that it would be clear when an answer was required of her. How luxurious, how relaxing.

He looked up at her, his head very slightly tilted, as if reading the progress of her thoughts through her

75

mind. Then he said, 'I want you to strip for me, Catherine.'

Strip? Her mind filled with images of tawdry bars, sequinned G-strings, spike heels, twenty-pound notes stuffed into bras and less printable orifices. And all the women in these images were skinny and had artificially inflated breasts. Stripping was not something she had ever seen herself doing. She said hesitantly, 'I, er, I don't think I'm really the right sort of –'

Mike moved his head a little, just a little. His responses were subtle, but the slight change in his expression was enough to make her stop speaking and wait.

'Whatever you're thinking of,' Mike said, 'forget it. I've seen your body, and I think it's beautiful. I want you to show it to me, slowly, just as you want to. If I don't like what you do, I'll tell you. Now, use your imagination.'

He settled back on the sofa and folded his hands behind his head, expectant.

Catherine glanced across at the window. Three stories below was Henry's Parade, full of people coming and going, into college, into the shops, and tourists too, who might at any moment look up and wonder what that blur of movement was behind the big windows at the top of that cute old building. Not that they would be able to see that far into the room, not really, but even so, perhaps if she pulled the curtains –

'Catherine.' She started, and Mike said, 'Leave the window alone.'

Was he a mind reader, or what? No, he was just watching her carefully. But even so, his prohibition made her even more conscious of the possibility of being seen. If someone in one of the gatehouse rooms looked out, they would certainly be able to see in. To be seen . . . She shivered, and was suddenly conscious that her arms were covered in gooseflesh and her nipples were hard and cold.

'I'm waiting,' Mike said softly.

Suddenly she was panic-stricken. She didn't know what to do. How terrible it would be, to disappoint him. Did Gaius Lucius Catullus ever treat Lesbia like this? No, she didn't think so. She was sure that Lesbia had always had the whip hand in their relationship. But if he had, how would Lesbia have responded? How would she have shown herself to her lover?

It helped, to think about Lesbia. Roman standards of beauty were not like modern ones, and it was good to make herself feel beautiful. Lesbia would have shown off her lovely, rounded arms, her smooth shoulders, the long white curve of her haunch and thigh. Catherine could do all those things, too. All those beauties were hers.

First, get rid of the fleece. It didn't suit this persona. She unzipped it and flung it away from her, beyond Mike, to the other side of the sofa. It was irrelevant. Mike watched its trajectory to the floor and then turned back, hawk's-wing eyebrows lifted in slight surprise. The stud gleamed. Had he had it put there just to accentuate the sardonic commentary of his beautiful brows?

Let him be sardonic, then. Catherine turned her back on him and went over to the chest of drawers which acted as her dressing table. She twisted her hair up behind her neck and fastened it there with a clip, then lifted the pashmina and draped it over her hair and her shoulders, like a Roman *stola*. Her hair, too, and the soft nape of her neck, could be the focus of his desire.

She returned to stand before the sofa, looking down into Mike's eyes. He nodded, acknowledging that the show was about to begin. Lifting her head against the unaccustomed weight of the stole, she turned away and began slowly to unfasten the buttons of her dress.

Silence from behind her. She unbuttoned the dress to just below her navel. Open like this, it could easily fall right to the floor. But it wouldn't, not just yet. She lowered her left shoulder and let the dress drop down, revealing her arm to the elbow. The dark russet of the fabric contrasted pleasingly with the paleness of her skin. She freed her arm completely and lifted it, turning her hand to call up the delicate curves of elbow and forearm, admiring the narrowness of her wrist.

What a strange, narcissistic pleasure this was. With her back to Mike, facing the fireplace, she could almost forget that he was there and undress purely for her own delight. But of course she couldn't forget his presence, not entirely. The knowledge of that masculinity behind her, cock thickening as she revealed herself, filled her with chill anticipation.

She unbuttoned the dress a little further so that it hung from her shoulder to her hip, a curve of fabric across the curve of her back. The straps of her black bra must look shockingly stark. She drew in a deep breath, feeling for herself how her breathing lifted her breasts, and rolled her head slowly to the right as she dropped her right shoulder and let the dress slide down and down.

It caught on her hips and hung, pooled around her feet. Perfect! She arched her back and lifted her hands to the ceiling, enjoying the soft touch of the pashmina on her shoulders and throat. Slowly she drew the ends of the shawl across her shoulders to lie over her front, and then she turned.

He didn't look relaxed now. His eyes were dark and bright, and he was sitting forward on the sofa. She lowered her hands, crossing them in front of her to press the fabric of the pashmina against her body, and watched his nostrils flare.

It was good to be wanted. It was good to be wanted by a man. It made her able to forget James' inexplicable silence. For a moment James was before her, fluent and charming, and then she touched her belly with her hands and he was gone.

A slight push dislodged her dress from her hips. It fell to the floor, and she was naked but for bra and panties and the pashmina, which draped across her whole body and hid her from Mike's hungry eyes. It was a wonderful, fluid shield. She lifted her hands behind her back and unfastened her bra, then drew it off, all without ever revealing her breasts to him. So if he had fancied another gloat over her French underwear, he would be disappointed. Her panties followed, joining the puddle of fabric at her feet.

Now for the real moment. She met Mike's eyes and began to let the pashmina slip from her hair and fall down her shoulders. That raised it at the front, but before anything was revealed she turned again, showing her back and shoulders, her buttocks concealed now by the drape of the shawl. Lifting her arms, she revealed her naked breasts to the mirror over the fireplace. Could Mike see her in the mirror? Perhaps; perhaps just tantalising glimpses. Smiling, she unfastened the clip in her hair and let it fall, swinging heavily on to her shoulders.

She had waited long enough now. She shook her head, so that her hair flew wild, and let the pashmina drop. Then she turned, naked, to meet Mike's gaze.

He nodded, and she realised that although she had been concentrating on performing, on putting on a good show for him, she had also become aroused. Her belly was tense with need. She hadn't even seen his penis yet, didn't know what he was like as a lover. She wanted to feel his cock in her, and she also wanted to suck him. To taste him, yes. She wanted to stroke her hands across his broad chest, feel the strength of him, learn his body.

Unwittingly she took a step towards him, then hesitated. But he was smiling, he must approve. 'Very classical,' he said. 'I can see that what you write comes from the heart.'

'I don't know about the heart,' she said. Her own voice surprised her. It was husky and dark with desire.

'Wherever it comes from, I approve,' Mike said. He sat up and reached forward with both hands, stroking her from her rib-cage down to her hip bones, trickling his fingers over her smooth soft flesh. She shivered. He held her more firmly, the tips of his fingers digging in, and pulled her towards him.

'Mike,' she began. She wanted to ask him to strip too, to show her his body as she had showed him hers. But the moment she spoke he looked up at her, frowning, as if he had already detected a different tone of voice. She fell silent, and he smiled.

'You seem very aware that you have a gorgeous and positively Romanesque arse,' Mike commented. 'Which is a recommendation, after all. Luscious, white haunches, just what the doctor ordered. Turn around, Catherine.'

He always sounded as if he was on the edge of joking, and yet not joking. Did he really admire her bottom? Flattered, wondering, she turned around.

'Ah, yes,' Mike whispered. 'Beautiful.'

His hands rested on her hip bones, holding her still, and then she felt his lips just at the top of her crease, soft, warm. She let out her breath in a quick long sigh and Mike's hands slid up her body to cup her breasts even as his tongue touched her, slipping downwards to enter her crease.

She stiffened with surprise. None of the men in her life had ever suggested or intimated a desire for anal sex, and none of them had ever tried to lick between her buttocks. Plenty of women found anal sex erotic, she knew, but she was prepared to bet that they thought about it a lot more than they did it. It was bound to hurt, and it would probably smell, and she didn't fancy it.

So she stiffened and pulled away a little as Mike's warm, questing tongue probed between her buttocks, slowly approaching her anus. He didn't stop what he was doing, but his hands left her breasts. With one hand he took hold of her upper arm, and the other returned to her belly, pressing hard, holding her still.

She didn't like the feeling of restraint. 'Mike,' she said.

His face lifted for a moment from her buttocks. 'Trust me,' he said.

Trust him? Why should she? That sounded like a command, as well. Didn't he know how to ask nicely?

But the sensation of his tongue squirming back between her buttocks, stroking softly and leaving a cool line behind it, was not exactly unpleasant. In fact, it was nice. She stood still, eyes closed, breathing shallowly. Mike's tongue moved down, down, and then it probed gently at her anus. She tensed, tightening her buttocks, and then, as he continued to caress, relaxed.

It felt wonderful, soft and delicious. She let her head fall back and found that despite herself she had let out a little moan. Mike went on probing with his tongue, and his restraining hands moved, sliding over her body to find her breasts and caress their aching points.

'Oh,' Catherine moaned, abandoned to the sensation now. She longed to feel something touching her clit, but she didn't dare move her hands herself in case Mike disapproved and stopped what he was doing. She knew how wet she was, how ready. She wanted to feel him fuck her.

As if he read her mind, one of Mike's hands left her nipples and slid down her belly. His fingers coaxed their way through the crisp curls of her pubes and eased between her legs. He began to stroke her and push his tongue further and further into her arse, and she moaned and moaned, shuddering with the urge to move and not knowing whether to push herself forward to rub her clit against his hand or backwards to take more of his tongue into her quivering anus.

'Mike,' she whimpered, 'Mike, I'm going to come. Please, Mike.' She meant please stop, because she didn't want to come this way again, like a sex object, stimulated by a man who hadn't even unbuttoned his trousers. She wanted to come with him inside her, feeling him moving. But she couldn't tear herself away from his hands, and when she said please perhaps he thought she meant yes, because he thrust his tongue even deeper into her and squeezed her breast and pressed his fingers hard against her aching clitoris and before she could stop herself the orgasm was there, shuddering through her until she nearly fell, making her cry out and stagger.

Almost at once he was on his feet, turning her so that she stood naked in his arms. 'Your arse tastes good,' he whispered. 'Almost as good as your cunt. You taste delicious.' And he leant down and kissed her, hard, and even as she accepted his tongue in her mouth she thought of his tongue up her arse and didn't know whether to struggle and spit him out or suck him in deep and relish the taste. If there was any taste. Her head was spinning, and she did nothing but hang in his arms and moan under his kiss.

After a moment he drew back, and as the dizziness of her orgasm receded she opened her eyes and looked up at him. He held her eyes, smiling lazily, drawing out the anticipation.

'Now,' he said, 'I think I want to fuck you.'

She closed her eyes in blissful relief. Thank God, he wanted just what she did.

'Well,' he whispered, and she opened her eyes again to look at him, because his voice sounded mischievous, somehow, even threatening. His eyes were narrow, glinting slits. 'Hmm,' he said, 'you thought about drawing the curtains, didn't you? To stop people seeing in through the window?'

She didn't nod, just drew back a little, apprehensive now. He smiled, then kissed her again, hard and deep. She couldn't help but respond, pressing her body against him, trying to feel his body through his clothes. His hands rested on her buttocks, caressing, making her hungry again. It was as if that first orgasm had been nothing but an appetiser, a delicious morsel to be savoured before the main course.

He pushed against her and she felt his cock through his jeans. She could actually sense the heat of it. It felt hard and big, and she wanted it. His lips brushed her ear, and he whispered, 'Go and stand in front of the window.'

She started and pulled away. 'What?'

'I want to fuck you against the window,' he said.

She shook her head, more and more firmly. 'No,' she said, when she trusted her voice. 'No, Mike, for God's sake. There's a bloody shopping street underneath us. No.'

He looked at her coolly, then shrugged and turned away. 'Okay,' he said, picking up his jacket from the chair. 'Your call.'

Did he really mean to go? He must be kidding. She had felt his erection, pulsing and hard. He wanted to have sex too, surely. They would be able to think of something they both wanted to do. 'Mike, don't be ridiculous,' she said.

He turned at that and regarded her coldly, and she felt more than just naked. He looked dangerous, angry. 'I am never ridiculous,' he said. 'I say what I want. If I don't get it, I leave. That's the way it is.'

Her head was throbbing with confusion and frustration. 'Mike, you can't just –'

'Then I go,' he said, and he moved again towards the door.

Did he want her, or not? Did he not feel any need at all? Why couldn't she match his self-control? Her pride struggled with her urgent need to be fucked and, to her shame, it lost. 'Mike,' she said, and he stopped with his hand on the latch. 'Please don't go.'

He came back into the room at that, slinging his jacket down again. He walked straight across to her, put his arms around her and kissed her mouth. She gasped and didn't resist him.

'Now,' he said, when the kiss ended, 'we'll go over to the window.'

He led her there, his arm around her waist. She didn't exactly resist, but as they approached the pool of light that would show her to anyone looking in from outside she stiffened. As if in answer Mike's arm tensed, guiding her forward. She thought that he would let her stop once they reached the brightness, but he didn't. What did he mean to do, take her on the desk?

A few paces from the window he stopped, and she stopped too, feeling a sense of relief, even of gratitude. Then behind her his voice said softly, 'Walk right up to the window.'

The sill was hardly higher than her knees. The whole of her body would be on show to anyone who cared to look up. 'Mike –'

'Walk right up to the window,' he repeated, and his voice brooked no disagreement.

She had never been so aware of the wooden struts between the panes, of the slight warping in the panes themselves, the only flimsy barriers between herself and the outside world. Looking down she could see the irregularities in the glass. But this would be more apparent to someone on the inside, looking out. Someone on the outside, looking in, would see a naked woman standing at the window.

Beneath her the crowds passed to and fro on Henry's Parade. But none of them looked up. She looked across at the windows in the gatehouse, but they were dark. It seemed that there was nobody to see her.

But they could. All she needed was for one curious tourist to turn their eyes from the towers of the chapel to the eaves of her building and she would be exposed to them. When she saw them looking, what would she do?

'Very good,' said Mike quietly behind her. His hands touched her shoulders, ran down her back, cupped the curves of her buttocks. She closed her eyes, shivering. Her desire had not gone away. In fact, the fear of being seen seemed almost to increase it. She could almost wish that one of the hurrying multitude would actually look up.

'Brace yourself,' Mike said. 'Lean forward.'

'The window –'

He pushed aside the curtain of her hair, then nuzzled the nape of her neck. Her whole body quivered with reaction. 'I want you to push your breasts against the window,' he whispered in her ear. 'I want you to feel the glass cold against your nipples. I want anybody looking up to see your breasts flattened, like two moons.'

For a moment she shut her eyes tightly and almost sobbed, not knowing whether she wanted to obey him or flee. But his body was big and warm behind her, and she did not want enough to escape. He leant against her, very slightly, and as if the pressure was the signal she had needed she leant forward, placed her hands against the struts between the panes of the windows, and rested her cheek on the glass.

So cold, unyielding. When her nipples touched the window she shuddered, unable to restrain the response. Mike's words echoed in her mind. Someone looking up would hardly see the shadowy figure of a man behind her. Their eyes would focus on her face, and on her breasts, flattened against the glass like two moons, her nipples like eyes.

He was close behind her, not touching her now. She heard the rustle of his clothes and knew he must be unfastening his jeans, taking out his cock. She wanted to see it, wanted to watch him preparing himself, but she did not dare turn her head. Another rustle must be a condom packet. Just as well he had remembered. She was so far gone with wanting him that she might even have said yes to unprotected sex.

Still the people passed by beneath her in an unending, unnoticing stream. She closed her eyes. Her sense of anticipation and need was so great it did not make sense that nobody else could feel it. She did not want to watch their indifference.

'Now,' Mike whispered behind her. His hands were on her haunches, pulling them a little away from the window. She began to move her feet apart, but he nudged them back together again, so that she was standing with her legs pressed together and her bottom stuck out.

God almighty, did he mean to take her up the arse? That would be too much, more than she wanted. She was going to say something, to protest, but then she felt the head of his cock nudging at her soft entrance and she moaned with pleasure and sheer relief.

She was very wet, and he entered her easily. As he slid into her she let out a long cry. He seemed to go on for ever, and the sensation of being filled was so blissful that for a moment she forgot about her strange position and the people below her. Then he withdrew, paused, and thrust into her again. And again. His rhythm was strong and slow, and it was wonderful. She groaned with each thrust, squirming to bring more of her body into contact with him. It was as if he was faceless, a stranger.

There was no pressure on her clit, but her legs were so tightly together that she found that by squeezing her thighs she could send a pulse of pleasure through her body. As he slid in and out of her she squeezed hard, regularly, and felt the waves of sensation begin to build that would lead to another orgasm.

Now the coldness of the glass on her breasts was an erotic spur, driving her towards climax. Whenever he thrust into her, her body was pushed against the window, flattening her nipples against the panes. Someone looking up would know immediately what was going on. They would know that she was being fucked, and that she didn't care if people saw.

She did care. She was ashamed and excited at the same time. It wasn't enough to stand there with closed eyes feeling Mike's penis slide in and out of her, she had to know if someone was looking. Still groaning with pleasure, she opened her eyes and looked down.

Below her, on the cobbles of the gatehouse, a young man in college rowing kit was standing, staring up, his mouth open. He had seen her, that was for sure. She felt as if she looked right into his eyes. He was nice-looking, with a shock of dark hair, and his expression was of disbelief and even wonderment.

Mike's hands grasped her waist to hold her steady as he began to move faster. He was really fucking her now, plunging into her hard, slapping his body against hers. She squirmed again and again to stimulate her clit, and without taking her eyes from the watching face she opened her mouth and moaned.

'Someone can see you,' Mike hissed behind her.

'Yes,' she gasped, 'yes.'

'He can see your breasts squashing against the glass. He can see you moaning. He knows someone is fucking you.'

The young man was still staring. His tanned cheeks were flushing slightly. Nobody seemed to have noticed his abstraction, but her eyes were fixed on his. 'Yes,' she moaned again, feeling her orgasm lurking in the pit of her belly. 'Yes.'

'He knows there's a cock in your cunt. He knows you're going to come soon.'

'Yes. Yes.'

It was as if the real sex was taking place between her and the watcher below her, as if Mike was nothing but the instrument of her pleasure. She felt her orgasm approaching, heaving in the pit of her belly and between her tightly-clamped thighs, and she opened her lips and cried out, wishing that the young man could hear her, wishing that he could really experience her climax. 'Yes,' she gasped again, all other words lost. 'Yes.'

Mike growled and held her hard and tight as he shafted her, so deep that it was almost painful. One hand released her waist and reached around in front of her, shoving between her legs so roughly that she flinched. Below her the young man watching flinched too, and knowing that he could respond to her feelings made her want to come, and as Mike found her clit with his finger and rubbed it hard she did come, spilling into an orgasm so strong that she slumped forward against the window, breasts and belly and face flattened against the glass, panting and whimpering.

She hardly noticed that Mike had finished too, but he

must have done because the next moment he withdrew from her. She gasped for a moment, then pushed herself away from the window, looking down, eager to make eye contact again.

But the young watcher had gone. She hadn't even seen which way he had gone, in to college or out. Had he known her? Had he recognised the writer in residence? What would he say to his friends? Horrified, she turned away from the window.

Mike had already removed the condom, disposed of it, and tucked himself away. She felt a flash of annoyance. Was she never going to get to see him? Was he in some way deformed, that he didn't want to show himself to her? He hadn't felt deformed, but why so shy?

He smiled at her. 'I'll see you soon,' he said.

Off already? Well, that was par for the course. She would have said something scathing, except that her orgasm had been so good. Perhaps this just went to prove that you could have sex without any sort of a relationship, and that it could be excellent, rule-breaking sex to boot. So all she said, as she went to retrieve her clothes, was, 'OK. Whenever.'

He picked up his jacket and went to the door without another word, without a kiss or a backward glance. Well, presumably he had got what he wanted. He was clear enough about it, for God's sake.

Catherine wrapped the pashmina around her. She could have put the same clothes on, but it would be just as easy to dress in jeans and go and see about that bike. She decided that that was what she was going to do. She felt as if she wanted to slump on the sofa and stare into the gas fire, recovering, but she wouldn't. If Mike felt able to jump up and walk away, then she damn well would, as well.

Odd. She had begun their encounter angry, and she was still angry. Normally after sex she felt mellow, but not now. Perhaps being dominated wasn't all that it was cracked up to be.

But those eyes below, looking up. That had been very

erotic. Very powerful. If Mike had any more tricks like that up his snake-tattooed sleeve, she was interested in finding out about them.

Dressed in jeans and a fleece, she went to turn off her computer. The icon at the bottom of the screen told her she had a new email, and she thought she ought to take a look.

Her heart jumped. It was from James.

For a moment her hand hovered over the mouse, ready to open the message and read it. But then she remembered how long she had waited, how many emails she had sent him, how deep and brown the silence had been, and she closed down the computer.

He could bloody well wait. She was going to buy a bike.

Chapter Six

*T*he bike shop on Henry's Parade was rather tatty, with peeling paint, but the bikes hanging up in the window looked shiny and new. In one window was a mountain bike, all aggressive paint job and handlebars turning up like a bull's horns, and in the other was a racer with sleek lines and tyres as thin as scissor blades.

Catherine reflected briefly on the fact that she knew nothing at all about bikes, then went in.

The place was full of bikes. Literally full. There were lines of bikes in racks on the floor, another set of them hanging in racks at head height, and even more of them suspended from gadgets in the ceiling. Only the wall by the door and the wall behind the till were free of them, and they were hung all over with gadgets, accessories and clothing. There was nobody in sight to advise her: the shop was empty. Catherine found herself staring at a set of Lycra cycle shorts about the size of a postage stamp, as unsuitable for a Roman arse as could be imagined. She shook her head and turned instead to browse along the rows of bikes.

Tourer. Off roader. Racer. Hybrid. What on earth? And the range of prices was mad, everything from £150 to thousands. She shook her head, wondering if this would all be too much trouble.

'Need any help?' said a voice behind her.

The voice came from a man in his early thirties, watching her with an amiable smile. Her first impression was of the way he stood, very straight, belly tucked in, shoulders back, like a fighter waiting to begin a round. Only afterwards did she notice that he was a little under middle height and stocky. She said, 'I think I want a bike. My friend told me I ought to get one.'

He rolled his eyes, which were hazel and fringed with bristly dark lashes. 'I suppose your friend told you all about them and just what you ought to get.'

'No,' she said, puzzled, 'just that it would come in handy here for getting around.'

He nodded. His face was heavy and oddly foreign-looking, but it was very animated, like a cartoon character's. It made her want to smile. 'Thank God for that,' he said. 'I get so fed up with people coming in here with second-hand information and thinking they know all about bikes. They don't. I know all about bikes. Pleased to meet you,' he added, with a charming smile, 'I'm Andy.'

'Catherine,' she said, accepting his extended hand and returning his smile without meaning to. This was a weird shop. Since when did shop assistants introduce themselves and shake hands with you?

'Right,' he said, 'so what do you want it for?'

She shrugged. 'I don't really know.' That sounded really feeble, so she explained, 'Riding from place to place, mostly. And when I'm back in London I suppose I might get odds and ends of shopping on it. And maybe ride on the tow path. I suppose.'

'Not triathlon or mountain climbing, then,' he said with a grin. 'Budget?'

'I don't want a crap bike,' she said. 'I think you get what you pay for.'

'Absolutely. If you want something decent, you'll need to spend upwards of £350. Is that OK?'

She liked his no-nonsense, no-bullshit attitude, and

she liked his face, too. He seemed like someone you could trust. 'What would you suggest?'

'I'd start off with a hybrid. Mostly for roads but it won't mind the odd bit of path riding. Something like this one.'

She looked at the bike he indicated and wrinkled her nose. 'It's purple.'

'Full marks for observation,' he said. 'Is that a problem?'

'I don't want a purple bike.'

'What is it about women?' Andy demanded. 'I show you a bike that's fit for the purpose and you complain about the colour? What difference does it make what colour it is?'

'I bet your bike isn't powder-puff pink,' she retorted.

'True,' he admitted. 'It's black. But what's wrong with purple?'

'I'd like a zippy colour. Like that one.' She gestured at a metallic orange bike above her head.

'Yeah, that one's horny, but it's a fifteen-hundred-pound mountain bike. Not worth all that extra for the colour, is it? Although, I mean, if you've got so much money that you want to buy one for the colour regardless of whether it's what you need, I'll take the money, it's no skin off my nose.'

She laughed. 'I just don't want a purple one.'

'Another fifty quid in my hand and I'll spray the frame for you, any colour you like.'

'Could be tempting.'

Were they flirting? They were just talking about bikes, but it felt as if they were flirting. His eyes were laughing at her, and there was something about the way he was standing that made her feel both self-conscious and incredibly conscious of him, of his body, of his proximity to her.

'Or spend a bit more and there's this one,' he gestured up at the racks. 'Nice bike, this one, hub gears makes it very simple, and it's a remarkably inoffensive black in colour. More profit for the shop, too, though speaking personally I'd go for the chance to spray your frame.'

Definitely flirting. Was this sensible, with Mike on the horizon and an email from James to read? Oh, bollocks to it. Flirting never did anyone any harm.

'Any colour you like as long as it's black,' she said. 'What else is good about it?'

'Woman's specific design and a nice low crossbar so you can wear a skirt if you want, mudguards, reliable, sturdy but not too heavy, it's a good 'un.'

She wrinkled her nose. 'I put on jeans specially.'

'Where would the world be if women couldn't wear skirts when they ride bikes? Think of all the inadvertent legs we wouldn't get to see.'

'Can I try it?' She decided to ignore the comment about the legs.

He shook his head. 'Nope.'

'What, you expect me to part with four hundred quid just because you say so?'

'No.' He grinned at her. 'It's the wrong size for you. Look, how tall are you, five five?'

She nodded. He was right to within an inch.

'And longish legs for your height. You need a much bigger frame than this one. Try this one out and you'll have your knees around your ears like a bloody heron and you won't buy the bike, will you? There's one in our storeroom in Cherry Hinton but I'll need to get it here and build it for you. Could have it ready for tomorrow first thing, if you want to come back and take it for a spin. Or are you in a rush?'

It was so pleasant to talk to someone uncomplicated. He came across as saying exactly what he thought. 'I'm not in a rush,' she said. 'I'll come back tomorrow.'

'Far to come?'

'No, no. I'm just in St Henry's, two steps really.'

'It'll be ready for you. See you tomorrow, then, Catherine.'

'Thanks, Andy.'

For a moment she thought that he would say something else to her before she left the shop, but then another customer came in and he turned to serve them, greeting them with the same attentive cheerful smile.

Just flirting, then. Nevertheless, she walked back to college feeling better, as if the lingering anger and resentment had been somehow tamed. Strong enough to read James's email, whatever pathetic excuse it might contain.

As she walked past the college gatehouse towards her stairs the slanting evening sun caught at her eyes and made her stop. She went back to the gatehouse, where the sun was pouring through, and stood beneath its shelter to look at the court. It was easy to forget, living and working here, how beautiful the surroundings were. The lawn was a square of perfect green, and the statue of St Henry in its centre was a pale gold in the fading sunlight. He held out his hands meekly, as if in protest, no doubt because last night yet another group of inebriated undergraduates had placed an upended beer mug on the top of his crown. Students and fellows walked past, ignoring the beauty of the evening, scorning the tourists who came in through the gatehouse and stopped as if struck, gaping before they dragged out their cameras and camcorders and eagerly began to film. Perhaps the tourists were right, appreciating what they saw. Certainly it couldn't be right to take it for granted.

Not for the first time, she wondered if perhaps she could seek a way to stay here, among all this. Surely she'd be able to do just what she wanted here, out of the way of London and all the business of the real world.

Then she laughed at herself. James was three times as productive as she was, and he didn't even have a real place that he called home. Okay, he was a journalist, not a novelist, but what had she produced since she had been here? What had the writer in residence written? Bugger all, basically. She was beginning to believe that her whole idea for the novel was useless, and as for

94

Gaius Lucius Catullus, well, the less she thought about him, the better.

Time to read that bloody email. She turned away from the sheeting sunlight and headed towards the little inconspicuous door that concealed the entrance to her rooms.

As she approached the door it opened and Maggie came out, very animated and ridiculously edible in combat trousers and a little fleece that showed her navel. She had been looking pale and a little abstracted recently, but now she seemed to be back on top form. She beamed when she saw Catherine, and said at once, 'Hey, do you want to come and have some fun?'

Catherine knew what that meant where Maggie was concerned, and although she was tempted she replied, 'Not right now, Maggie.'

'No, I don't mean you and me, not this minute. I've got a cunning plan.' Maggie shook back her hair, revealing her earrings, which today were a pair of very small sheep, complete with black faces, little stick-like black legs, and wool. 'There's a few guys I've been meaning to introduce you to, and I thought I might have a little party in my room tonight. Just a few drinks and bites and we'll make our own entertainment. Want to come?'

Catherine made an uncertain face. 'I don't know, Maggie.'

'Hey, why not? It'll be fun.'

Why not? Because I'm thirty-something and your male friends will all be in their early twenties, and they'll be after your little blonde body, not me. 'I think I might be a party pooper.'

Maggie raised her eyebrows. 'I hardly think so. Oh, go on.' Her voice changed to a wheedle. 'Please, Catherine. I want you to be there.' She came closer, too close for friendship, and looked up at Catherine beguilingly. 'At least if you're there I'll know that there'll be some half-decent company.'

'Well . . .' Catherine hesitated. 'Well, maybe. Perhaps.'

'Great.' Maggie stood on her toes to kiss Catherine's

cheek, a very chaste kiss, nothing the street need be ashamed of. 'I'll get working on it. See you later.'

And she was gone. Catherine watched her bounce across Henry's Parade, then pushed through the door and headed up to her room.

Why was she so reluctant to open James's email? Was she so angry with him, after a fraught silence of nearly two months? Perhaps she ought to ignore it, leave it for another time.

But putting things off rarely achieved anything. She sat down at her computer, switched it on, launched email straight away and clicked on the new message.

> Hi C
>
> Sorry havnt emailed u for yonks. Really sorry. Have read yours, glad re Cantab, but have been v preoccupied. Not just work. Ready? Am in love.
>
> Seriously. I'm in love, Catherine. She's a Malay girl, her name's Elaine. I've never met anyone like her. She's – perfect, I suppose. Can you tell how serious I am? I'm writing in connected English, for once.
>
> I'm trying to get a permanent post out here so we can get married. There might be a few problems, she's part of an anti-government faction, but I'm sure I've dealt with worse things. I just want to be with her.
>
> Sorry again about the long silence. I'll let you know how I get on over here. Do you want to come to my wedding? It'll probably be in Kuala Lumpur. It would be good to have it on the walkway between the twin towers, 400m up in the air. That's how I feel at the moment, all the time. If you want to come, I've got plenty of air miles for your ticket, it won't have to cost you a penny. It would be good to see you, and you could meet Elaine.
>
> Write soon, Catherine.

The words on the screen seemed to move and shimmer, as if they had a life of their own. Catherine sat back a little, her eyes glazing.

Had she missed something? Should she have seen

this coming? But he'd been out of touch before, and there had been no reason to suppose that this was any different. And he'd had flings before, and so had she. It was just that all the time there had been this unspoken arrangement, convenient for both of them, that at some unspecified future time they would be together.

And now he was getting married. To a stranger.

Moving blindly, she got up from the desk and went over to the cupboard where she kept a bottle of wine. Red wine, sealed with a Vacuvin. She poured herself a large glass, amazed that her hands were steady, and sat down on the sofa.

Why hadn't he warned her? Why hadn't he told her what was happening to him? Why wait until this point and then drop it on her like a bucket of ice down the back of her neck? What had she done wrong?

Time passed. She did not notice the light dying outside the window. Her wine was gone. She poured another glass and returned to the sofa. When someone knocked on the door she ignored it, and jumped when the door opened anyway and Maggie's voice said, 'Catherine?'

She didn't want to tell Maggie about this. Maggie was just a girl: she thought nothing could hurt her, she would laugh. Swallowing her wine, she turned with a half smile and said, 'Sorry, miles away.'

'They'll be here in about an hour,' Maggie said. Her little face was bright. 'They really want to meet you, Catherine.'

'Who is they?' Catherine was playing for time.

'You've met Ash, of course. And a fresher, Dave, I met him rowing, and another friend of mine, Bill, he's a graduate student.'

Perhaps this could be something to take her mind off James. Catherine turned round, resting her chin on her hands on the back of the sofa, and frowned at Maggie. 'Maggie, what exactly are your intentions for this evening?'

Maggie's eyes became big and round. 'To have sex with them, of course. Obviously.'

'Obviously, yes. And what about me?'

'Oh yes, I want to have sex with you, too.' Maggie grinned.

Catherine sighed and shook her head. Her mind was full of that bloody email. The prospect of an evening of sex didn't even seem real, never mind attractive. 'Maggie, I just don't think I can,' she said, and suddenly her eyes were full of tears and she couldn't hide them.

Maggie's face changed. She looked older in an instant. She didn't say anything, just walked over to Catherine's desk and read what was on the screen. Her lips compressed, and when she came back to Catherine she looked resolute.

'Look,' she said, 'whatever he's done, you won't help yourself by sitting here and drowning in a bottle all on your own. Catherine, these guys really do want to meet you. They're just boys, they think older women are really horny. Come and knock them dead, have some fun, prove that you can enjoy yourself without James, or whatever his name is.'

Maggie pretended to be an airhead, but under the surface she was shrewd. There was something in what she said. Catherine wiped her eyes with the back of her hand and said, 'Well.'

She had a sudden image of her feelings, like a table set with a beautiful white tablecloth and silver and fine glass and china, and then some magician comes and whips the tablecloth away. The place settings all remain where they are, but without the tablecloth everything looks completely different, and every item is shaking, as if it could fall over at any minute.

But what was she supposed to do? Go into mourning? No. She wasn't going to take the blame for James. She drew in a deep breath and looked up. 'All right. All right, Maggie, I'll come.'

'Good.' Maggie nodded, not smiling yet. 'Get ready,

then, darling. Take your time. Make them sweat for it. I'll keep them hot, don't worry.'

So what does one wear for this kind of occasion? What does one wear to a sex party? Catherine looked at her clothes with a sense of discontent. She didn't own anything made of rubber or even leather, apart from shoes, and she did not own a single spike heel. So what would she wear?

Something, obviously, which would make her look attractive and feel sexy. She couldn't hope to look petite and fragile, like Maggie, so why try to compete? She would show off what she had to offer, a splendid body, fine breasts, and a Roman arse.

She pulled out a long, straight wrap skirt made of silky jersey and a matching ballerina top. The fabric was soft and smooth and it would cling to every curve she possessed. It was also simplicity itself to remove, held together by no more than a knot for the skirt and another for the top. It would require carefully chosen underwear, a bra with a hint of uplift, a pretty thong. Fortunately she had just the thing, black and amber lace, expensive undies bought with an unexpected cheque from a magazine. They looked the part. She doubted that Maggie's friends would be accustomed to such costly gift-wrapping.

Time now for a long, luxurious bath, something to get her into the right mood. Not for the first time, she blessed the college authorities for having given her a room with its own bathroom. Many of the older building still had shared bathrooms, and in fact Maggie had to go down a corridor and up three steps to hers. But the room allocated to the writer in residence had a bathroom, small, but equipped with a full size bath, a telephone-handle shower, and ample hot water.

She put on some music: Elisabeth Schwarzkopf singing Strauss's *Four Last Songs* a shimmering, ethereal voice in music of such density and texture that it was like a whole landscape. Surrounded by the richness of

Strauss's sounds, she started the bath running and added essential oils, a drop at a time. Rose, because nothing smelt quite so beautiful. Vetiver, because its earthy, woody tones reminded her of the odours of sex. And frankincense, because its smoky ancient smell would make people think of churches and museums and ancient Rome.

The warm, silky water welcomed her. She lay back in it, resting the weight of her head on her coiled and pleated hair, letting out her tension with a long sigh.

And as she closed her eyes, James came back to haunt her.

Perhaps because they met so rarely, James liked to make an event of sex. They would stay in bed all day, making love from the moment they woke in the morning until they fell asleep. Once or twice he had fallen asleep with his softening cock still buried inside her, and when he woke he began to move again almost at once, so that she woke to feel his penis stiffening and thickening actually within her, moving from sleep into sexual pleasure as if it were a waking dream.

He used to love to lick her, slowly, gently, exploring her throat and shoulders with his tongue, wetting her nipples with his saliva, sucking slowly on her engorged clitoris until orgasm was inevitable. She had known him a long time, and she was always completely relaxed, knowing that she would come, knowing that her pleasure was important to him, able to give herself over to the sensations utterly and float in bliss as in a warm sea.

Was he doing that now, to his new woman? Was he lying in bed with Elaine, touching her, sweeping his tongue across her flesh, making her cry out?

For a moment she felt black misery descending. But she was not going to allow it. What if he was with someone else? She was about to go to – to what? To a Roman orgy? Yes, maybe. She was going to enjoy herself.

She didn't want to think about James any more, but

100

she did want to think about sex. She wanted to get herself in the mood for the party. She wanted to arrive on Maggie's doorstep with her cheeks slightly flushed and her eyes sparkling, looking the part.

So what should it be? She ran a little water out of the bath, then lifted the telephone-handle shower and adjusted the water to the right temperature. When it was warm enough, she let it begin to pour on to her body, her breasts, her throat, her thighs. She closed her eyes and let her mental file spin open, looking for the right fantasy. Not the one she told Mike. That was always her favourite, but it wasn't right for now.

Perhaps it was the woody smell of the vetiver, or the rich shimmering sweep of Strauss's musical landscapes, but she was outside now, walking in the foothills of high mountains on a spring day of such glowing perfection that it was like another Eden. She was Eve, naked, barefoot on the new grass. When she looked down, tiny mountain flowers sprang between her toes like jewels. The sun was warm on her pale skin, but there was enough of the snow-chill in the barely stirring air to make her backbone shiver and her nipples tighten. She crossed a little stream, swollen with milky snow-melt, and its kiss on her ankles was icy. When she stooped to cup the water to her lips, the taste was sharp and smooth, like lemons and stones.

The sun grew stronger, warming her through and through. She wandered onwards, looking up to the blue sky, feeling beneath her feet the grass softer than down. The greenness and growing things filled her with joy and a sense of her own belonging to the world. She touched her breasts, and the sweet tang that darted through her was like the pain of growing which makes the trees spring into leaf, as if her breasts were the buds that would burgeon new life.

A little way on she found a tiny green meadow beside the stream, below a leaping waterfall where the spray made rainbows. There were tall trees on the other side of the stream with bluebells beneath them, but the meadow was starred with daisies and celandines and brilliant blue flowers like fragments of the sky scattered on the grass. She sat down, and the grass stems prickled against the backs of her thighs and reached up between them as if they wanted to arouse her. Her juices woke and stirred, but for now she did nothing to assuage them. She reached out around her and picked the flowers, one by one, and sitting in the glowing sunshine she made them into a garland of white and blue and gold and set it on her dark hair.

The sun caressed her. She lay back on the soft grass, feeling the warmth like great soft hands running up and down her body. Beneath her the grass was cool, and the contrast of temperature was itself an arousal. Her own hands followed where the sun's hands guided them, cupping her breasts, sliding over the soft plain of her belly, skimming her pubic hair, pressing between her legs.

Then something made her stop and sit up. Her eyes were dimmed blue with the sun. As they cleared, she looked into the shadows beneath the trees beyond the stream. There was a deer there, come down to drink with its little spotted fawn. They saw her move and took fright, bounding gracefully away on slender legs. Had it been their movements that she heard?

No. A little way upstream from where the deer had stood there was a figure, a human figure, a man. A man, watching her as she lay in the sun and stroked herself. He was naked also, and his body was strong and hard. His rough curling hair hung on his shoulders and his eyes were bright in the shadows. There was a thatch of dark hair at his crotch, and within it his penis was already erect, thick and firm and ready.

She was not afraid. Why should Eve fear Adam? She got to her feet and walked towards him, and saw as she approached him her own glory reflected in his eyes. She was Eve, the only woman, naked and bathed in sunlight, crowned with flowers, shimmering with the power of her beauty in the morning of the world. Adam would do anything for her. He would give up Paradise for her.

There were boulders in the bed of the stream, and from one to another she crossed dryshod, laughing as she balanced. Adam stood on the other side, waiting for her, bright eyes yearning. When she stepped up on to the bank he reached out for her. His hands were rough and strong. They found her breasts and squeezed them, tightened on her pointed nipples, made her gasp. He did not speak, but guided her over the moss and the bluebells to a great smooth-trunked tree and made her lean against it, legs apart. He leant against the trunk, hands braced on either side of her head, and the head of his penis nudged between her legs, finding its way as if her vagina were a strong magnet. She was already wet, and when it found the notch the broad smooth head slipped up into her without hesitation, stretching her, filling her.

He was big, and he gave no quarter. He fucked her as if he had been waiting for her for a thousand years. She held on to the trunk of the tree to steady herself, gasping with her eyes open, watching his brow furrow and his nostrils flare as he ploughed his way into her. She was soon almost at the point of orgasm, but it would not come, and she hung there, waiting, crying out with every fierce stroke, and then at last he took his hands from the tree and instead took hold of her breasts, pinching her nipples hard as his plunging became fast and irregular, and she put a hand down between her legs, and her orgasm took her just as she felt his cock jump and spurt within her, and then he leant forward, his hot body against her cool one, holding her against the tree, his mouth caressing the soft skin beneath her ear . . .

Catherine moved the shower away from her pubis. This was too good, too beautiful, she didn't want to come yet. She wanted it to last.

They kissed, and kissed, and kissed until his softening cock slipped out of her, and then they went hand in

103

hand to the pool beneath the waterfall and walked into it, laughing and shivering at the bitter chill of the water. They clung together for warmth, and then she was hungry for him again. But it was too cold in the water, and so he laid her on a flat rock in the sun with the chill droplets flickering against her skin and knelt between her legs and licked her, worming his tongue up within her until he had sucked out every drop of his own juice, then flickering against her clit and mouthing it until she came with a cry, staring open-eyed up into the blueness of the sky and the bright sunlight.

She couldn't wait longer. Her body writhed and contracted in pulses as her orgasm flooded through her, leaving her drained and quivering. She turned off the water and lay still, eyes closed, wondering.

Where had that fantasy come from? It was new, she had never dreamt it before. Who was her Adam? Who did he look like? Certainly not James. More like Mike, but she hadn't really seen Mike's body, so she couldn't say if he was built that way.

It seemed good to her that she had not fantasised about James or anyone like him. Strengthened by the thought, she got out of the bath and towelled herself dry, then softened her skin with a moisturiser scented with the same essential oils.

Then she looked in the mirror. Her face looked back at her, eyes wide, lips slightly parted, a flush on the cheekbones. She looked as if she had just been soundly fucked and was ready for more.

That was the right look, the right look entirely. And now, it was time to get dressed and go to Maggie's little get-together.

Chapter Seven

Dressed, scented, ready, she approached Maggie's door. She stood for a moment in the gloom of the corridor, listening, wondering.

Outside it was already dark, and not much light glimmered from under the door. Candlelight, perhaps. The music was clearer: Tom Jones singing 'Mama Told Me Not To Come'. Well, that was probably quite suitable.

A deep breath, a look down at her body, and she knocked on the door.

There was a sound of scurrying, and the door was flung open to reveal Maggie, resplendent in a little beaded halter and a scrap of handkerchief skirt, a dizzy outfit completed in its dizziness by high, strappy, transparent-heeled mules. Pop stars would have killed to look like her.

'Hi, Catherine, welcome,' Maggie exclaimed, and she reached out to catch Catherine by the arm and draw her in. Her smile was infectious, suggestive of good times to come. 'Want a drink? We're all on Jack Daniel's here.'

'Yes, sure,' Catherine said.

The room was lit only by candles, which burnt over the fireplace, on the low table in front of the sofa, in sconces on the walls, and beside the bed. The gas fire was on low, giving out a delicious gentle warmth and a muted orange glow. Maggie had tidied up the layers of dirty clothes – probably shoved them just as they came into a cupboard and shut the door – but the room looked warm, sensual and inviting. There were soft throws on the sofa and the bed, and Maggie had even gone to the trouble of plumping up the cushions.

There were also three young men in the room: two were getting up to face her with welcoming smiles and one was busy pouring a glass of Jack Daniel's for her.

Maggie closed the door. 'Let me introduce you. Ash I think you've met –'

A cool-looking young Asian: a face straight out of the *Arabian Nights*, a carefully trimmed beard at the edges of his chin and trailing smooth lines down either side of his thin mouth. Yes, they had met, when Catherine had been walking along the corridor and Ash had been trying to make his way back from the bathroom with nothing but a flannel to preserve his modesty. 'I don't think we spoke on that occasion,' Catherine said, unable to restrain a smile.

'It's a pleasure to be properly introduced,' Ash said, smiling in return. His voice was very cultured, very charming.

'And Bill,' Maggie said. The next face was older, late twenties perhaps, and it belonged to a rather ordinary-looking chap of middle height. Catherine said, 'Hi,' at the same time that Bill said, 'Pleased to meet you.' He had a nice voice and a nice smile, but otherwise she wasn't quite sure what Maggie saw in this one. However, Maggie's taste in men was eclectic, so she decided to suspend judgement for now.

'And here's Dave with your drink,' Maggie said. The last of the young men turned, holding out a glass. Their eyes met.

'Oh,' Catherine said, feeling the blush rising, unstoppable. She did not take the glass, and the young man stood there holding it as if paralysed. He was blushing, too.

106

It was the young man who had watched while Mike fucked her against the cold glass of her window. The same bright eyes, the same dark tousled hair, and at the moment the same expression of incredulity. Her stomach lurched with disbelief and the sudden memory of how aroused she had been.

'Hello there,' said Bill, his smile turning into a grin. 'Is there something here we don't know about?'

'Dave, you never told me,' said Maggie accusingly.

Catherine pulled herself together. After all, what was she here for? 'We haven't exactly met,' she said with a slight smile. 'We've just – seen each other around.'

She reached forward, took the drink from Dave's unresisting hand and sipped it. He lifted his eyebrows, then grinned, charmingly. 'I suppose you could say that,' he said.

'Hey, come on, no secrets!' Maggie exclaimed. 'What's going on?'

'Maggie, secrets are what it's all about,' Catherine said. She'd never had the chance to play the siren, the mysterious older woman, and she was looking forward to it. She drank a sip of the bourbon and rolled it around her mouth. It was neat, chilled to almost freezing by the ice, and it made her shiver and warmed her at the same time.

Tom Jones had moved on to 'Baby, It's Cold Outside.' Maggie danced in front of the fire, her beaded halter glittering. 'I vote we tickle Dave's feet until he tells us.'

'Hey, no!' Dave said, looking startled.

Another sip of bourbon, and Catherine was ready. 'Dave actually provided me with an extremely sensual experience,' she said, smiling inwardly at the way every face, including Dave's, swivelled to stare at her.

'Do tell,' Maggie said, breathlessly.

'He was there at the right moment,' Catherine said. 'I opened my eyes, and there he was.' There he had been, looking up at her, eyes fixed on hers as Mike's plunging cock brought her towards orgasm.

107

'What did he do?' Ash asked, curiosity naked in his voice.

'He watched me,' Catherine said. Sensing a tinge of disappointment in the room, she added, 'Watching can be very erotic, believe me.'

'It certainly can,' Dave said, his voice thickened with memory.

Maggie tipped her head to one side in an attitude of thought. 'Well,' she said, 'why don't we test that out?'

They all looked at her. She smiled. 'I'd like to play a sort of game,' she said. She reached under the table and brought out a jester's hat, made of multicoloured felt and complete with bells. It jingled as she moved it. 'A bit like forfeits, but not entirely. We'll play it with themes. So the first theme is Watching. What you do is, you write on one of these pieces of paper that I made earlier –' a pile of paper slips emerged from below the table '– something that you would like to watch, and you fold it up and put it in the hat. Then one of us pulls one of them out, and whatever it is happens.'

'What if one of us doesn't want to do what it says?' Dave asked, cautiously.

'Then there are forfeits.'

'Who gets to say what the forfeit is?'

'Me,' Maggie said, with decision. 'It's my party, and I know you all.'

The men exchanged glances. Catherine looked at Maggie and found her look returned. Maggie's eyes were sparkling. Catherine knew that if she wanted to change her mind, chicken out, she ought to say so now.

But she didn't want to. She wanted to dive into the evening like a warm sea, not return to her empty room and thoughts of James.

'OK,' Bill said at last, and the others nodded.

Maggie grinned and handed out slips of paper and things to write with. There was a short silence while everybody thought, chewed the ends of pencils, and wrote. Catherine looked at the other people in the room and looked at Maggie whose idea this was and wrote, *I would like to watch Maggie pick one of the men and do whatever she wants to him.* She folded up the piece of paper small and dropped it into the hat when Maggie held it out.

'So who gets to choose?' Ash asked, looking at the hat with an eager eye.

'Catherine,' Maggie said. 'She's our guest of honour.' And she held out the hat.

Suddenly Catherine wondered if this was a fix, a joke, a put-up job. Were all the other bits of paper in there the same? Did they all suggest something that she should do, something hideous and humiliating? But there was her piece, anyway. She might pick that. She reached in and found a folded slip and drew it out.

She knew before she unfolded it that it wasn't hers. The writing was small and hard to read in the gloom: she had to hold it up to a candle.

'What does it say?' Maggie demanded.

Catherine swallowed. Her mouth was dry, her tongue felt unwilling to move. She forced the sounds out. 'It says, I want to see Maggie and Catherine getting it on.'

The men growled, a deep susurration of approval. Catherine looked from the piece of paper up to Maggie and wasn't surprised to see her smiling. 'Well,' Maggie said, 'that gives us a lot of latitude.'

'But what I meant was –' Dave said.

'If you meant something specific, you should have written it down,' Catherine cut in, determined not to let Dave impose something on her. 'As it is, we get to use our imaginations. Isn't that right, Maggie?'

'Absolutely right,' Maggie said. She looked surprised and pleased, as if she hadn't expected Catherine to take the initiative. 'Did you have something in mind?'

Catherine did have something in mind. It was something she wanted to do, but it also had the advantage of making Maggie the main focus of attention, at least to begin with, while she got used to the idea. 'Yes,' she said, putting down the slip of paper. 'Yes, Maggie, I have.'

She came close to Maggie, close enough to feel the warmth of the fire. She could sense that the men were staring, as if they were hardly able to believe that something was going to happen, but she didn't want to look at them. This time she didn't need to see their hungry eyes to know that they were watching her. 'My idea is about that skirt,' she said, and Maggie glanced down at the little scrap of fabric that draped over her slender thighs. 'It's just irresistible, Maggie. It invites someone to put her hands on your thighs and slide them upwards, doesn't it?'

Maggie's eyes were fixed on hers, dark and eager. It was surprisingly easy to ignore the watching men, and almost equally easy to speak her desires aloud, so that the audience could share them. Catherine took a final step and slipped her hands under the hem of the skirt to touch Maggie's legs.

Maggie shivered and let out a little sound, as if she was cold. Catherine let her hands slide up under the skirt, towards the top of Maggie's thighs. The flesh she touched was warm and smooth. She hovered her lips in front of Maggie's mouth, then, very softly, kissed her.

It was a long, slow kiss. Catherine's hands rested at the hollow of Maggie's hips, her thumbs just brushing the edge of a tiny pair of knickers, feeling the swell of the soft pubic mound. She edged her thumbs a little closer, pushing, and Maggie moaned into her open mouth.

'I'm going to make you come, Maggie,' she whispered as the kiss ended. She was filled with a reckless eagerness to show these young men something they would remember all their lives. 'I'm going to make you scream. Tell me where the toys are.'

'Under the table,' Maggie muttered. 'Everything's under the table.'

Catherine nodded, then nudged closer with her thumbs. Maggie's panties were already very warm and beginning to feel damp. She squeezed Maggie's mound between her thumbs, kneading it, avoiding a direct touch on the clit. Maggie closed her eyes and pushed her hips forward, inviting more.

'Not yet,' Catherine whispered. 'Not yet.' She took her hands away and reached behind Maggie's neck for the fastening of her halter. It was a single button and loop. As it came loose she held the halter in place, then kissed Maggie again, quickly, to get her to open her eyes.

'Maggie,' she whispered, 'I'm going to suck your breasts now. Afterwards, when your nipples are wet, I want you to pinch them and squeeze them, just the way you like it.'

'Yes,' Maggie breathed, her eyes slipping shut.

Catherine let the little halter loose and it slid down to hang around Maggie's waist, revealing her soft buds of breasts. She cupped one breast in her hand, smoothed the skin, pressed its curve with her palm, then stooped to take the tight nipple in her mouth. Maggie whimpered as she sucked on the swelling flesh, and cried out loud when she nipped it between her teeth. When it was fully erect, swollen and hard, she turned to the other breast and sucked again. Then she slipped to her knees and pushed her hands once more beneath the hem of the little skirt, caught hold of the string of Maggie's panties and pulled them down. For a moment they sat at Maggie's feet, then she lifted one crystal-shod heel after the other and kicked them away.

Catherine raised her arms, letting her wrists lift the skirt so that the whole length of Maggie's slender legs was exposed. Maggie whimpered, and glancing up Catherine saw her caressing her own small breasts with her hands, catching her nipples between her thumb and the underside of her stiffened forefingers, pressing as if she were trying to expel drops of milk from her little teats. Behind her from the watching men came only silence, but she did not need to look at them to be assured of their attention.

She leant forward, towards the neat blonde curls that adorned Maggie's pubis. Pursing her lips, she blew gently, stirring the golden fur. Maggie gave a whispering moan. Catherine slid her hands around the slender haunches to grasp the cheeks of the little tight arse, because she knew that when she touched Maggie with her tongue she would stagger. Holding her firmly, relishing the round firmness of her buttocks, she pressed the whole of her open mouth against Maggie's mound, squeezing with her lips as she had squeezed with her thumbs. Maggie whimpered, 'Oh, please, please, Catherine.'

Catherine brought her lips to a narrow O as if to blow a kiss, and trapped in the narrow O was Maggie's clit. She mouthed it, fondling it with her lips, not yet touching it with her tongue. Maggie gasped and sighed, tightening her buttocks to try to push herself against Catherine's mouth, but Catherine meant to make her wait. She held on more tightly to the tight buttocks, pulling them slightly apart now and probing between them with her fingertips, seeking the soft clenched anus. She found it, and as she pushed one finger into the tight hole she pressed harder on Maggie's clit with her pursed lips and Maggie shuddered and cried out.

It was time to make her come now. Catherine pressed her face hard into Maggie's body and let her eager tongue do its work, lapping slowly against the swollen clit, sliding back to probe into her wet vagina, increasing the speed and the pressure of her caresses as Maggie shook and trembled and groaned with pleasure. She twisted the finger that was buried in Maggie's anus, forcing it further and further in until it was buried beyond the knuckle.

'I'm coming,' Maggie wailed. 'Oh, Catherine, I'm coming, please don't stop, please don't –' and Catherine felt the spasms shudder through her.

After a few seconds she drew back, wiping her face with her hand and looking up with a smile. Maggie shook her cloud of hair, then smiled down at her. 'Lovely,' she said. 'And now it's your turn.'

Catherine hesitated. She had meant to avoid that. She

glanced over her shoulder and looked at the men, all three of them staring at her. Ash was standing behind the sofa, Bill sitting in the chair, Dave perched on the arm. All of them were still buttoned, their pricks firmly within their trousers, although she could practically smell their excitement. Dave caught her eye and said, 'It has to be both of you getting it on,' and there was a murmur of agreement from the others.

She could refuse and accept a forfeit. But, she realised, she didn't want to. Making Maggie come had aroused her ferociously, and now she wanted some satisfaction too. She took Maggie's hand and stood up. 'What did you have in mind?'

Maggie moved close to her, hands resting on her waist, naked breasts brushing against her. 'I want something in my cunt,' she said, 'and I bet you do too.' She lifted her eyebrows in arch curiosity.

Catherine wondered for a moment what Maggie was suggesting. Then Maggie reached beneath the table and with a wicked smile held something out.

It was a thick, fat, double-ended dildo. Catherine stared at it, gasping. Part of her mind screamed at her that she couldn't possibly, she must be mad, what did she think she was doing? But she silenced it, because the thought of that fat shaft in her made her shiver. She kissed Maggie slowly and simply said, 'Just get me ready first, sweetheart.'

'Delighted,' Maggie whispered. She slid her hands across Catherine's back, up to her shoulders, down to the swell of her breasts. 'Mmm, lovely top. But let's show them how gorgeous you are.' She found the knot of the sash which held the top closed and unfastened it. Catherine looked down into her eyes, holding her gaze to keep her confidence. Her breath was cold between her lips. In a moment these three strangers were going to see her breasts, going to assess her naked body. She didn't really believe they would laugh, but perhaps they might not think she was attractive.

Maggie pushed the top back and cupped Catherine's

113

breasts through her bra, then reached around to the fastening of the bra and unclipped it. In the same movement she unfastened the skirt and pushed it off. Catherine closed her eyes as she felt the fabric slither across her skin and fall to the ground. She was naked now, naked except for a thong. There hadn't even been time for the men to admire her beautiful bra. She felt Maggie turning her and then standing behind her, pressing her body against her, her hands reaching around to cup and lift her breasts. She took a quick, sharp breath and opened her eyes.

The men were gazing at her, eyes darkened with desire. Dave's lips were open and Ash's nostrils were flaring, while Bill had his hand pressed tightly across his mouth as if to prevent himself from speaking. They did not look as though they disapproved of her body. On the contrary, they looked as though they could not wait to fuck her.

A sudden sensation of power swept through Catherine. She lifted her arms and reached behind her to encircle Maggie's neck, and the men's heads turned to follow the movement, then swung back as their eyes fastened again on her naked breasts. How they wanted her!

She felt Maggie's smile, and then Maggie's lips were on her neck and Maggie's hands were sliding down her body, lifting the lace fabric of her thong, insinuating themselves beneath it. In her ear Maggie whispered, 'Let them see you,' and then one hand was between Catherine's legs, one finger slipping across her wet flesh, probing into her, then finding her clitoris and rubbing it gently. Pleasure flashed across Catherine's brain and she flung back her head, arching her back and thrusting her breasts forward, moaning with delight as Maggie touched her. The watching men were in her power now, their wide eyes adding to her pleasure as Maggie frigged her expertly, touching her just enough to drive her mad. She never doubted that she would come, and in only a few moments she did, crying out her pleasure and jerking her hips against Maggie's hand with eager abandon.

They slid to the ground, and as Maggie reached for the dildo that was still resting on the table Catherine fumbled for the second fastening of Maggie's halter, found it, pulled the inconsequential garment off and flung it away. Now they were both almost naked, Maggie with her little skirt up around her waist, Catherine clad in nothing but her thong, and they moved together and clasped and kissed and Maggie pressed with the fat cold head of the dildo against Catherine's pussy, pressing, pressing, until she found the spot and pushed and the thick shaft began to slip inside.

Catherine moaned with pleasure as she felt herself penetrated. She leant back on her hands, breasts thrust towards the ceiling, squirming with shameful pleasure as she thought of the picture she presented, thong wrenched aside to allow the dildo to protrude from her cunt, sticking upwards like a man's erect cock, unnatural and lewd.

'Oh, Catherine,' Maggie whispered, her voice shaking with excitement, 'hold me, hold me while I sit on it, God I want to feel it.'

Catherine sat a little more upright and put her hands on Maggie's waist as the girl squatted over the dildo, presenting its tip to her wet ready hole. She helped Maggie support her weight as she slid down on to the fake cock, and the pressure of Maggie's impalement pressed the fat head that was already buried inside her further up and further in, penetrating her deliciously.

Now Maggie was penetrated too, sitting in Catherine's lap, their legs spread and entwined, the double-ended dildo filling them both. They wriggled closer together to bring their clitorises and breasts into contact and then began to move, a slow, gentle writhing that shifted the fat shaft inside them and allowed a gentle, delicious pressure on their most sensitive spots. It was lovely, not remotely like being fucked but lovely all the same. Catherine rose and fell a little, knowing that as she fucked herself she would also force the dildo further into Maggie's quivering body.

Suddenly she sensed movement behind her. She began to twist round, but before she could turn fully she felt hands beneath her arms, hands moving on to her breasts. They were slender, dark-skinned hands, Ash's hands. He whispered quickly in her ear, 'Don't move. Don't worry. I just want to touch you. Let me touch you.'

She leant back, letting him take the weight of her body, and gasped as his clever hands cupped and caressed her breasts. Maggie moaned, and Catherine saw that Dave was kneeling behind her, stroking her hair. Dave's hand slid down Maggie's body towards the point where her clit touched Catherine's, and his fingers probed into the darkness between them, exploring the cool thickness of the dildo where it entered Maggie's body, where it entered Catherine's, slipping over their wetness, seeking out the stiff stems of their clits to touch and tease them. Maggie cried out and began to heave, more and more quickly, and the speed of her movements thrust the dildo harder and harder into Catherine's aching cunt. She felt another orgasm hovering, and she let herself lie back into Ash's arms and cried out as it swept towards her. Her body was filled, Maggie's cries of pleasure were trembling in her ears, Ash was pinching her nipples, Dave was stroking her clit, and at last she felt herself shaken with violent shudders as she came.

After a moment Maggie crawled out of her lap, withdrew the dildo and kissed her. 'Excellent,' she whispered.

Dave wrapped his arms around Maggie and said, 'That was amazing.'

'I think it entirely unfair that you two can get up to more or less what you like and never have to have recourse to condoms,' said Ash, grumpily.

Where was Bill? Catherine turned her head and saw him still sitting in the chair, hand across his mouth, as if

116

he hadn't moved all through their performance. What was it with him?

'Now what?' Dave asked Maggie.

Maggie twisted round to face him. 'I'm so horny,' she said, 'I can't sort out more games for now. Come here.'

She grabbed him and they fell to the rug in front of the fire. Dave was kissing Maggie and biting at her breasts, and she was frantically scrabbling at his clothes, pulling off his shirt, wrenching down his jeans, getting him naked as fast as possible.

Ash pushed a little closer to Catherine and whispered in her ear, 'If you would like to go down on me . . .'

Catherine glanced up at him, weighing up the options. Her hand rested on his thigh and she could feel beneath his chinos his cock, stiff and hot. It would be nice to taste it. In fact, she would love to taste it. She had wanted to suck Mike off, and hadn't got a chance. It would be a real pleasure to feel a man in her mouth. She smiled and said, 'Love to.'

Ash smiled at her, then pulled himself up on to the sofa and tugged his polo shirt off over his head. He reached to pull his chinos down, but Catherine shook her head and prevented him. She wanted to suck him off through his fly, trousers open, as if they had simply been overcome by sudden lust.

She glanced around as she rose to her knees and saw Maggie rolling a condom on to Dave's scarlet cock, then lying back on the rug. Dave flung himself down on her and she lifted her legs and wrapped them around his waist. The soft flesh between her legs gleamed with the juices of her orgasms. He pushed his cock against her and it found the spot almost at once and slid right up inside her.

'Yes,' Maggie moaned, and Dave made a strangled sound. 'Yes, Dave, fuck me now. Give it to me now.'

Dave obliged, bucking his body against hers in a frenzy. Catherine couldn't take her eyes away from the sight of his thick penis sliding in and out, in and out of Maggie's slender body. He was fucking her hard, violently, it seemed almost impossible that she should enjoy it. But she was enjoying it, writhing around, bucking her hips up towards him to meet his fevered strokes, urging him on to do it harder, deeper.

Ash's fingers moved against her hair. 'Indulge me,' he said in a low voice.

Catherine turned reluctantly from the spectacle of Dave and Maggie and unfastened Ash's fly. Almost before the final button was undone his cock sprang free, and she could smell the hot musky scent of him.

She leant forward, forgetting about what she was missing, riveted by the sight of Ash's cock. It wasn't that it was particularly large or especially thick. It was, simply, very beautiful.

A satin-smooth column of brown rose from black pubes so glossy that they looked as though they might have been oiled. The cock itself was an attractive shape, even in thickness right up to the swelling tip, then smooth and rounded like a ripe fruit. The velvet softness of coffee-coloured skin was adorned by delicate twisting traceries of blue veins, like lapis inlaid into dark stone. The very tip was adorned by a single clear teardrop of fluid, transparent and pure. The whole thing might have been made of marble by a great master, by Michaelangelo or Henry Moore, it was so smooth and perfect.

And it smelt wonderful, rich and eager. Catherine brought her face very close to it and drew in a deep breath, relishing the dense perfume of aroused male. Ash caught his lower lip in his teeth and breathed in deeply as she extended her tongue and gently licked the bead of fluid from the tip. It tasted, very slightly, of salt. She brushed her cheek against the shaft, enjoying its touch of smooth hot satin. She nuzzled into the dark curls at the base, ascertaining that their glossiness was natural, for they were silky and crisp, not oily.

And now Ash's hand became insistent, pressing her head towards the tip of his cock, urging her to take it in her mouth. So she opened her lips and let the shiny head slip inside them, wrapping her tongue round it, coating it thoroughly with her saliva so that she would be able to suck at it easily. It was such a delight to take it in her mouth, feel it twitch and surge with the pleasure of what she was doing. She moaned a little as she moved her head, lapping with the tip of her tongue at the special place where his foreskin was attached, opening the tiny split in the top to suck out the rest of his preparatory juices.

'God, that's good,' Ash whispered. 'Oh, that's good.'

Now there were hands on her body, reaching around to cup and squeeze her dangling breasts. For a moment she thought the hands were Ash's, but then she saw them out of the corner of her half-closed eyes and realised that they were white.

She could still hear Dave and Maggie fucking like minks, so the hands could only belong to Bill. Well, she was glad that something had excited him enough to get him out of his chair.

'Oh, God, I'm coming,' Maggie wailed. 'Now, now, now, Dave, come now,' and a sudden anguished cry from Dave announced that he had obeyed her.

Catherine continued to suck gently at Ash's cock, enjoying the feel of the firm shaft sliding in and out of her mouth. Bill was fondling her breasts very gently, weighing them in his hands and teasing her nipples. His body pressed close behind her and he whispered in her ear, 'I want to fuck you.'

Mmm, that would be nice. Catherine lifted her mouth from Ash's cock just long enough to reply, 'Don't forget the condom,' and then she returned to her pleasant duty. Ash was beginning to moan now, shifting his hips and occasionally thrusting up towards her. She felt Dave's hands on her hips, easing down the thong. Then he began to stroke her bottom, running his palms all over its full curves. That felt very nice, and Catherine purred and lifted her arse a little towards him. Something nudged between her legs, something hot and smooth, and she gasped a little and pushed out her backside, showing her willingness.

119

The thing nudged again at her. What was it? It felt bigger than a fist, but it was so hot. One of the toys, or –

Then the thing found her entrance and pushed at it. She gasped and almost gagged as Ash took the opportunity to push his cock deep into her mouth. Again and again it nudged at her and then it stuck and began to force its way in, and she would have screamed except that her mouth was full of Ash and he had his hands in her hair, holding her mouth on to his cock, not letting her go. Ash's voice hissed, 'Go on, Bill, go on.'

Could it be Bill's cock that was trying to enter her? It couldn't, surely not, it was just too big. She moaned again and writhed, trying to get away from it, and managed to pull herself back until the head slipped out of her. She whimpered against Ash's cock and suddenly Maggie was kneeling beside her, stroking her body, reaching beneath her to tickle her clitoris with eager fingers and whispering, 'Just relax, Catherine, relax, let him get inside you, it'll be great.'

So this was the reason that Bill was invited to Maggie's party! Catherine tried to do as she was told and relax, but how could she? It felt as if he was trying to push a bowling ball inside her. She arched her back, not knowing whether to resist or escape, and then Maggie's fingers were between her legs, prising open her labia, using her juices to moisten the massive head that was pushing at her, and then it was firmly lodged at the entrance to her cunt and then she heard Bill grunt with effort and the head was inside her.

She cried out, the sound muffled by Ash's thrusting cock. The giant penis inside her was stretching her so wide she thought she would burst. It felt like pain, and yet she couldn't help pushing herself backwards, bearing down on the huge thing as if she wanted to be split limb from limb. Gradually, inch by inch, it slid up inside her, cramming her so full she could not think of anything else. She could barely feel Ash's cock in her mouth, even when he grabbed her hair and began to jerk his hips savagely against her face. His cock jerked and spasmed and her mouth was full of his come, but she couldn't even swallow, just let the come dribble out and moaned as Bill forced his cock ever deeper inside her.

'Turn her over,' Maggie whispered. 'Bill, I want her to see what you're doing to her. Turn her over.' And the men's hands were on her, lifting her, sliding her body on to the sofa. They placed her with her body on the cushions, her lower back raised on one of the low arms. Bill was holding her hips, fingers denting her white flesh, his cock still deeply imbedded in her as she was arranged. It filled her so tightly that she could almost believe that it would never come out.

They stopped moving her around. She opened her eyes and looked down the length of her body and gasped.

Bill's cock was as thick as her arm, as thick as her upper arm. Its root was still clear of her body, sprouting from between her legs like the limb of a tree. She tried to move her hips, tried to escape this massive thing that held her, but she couldn't move. Bill was watching her with a look of fierce, determined lust, and just behind him Dave was standing, still panting from his eager fucking of Maggie, staring wide-eyed.

'What do you think?' Maggie whispered, her face close to Catherine's, her voice dripping with lust. 'What's it like, Catherine? Do you like it?'

Catherine turned her head helplessly from side to side, moaning. Maggie liked to talk during sex and enjoyed a running commentary, but with that thing inside her she was incapable of speech. The sensation was unparalleled, more like pain than pleasure and yet irresistible. She wanted to cry out, 'Don't, don't, don't,' knowing that she didn't mean it, wanting him to ignore her and continue to root at her with that great trunk of flesh.

'Catherine,' Maggie whispered, 'let go, let go. Don't fight it.'

How could she not fight it? But she tilted her head

back and flung up her arms, letting out another long aching cry as Bill grunted and tried to thrust himself deep inside her.

'God, you're so tight,' he hissed. 'Relax.'

'Ash,' Maggie's voice whispered, 'touch her, help her out.' And suddenly there were hands on her, running over her trembling body, soothing the pain of Bill's penetration and arousing her. Maggie's hands were on her shoulders, little fingers slithering down the curve of her breast, teasing the flesh into goosepimples, the nipples into tight swollen points. And Ash's hands were caressing the skin of her thighs, skin she had hardly known was sensitive until his long fingers stroked and pressed it. Her cry turned to a shuddering moan, and as the tension left her body Bill gave a guttural huff of satisfaction and screwed his massive cock right into her, filling her, stretching every particle of her.

'That's it,' Maggie whispered. She pinched Catherine's nipples between finger and thumb, wet them with her saliva, drew circles around them, pinched them again. 'That's it, Catherine. Let him fuck you, sweetheart. Let him fuck you.'

At last Bill's jerky thrusts settled towards some sort of rhythm. He clutched tightly at Catherine's haunches and shafted her hard, strong and slow. She groaned and looked down at the appalling, wonderful sight of that giant cock sliding in and out of her, gleaming with her juice. Then she closed her eyes, seeing stars with every stroke of his cock. The touch of Maggie's hands on her breasts was delicious, a delicate refinement of sensuality, overlaying a shimmering counterpoint on to the coarse brutal driving of Bill's penis, and Ash's hands moving on her thighs and arse added yet another dimension.

'Do you like it now?' Bill hissed, leaning forward over her, holding her still to receive his savage thrusts. 'Do you like it?'

'She could like it more,' said Ash's cultured voice. 'Dave, do something.'

What more could be done to her? Surely there wasn't anything. But as Bill began to increase his speed, screwing himself into her faster and faster, she felt someone take hold of her feet, very gently, very firmly. And then she felt Dave's tongue against her ankle, cool and soft, moving down towards the arch of her foot. It was so unexpected and yet so delicious that she gave a high, startled cry.

'Great stuff,' Ash said, a laugh in his voice. 'And now the final touch.'

Those long, sensitive hands began to move up to her hips, sliding beneath her arse, to the crease of her bottom. It was wet there, wet with the trickles of her juices. She turned her head, pressing her eyes more closely shut, whimpering, 'No.' But she didn't mean it. She arched her back and her neck writhed as Ash found her anus and pushed first one long finger, then another deep inside her, fucking her arse with his fingers, matching the rhythm of Bill's plunging prick.

'Catherine,' Maggie whispered, pinching her nipples so hard that it would have hurt if Catherine had not been on a plateau of excitement so high that she could barely feel pain. 'Come now, Catherine. Come now.'

It was going to be so easy to come, so easy. Catherine cried out, her head rolling, limbs quivering with spasms as the feelings overwhelmed her. Bill bruised her hips with his fingers as he drove himself into her, faster and faster; Dave's soft lips and tongue nibbled at her toes; Maggie's clever hands teased her breasts, and Ash slid his fingers into her anus, over and over again, until each separate sensation merged into a brilliant rush of sound and a wave flowed up her body and she came violently, screaming, beating her head on the cushions, her whole body jerking and twitching around Bill's buried cock.

And then it was over. Bill and Ash withdrew from her and she found herself cradled in Maggie's arms, receiving soft kisses on her forehead and cheeks, shuddering and panting with reaction and delight.

'Music,' Maggie whispered over her shoulder, and

123

Dave headed towards the CD player. A few seconds later music started. Catherine didn't recognise it, but it was a black woman singer, her dark smoky voice perfect for the glimmering candlelight and the afterglow of orgasm. Bill and Ash were slumped on the floor beside her, rubbing their faces with their hands and avoiding each other's eyes. They were still half dressed, shirts and trousers unfastened, and as Catherine watched Bill tucked his penis back into his trousers and zipped his fly. Catherine looked up at Maggie and smiled. The men seemed to want to avoid any connection with each other, even to the extent of avoiding eye contact. They didn't know what they were missing.

Dave returned, sipping another drink and carrying a number of other glasses clustered in his hands. He passed them out. Bill and Ash said 'Thanks,' and 'Cheers,' and Maggie just smiled up at Dave and held the glass to Catherine's lips, letting the fierce tang of the bourbon do its work.

Catherine made herself sit up and looked again at Maggie. Her friend seemed to have lost the glow of excitement that she had had at the beginning of the evening; she looked almost disconsolate. Perhaps everybody concentrating on someone else had bothered her: she loved to be the centre of attention. Catherine reached up to stroke Maggie's cheek and said softly, 'What about you, sweetie?'

Maggie frowned and drew in a deep breath, almost as if it was an effort to focus on what she wanted. That was very unlike her. But before Catherine could ask again she let out the breath quickly, smiled brilliantly and said, 'I want everything, Catherine, didn't you know?'

Pushing the glass into Catherine's hand, Maggie got up and crouched down in front of Bill, leaning so close that her naked breasts touched his shirt. 'Bill,' she said wheedlingly, undoing a couple of buttons and running her hands across his naked chest, 'I want you now, you know that, don't you? I know you can get it up again,

124

Bill, I know you can. Let me fix it for you, you know you want to.'

Bill glanced around the room almost apprehensively, but then he nodded and sipped his drink and began to unfasten his trousers. Maggie grinned, like a child who has got its way, and her fingers leapt to the remaining buttons on Bill's shirt. 'OK,' she said over her shoulder as she unbuttoned. 'This scene is written for me and Bill and Ash, and Dave and Catherine can watch us. And amuse themselves,' she added, flashing Catherine an arch smile.

Catherine was interested to know what Maggie had in mind for Ash and Bill, but she also wondered what Dave's reaction would be to this suggestion. She looked up at him curiously. He was the youngest of everyone here: he didn't look a day over nineteen, and he had a certain callow, gauche quality which was very attractive but also made her feel that he might not always say what he wanted or didn't want. He might not fancy having a woman in her mid-thirties, a woman almost twice his age. He might just resist by not getting an erection. How embarrassing that would be. 'You sucking my toes was lovely,' she said, rather lamely, she felt.

Dave hesitated, then knelt quickly down beside her. His smooth shoulders and chest made her want to run her fingers over them. 'I,' he said, and licked his lips, and tried again. 'I'd really like to, to, to have sex with you.' He looked as if he wasn't accustomed to saying things like that. That made two of them, but Catherine was pleased he had made the effort. However, there seemed to be something else on his mind. 'It's just,' he said, 'I wondered, would you mind if we, if we watched?'

Would she mind? Catherine wanted to laugh, but she thought that it might upset him. Instead she smiled and said, 'I was hoping we would,' and reached out for him.

He seemed to be fascinated by her body, and especially by her breasts. He nuzzled them, pushed his face between them, held them in both hands while he suckled on one nipple and then the other. This outright

125

worship was delightful, and Catherine leant back on her hands and gave herself up to enjoyment while she watched Maggie work on Bill.

Bill was sitting on the floor leaning against the sofa. His huge cock was limp, as deflated as a pricked balloon. Maggie knelt in front of him and leant forward to fellate him, and Ash sat himself down behind her, naked now, probing at her arse and vagina with his long fingers. Maggie gave a little whimper of pleasure to encourage him.

At first it didn't seem that she was having any luck at reviving Bill's cock. But then she stopped licking the shaft and sucking the head and turned her attention to Bill's heavy, hairy balls. When she touched them he groaned and spread his legs wide apart and Catherine saw his slack penis twitch with renewed life. Maggie drew one ball into her mouth and as she sucked it she slid her little hand between Bill's legs, feeling for his arsehole, fingering it. He gave another cry, louder this time, and his cock tautened and thickened. It looked as though Maggie was going to get whatever it was that she wanted.

She opened her mouth as wide as she could to suck on the glossy, swelling head and as she did so Ash began to lick her, pushing his tongue deep into her cunt, then fingering her clitoris while he sucked her anus. She moaned with delight, then lifted her mouth from Bill's cock for long enough to say, 'Ash, that's lovely. Make me nice and wet. I want you to fuck me in the arse.'

Catherine wriggled with excitement. She had often thought about anal sex, never done it. The thought of watching it aroused her enormously.

It also seemed to have the same effect on Dave. He whispered, 'Jesus,' and got to his knees, wrapping his arm around Catherine so that he could still fondle her breasts. She reached down and found his stiff cock and began to masturbate him, rubbing him hard. He moaned with pleasure and with his free hand reached down to touch her between her legs, exploring the wet folds until he found her clitoris and rubbing one finger against it with such gentleness that she pushed her hips towards his hand to get him to do it harder.

Before them Maggie got up, pulling herself away from Ash's worming tongue. She caught the men by their hands and dragged them up. 'I want you to make me into a sandwich,' she breathed. 'That's what I want, a Maggie sandwich.'

'You're a bit short, Mags,' Bill said uncertainly as she tore the top of a condom packet and forced the condom over his cock.

'I'm light,' she said eagerly. 'Hold me up.' And without another word she jumped on to Bill, caught him around the shoulders and wrapped her legs around his waist. He looked startled, then laughed and held her and began to nudge his way between her legs.

'Jesus,' Dave whispered again. Catherine glanced at him and saw that his tongue was practically hanging out. He caught her eye and said, 'Christ, I'm so horny, can you think of how we can do it and still watch?'

That suited Catherine very well. 'I'm sure I can,' she said, reaching out for a condom.

When he was rubbered up she said, 'Sit in the chair, on the edge. Let me sit on your lap.'

'Yeah!' he said. Then he looked hesitant. 'I mean, if you want. After Bill, I mean.'

Was he feeling inferior? He didn't need to. Catherine squeezed the shaft of his hot penis, looking for the right words. She wanted to explain that it had been really amazing to feel the size of Bill's cock, but that she didn't mind in the least enjoying an ordinary one. After a moment she said, 'Look, it's like a really hot curry. It's great once in a while, but you wouldn't want to eat it every night.'

Dave looked anxious, as if he wasn't sure that he should laugh. Then he smiled, that lovely boyish grin. It really suited him. 'Chair it is, then,' he said, and moved swiftly to sit, legs spread, penis erect and lifting from his lap.

'Quick,' he said. Catherine knew why. Maggie had sunk down on to Bill's giant cock, groaning with delight as it filled her, and now Ash was coming up close behind her, his dark penis sheathed in pale rubber, ready to fuck her in the arse. Catherine didn't want to miss this, and she wanted to feel Dave inside her while she watched it.

She turned her back to him and put her feet on either side of his, ready to sink down on him. He ran his hands over her backside and said softly, 'Jesus, I won't know where to look: at Maggie, or at your arse.'

That was such a wonderful compliment that Catherine glowed even as she lifted the head of his prick towards her body. Ash was touching Maggie now, his cock sliding up between the cheeks of her bottom, ready to penetrate her even while Bill was fucking her. Catherine poised herself and let Dave's cock slide up inside her, sighing as she took him completely in. Rather to her surprise, it felt pleasantly tight, almost as if she had not been so thoroughly reamed by Bill not half an hour ago.

'Ah,' Dave sighed, and Catherine watched as the head of Ash's cock found the place and began to disappear into Maggie's anus. Maggie didn't seem to feel pain. Far from it. She reached back, clutching at Ash's hips, and her head rolled from side to side. 'Oh, God, yes,' she called out. 'Both of you, do it hard.'

They obeyed her, sharing the task of holding her still between them so that they could each fuck her. Her small pale body was almost invisible between Bill and Ash, but her white thighs wrapped around Bill's haunches and the golden froth of her pubic hair were like a beacon, drawing Catherine's eye irresistibly to the wet red lips where Bill's cock plunged, to the smaller, darker aperture where Ash was lodged.

She put her hand between her legs and touched herself, then rose and fell on Dave's cock. She didn't feel the need to worry about him, he could look after himself. It was almost like masturbating, only with the

128

pleasure of having a real cock inside her, and a real pornographic film unspooling before her instead of her fantasies within her head. It was wonderful. She touched herself gently at first, then gradually built up speed until she was rubbing really hard, the eager movements of her hips mirroring the thrusts of Bill's and Ash's buttocks as they continued to fuck Maggie. Maggie was crying out now, and her face was a beautiful picture of sexual arousal, eyes just dark quivering slits, lips parted, her tongue visible in the soft O of her mouth. Catherine suddenly thought how wonderful it would be if only there was a cock in that soft mouth, and she imagined Maggie penetrated everywhere, fucked in every orifice, and her orgasm was on her before she was ready, before she intended it. She shuddered and moaned and then leaned forward, still touching herself, letting Dave push up into her harder and harder, and his movements kept her on the edge, kept her spasming until in front of her Maggie's heels drummed on Bill's working buttocks as she came. Then it was the men's turn, first Ash, thrusting his way to orgasm in Maggie's arse, then Dave, groaning and heaving himself up so that he could bury himself deep in Catherine's wetness as his semen spilled, and finally Bill, pulling Maggie's hips closer to him as he gave a final convulsive jerk and staggered with the shock of it.

Catherine leant back, letting Dave's body cushion her, and watched as Ash and Maggie and Bill subsided to the ground, still intimately entwined. Maggie gave a sigh, and Bill's voice said from the tangle, 'Fucking excellent.'

'Fucking excellent indeed,' Ash agreed in his quiet, precise way.

After a moment Maggie said, 'I'm really hungry. Do you think we could get in a pizza?'

'By all means,' Ash said. 'Fuck the delivery boy if you like. It'll give us a chance to get our breath back.'

'And then,' Maggie said brightly, 'round two. More games!'

Chapter Eight

Catherine couldn't quite remember how she had got back to her room, but she must have done, because she woke up in her own bed. The curtains were only half closed, and a bright shaft of morning sunlight was lying across the floor, making her squint.

She didn't feel as ill as she expected. Somehow she had imagined that an evening of total debauchery would have left her feeling worse than this: sick, dirty, wicked. But actually, she felt all right. A bit puzzled, a bit tender between the legs, but basically all right. Of course, they had been so busy having sex that she hadn't had time to drink much, so at least she didn't have a hangover.

What would James think of what she had done last night? Was he open-minded enough to see it for what it was, just a bit of harmless entertainment? Maggie had the right idea about things like this, almost a man's attitude, following her sexual urges and not worrying about all the relationship crap. James would see it differently. He liked to be alone with her.

He had liked it, once. Now he liked to be alone with someone else: with Elaine.

Catherine frowned, trying to drive the thought of James from her mind. He wasn't hers any more; perhaps he never had been. She couldn't go on tormenting herself by thinking about him. Why did she? She had to think about something else.

That was easy enough, for now. Last night she had got an idea of what a Roman orgy might have been like. Although, mind you, in an orgy there would be bound to have been slaves involved. How would that have changed things? What would that power differential have done to it? Mm, an interesting speculation. Perhaps worthy of something in the novel.

The bloody novel! She needed to get something down on paper today. Perhaps unsurprisingly, she had woken late, and she had to host a writing workshop at three, but that gave her a couple of hours to head over to the UL and really try to crack this opening chapter.

But she had meant to test the bike in the morning. Maybe she could go there instead? But that was just putting off. It would have to wait. After class would do. She really had to get some work done.

In the shower she washed between her legs and felt how sticky it was there, as if she had scarcely dried out since last night. Tentatively, she parted her labia and felt between them, wondering if Bill's massive cock had caused some damage, some tearing or stretching that she hadn't noticed yet. It didn't seem to have done anything, though, other than leave her a little pulpy and tender.

Touching herself felt good. She ran one hand over her breast, guided the stream of water from the shower between her legs, and brought herself to a quick orgasm, still standing, just catching her breath when the spasms took her. Then she washed herself again, gently but thoroughly, enjoying the sensitivity of her flesh following her climax.

It was bright outside, but when she opened the window there was a chilly nip of autumn in the air. She dressed comfortably, in soft shoes and a jersey skirt, and wrapped herself in a warm fleece.

On the way down the narrow stairs she met Maggie,

who was dressed for sport, as if she were returning from a rowing outing. Catherine said a cheery Hello, but Maggie looked distracted, almost woebegone, and barely responded. 'Maggie,' Catherine asked anxiously, 'are you all right?'

'Mm?' Maggie hesitated, then shook her head. 'Oh, I'm fine. I'm just a bit tired after last night, know what I mean?'

'Well, yes. But you look sad, Maggie.'

'Me? Sad? Not a chance.'

They passed, and Catherine made her way across the court and onwards towards the University Library.

It was a beautiful day, and she didn't want to bring back her post-James melancholy by having uncomfortable thoughts.

But Maggie had looked sad.

Maggie closed the door of her room and immediately began to strip her clothes off, trying to ignore the smell of incense and booze and sex that still lingered on every soft surface. She'd spent ten minutes this morning clearing away the used condoms, and she didn't want any further reminders of last night's party.

Because she hadn't enjoyed it.

Oh, she'd enjoyed it in the sense that she had enjoyed having sex with all those different partners, and putting on a show, and setting up an event which had distracted Catherine from her problems and which she was sure the guys would remember for the rest of their lives. But she had thought it would be a real high spot for her too, something that she had been building up to, and instead it had been a disappointment. An anticlimax.

Was there something wrong with her? She had been looking forward so much to this term, to the opportunity for licentious high jinks, and she had wanted to set up something like an orgy for ages. Why wasn't she revelling in memories of last night, eager for a re-run as soon as humanly possible?

Surely she wasn't starting to go off sex?

132

No, that wasn't possible. After all, sex was a physical thing, and some of the things that had happened last night were still so fresh in her mind that they made her shiver. Having two men at once, for example, getting fucked in the cunt and the arse at the same time. That was something everybody fantasised about and very few people had the nerve to try. Well, she'd had the nerve, and it had been great.

So why didn't she want to do it again? Was she getting blasé?

She stood with her hands locked behind her head, frowning as she tried to puzzle out the conundrum of her own ennui. It didn't make sense. Nothing made sense, and instead of worrying about it she decided to go and have a shower and then head down to Hall for a bite to eat. She was probably just tired, after all. Last night had been extremely energetic, and then she'd been off to cox the first eight, and altogether she was probably just knackered and wouldn't feel like an orgy now even if the participants were Brad Pitt, Ewan McGregor and Kirk Douglas in his prime.

That was definitely it, she decided as the shower washed away the last traces of the previous night. Just tired. Things would look different after a meal and a bit of a rest. Perhaps she would go out and wander around the shops, or head over to the Department of Chemical Engineering and find out how her hapless project partner was getting on with their work.

She dressed in trackies and a baggy sweatshirt, scrubbed her hair dry with a towel, and glanced at her face in the mirror. She looked odd; pensive, that was the word. She looked as though everything was not right with her. Even though it was.

She had to walk through the bar to get to Hall for lunch. It was crowded with people, many of them boozing already. A few friends enjoying a pint in a nearby booth called out to her to join them, but she wasn't feeling particularly sociable and waved and smiled and walked straight past.

133

Then there was somebody beside her, and when she turned and saw who it was she nearly fell over. Ben! Gorgeous blond Ben, looking down at her with a pleasant smile on his sculptured face. He had never once even opened a conversation with her, let alone fallen into step with her. Things were looking up.

'Hi,' she said, congratulating herself on sounding restrained when her whole body was leaping with eagerness to get this glorious man into bed.

'Hi, Maggie,' he said. He was still smiling. 'You going into lunch?'

She nodded. He said, 'Me too. May I join you?'

And it was as easy as that. Five minutes later they had negotiated the cafeteria and were sitting at a corner of one of the long wooden tables. Maggie had got herself a big salad, and Ben was forking his way into an enormous plate of pasta. Rowing blokes needed lots of calories, and he seemed determined to get them.

'Sculling again this morning?' she asked him.

'Yes, there's a regatta in a few weeks and Richard's put me in for it. I don't think I stand a chance, personally, but mustn't let the side down, all the same.'

His voice was lovely too, warm and deep, just right. She'd hardly ever heard him talk for so long. And he was talking to her!

Now he was saying, 'You're looking a bit tired this morning, Maggie.'

'Am I?' Oh God, did she look horrible? No, she'd checked in the mirror, it hadn't been that bad. How did he know that she was feeling low? 'Well, I had a bit of a heavy night last night.'

He smiled. 'I heard.'

He'd already heard about her party? God, the Boat Club was worse than a harem for gossip. That must have been Dave, curse him. Ash and Bill weren't in the same college, never mind the Boat Club. Dave had been down there this morning already shooting his mouth off! That was the last time she'd ask him to an orgy. Not that she had anything to be ashamed of, anyway.

She realised that although she didn't think she had anything to be ashamed of, she was blushing. All Ben had said was, 'I heard,' and she was blushing! It was ridiculous.

'Anyway,' she said, trying to brush it off, 'there was an outing this morning as well, and I guess I've just been overdoing it a bit, burning the candle at both ends, you know what I mean.'

'Not personally,' Ben said, forking up another bite of pasta and smiling at her. 'I don't think I'd ever have been able to keep up with you, to be honest, Maggie.'

There was something irresistible about his smile, something slow and warm that made her stomach feel odd. It had to be lust. After all, she'd fancied him for years. And now they were having lunch! She couldn't wait.

'Well,' Ben said, 'when I heard about your little soirée last night, I thought I ought to make my move before you took yourself right out of my sphere of influence.'

What did he mean? Why should hearing that she'd had a sex party change his mind about anything?

'I wouldn't want you to get a taste for that sort of thing,' he said, still smiling. 'Why don't you come out with me this evening instead? There's a new Thai restaurant opened on the market square and I've been waiting for a chance to try it out.'

Was he joking or was he serious? It didn't matter. He'd asked her out, that was the main thing. She opened her mouth to accept, then remembered her policy of not going out with anyone, just sleeping with whoever she fancied. She frowned, because she really didn't want to rebuff this one, and ventured tentatively, 'Wouldn't you like to stay in instead? I'm sure they'd do a take-away.'

He shook his head and met her eyes. 'Afraid not. I want to eat there. If you don't fancy it, we could always do something another time.'

He'd turned her down! She'd offered him an evening in, a prospect which any red-blooded college male

135

would view with eagerness, and he had preferred a Thai meal to her! She didn't know where to put herself.

'Well?' he said, as she gaped. 'Do you want to come?'

I want to come screaming, with your cock inside me, she thought. She knew she ought to stick to her guns, say no, make him come to her offer. She even opened her mouth to say as much. But what she actually said was, 'Well, yes, OK.'

Catherine sat at her usual desk in the quietest wing of the UL and spread out her books and papers and laptop. For a moment she looked out of the window at a blustery autumn day. Then she lowered her head and rested it in her hands, pressing her fingers tight against the bridge of her nose as if she was trying to squeeze the thoughts out.

James, lost to her. Why had she never realised how much she wanted him until he was gone? Last night's sex was excellent, but where was the connection? Where was the mutual liking that allowed you to talk and laugh, as well as fuck? The tolerance that meant that a failure of orgasm or a slack erection wasn't the worst thing in the world?

She had come here to get her life sorted, and it was not sorted. It was worse than it had been. The translation was nearly finished, but that was always going to be the easy part. She had failed to get her book going, and James was gone, and she would go home at the end of term alone. Really alone, unable to say to herself in the middle of the night that there was someone, even though he was a long way away.

She tilted her head back and sighed heavily, then looked guiltily around in case she had disturbed someone. But she hadn't. There was nobody in sight, not even anyone walking around the stacks looking for a book. She was really alone.

Where did all this feeling sorry for herself take her? She needed to concentrate on this damn book, and at last she had an idea. The book was going to be about

136

Catullus and his Lesbia, about their affair and its ending, so she could add some spice to it and maybe even kick start it by finding the juiciest quotes from the poems. Catullus in his own words. And scurrilous words too. There was no shortage of scurrilous words in Catullus.

She had spent months translating the poems, and she didn't need to open her text to extract a few choice phrases:

> It's not just the great and the good who are
> Her lovers, no, it's worse than that; the small-time
> Backstreet lechers screw her too, and you,
> Ignatius . . .

And here was another, even harder to take:

> Take this message to her from me,
>   Few words, and bad.
> She lives and thrives with her adulterers,
> Holds them three hundred in her arms at once,
> Loves none of them, but fucks them all alike,
>   Breaking their balls.
> She can't expect my love now as before.
> Her sins have made it die, like the sweet flower
> At the meadow's end; touched by the plough
>   It falls.

She meant the quotes to be ribald and racy, but she had moved unerringly to the poem which flung out sexual accusations like weapons, only then to reveal the writer's desperate vulnerability. She was choosing poems which showed her own feelings. How psychologically appropriate. And what a bummer.

It didn't seem that this was going to work, either. Her mind was too distracted, too focused on itself. Or was she just bored with Catullus, his self-absorption and self-pity? No, that couldn't be right.

She drifted off, away from the UL and back into

memories. She'd told James about her plans for this book once, the last time he was in England, the last time they had made love. He'd listened, made some intelligent remarks about the way she could tie the themes from the poems into the story, approved of her choice of subject. He certainly had sympathy with Catullus, with the betrayed man.

He'd listened. And then they had made love. They'd stayed in bed all day, the way James liked it, making love and then resting, talking, touching, starting again. He'd had a book with him that time, a book of erotica written in English and printed in Germany. They'd looked at it for light relief, really, and to get their interest back again when they were tired. It wasn't that they had wanted to do the things in the book. It had had a heavy emphasis on bondage, and James never really got any closer to that than the odd silk scarf. But it had been exciting to look at, and interesting to wonder whether some of the things were actually possible.

That picture, for example, of the girl with her ankles and wrists fastened together behind her back, resting on the fastenings like a crab, knees wide apart, head tilted back, ready to be fucked in any available orifice. Surely only a committed yoga practitioner would be able to do that. And even if she bent that way, she wouldn't enjoy it, would she?

There had been another couple of pictures that Catherine had liked very much, found very erotic. She thought of them now and felt the familiar shiver of arousal passing through her. It made her want to look at them. But the book had been James's, and he had taken it away with him. Presumably he was enjoying it now with Elaine. Perhaps her lithe Oriental body was limber enough to be tied up like a crab so that he could fuck her. Perhaps that's what he had always wanted, and that's how Elaine had got him, because she could do those exotic things. Perhaps she had a really small pussy, so that she gripped his cock tightly. Didn't people say that about Asian girls, that they were built small? Was that what James had fallen for?

She pushed her mind away from those self-destructive thoughts and thought about the book again. And then it struck her. She was sitting in one of the major libraries of Europe, one of the major libraries of the world, and it was a copyright library, and if that book was copyright in the UK it would be here somewhere. Why not find it, and remind herself of those pictures and why she had enjoyed them so much?

It was just the right thing to take her mind from her troubles. She had to ferret through her brain until she remembered the exact title of the book. She couldn't remember the author, but that wouldn't matter. She knew that it was a foreign publisher, and at a nearby terminal she searched for it and after only a matter of minutes tracked it down.

Interestingly, it was on the open shelves, classified as History of Art. It also appeared to be in stock. That was a surprise, too. She half-expected some doddery old don to have it on permanent loan on his bedside table, ready to help him come up with something hard enough to wank in the middle of the night.

Time to look for it, then. It was quite a long walk. She made a note of the shelf reference on a scrap of paper, locked up her laptop, as many had gone missing when left unattended, and headed for the stairs. She thought of going to the coffee lounge on the way, partly because she was hungry and partly as a way of delaying her gratification, but decided against it.

The book was there, on the shelf, but she didn't recognise it. James's copy had had a bold, coloured cover, a reproduction of one of the tamer works inside it. This one was bound in plain green boards with the title and author stencilled in black. Very correct, very plain brown wrapper. She pulled it off the shelf and flicked through it.

Oh yes, it was definitely the same book. Some of the pictures were plain weird; others made her shiver. She snapped it shut and glanced around, as if someone might have seen her reading it, then carried it back to her desk.

Back in the stacks, in the quiet, sure that nobody was watching her, she opened the book and turned the pages. She knew where to find the pictures she was looking for; towards the end. She flicked past a Victorian representation of gang rape which half-aroused, half-disgusted her, past Decadent images by Beardsley and von Bayros, past gangster-period French watercolours, and there they were.

Two drawings, both by the same man, both of the same girl. She was idealised, but she was clearly based on a real woman. More than anything she resembled the 1940s cartoon heroine Jane; tall, long-legged, with high full breasts, shoulder-length blonde hair in 1940s waves, a pretty but unremarkable face. A male fantasy girl in every respect.

In the first picture she was naked except for her five-inch spike heels. She was seen from the side, in profile. Her ankles were tied together with soft rope, and she was bent forward at the hips to form a perfect right angle. Her back was flat, bare breasts dangling, nipples erect, and her arms were pulled up behind her back, suspended from some invisible point, so that they also formed a perfect right angle with her body. Her wrists were tied tightly with the same soft rope. Long straight legs, straight back, straight arms formed a zig-zag of bare flesh. She wouldn't have been able to move, and as Catherine knew from experience, it was possible to penetrate a woman easily even though her feet were close together, as long as she was bent forward far enough to reveal her vulva. So this girl was available, mouth and vagina, to anyone who chose to take her, and there would be nothing she could do about it.

The girl in the first picture seemed unmoved by her predicament, but the same could not be said of the second picture. In this she was clothed in what looked like the rags of an army uniform. She was standing very straight, because she was tied to a pillar. Her arms were bound behind the pillar, and there were ropes at her waist and again at her ankles, holding her spike-heeled feet closely together. Her skirt was torn to reveal her pubic hair, and her blouse was also ripped so that her dark nipples protruded through the fabric. She was gagged, and her head was tilted back as if she were in agony, as if she were screaming against the gag for rescue.

This picture was very erotic. Catherine's pulse beat hard in her ears as she considered it. But what would be the good of a girl tied to a pillar in this way? How could she serve a ravaging male? He would be able to lick and suck at her nipples, push a finger or two between her legs and fondle her, but would he actually be able to fuck her? It seemed, frankly, unlikely. But –

'What exquisite taste you have,' said a male voice softly in her ear.

Catherine started and tried to pull away, but Mike was leaning over her, arms planted on the desk on either side of her, holding her down as he looked over her shoulder at the book. He was smiling. 'I thought you were working,' he said. 'How wrong I was.' There was a pause, while he examined the pages. She would have liked to say something, but couldn't think of anything. She felt guilty, as if she had been caught stealing, and at the same time she was aroused.

'You like these pictures,' he said. It was not a question.

She nodded, then found her voice. 'But I don't exactly – I mean, I don't think that it would be possible for anyone actually to, to have that girl, tied the way she is.'

Mike put his head on one side. His eyebrow ring caught the light. 'Don't you?'

'Well –' She hesitated.

He stood up, then rested his hands on the upper surface of her breasts, slid them down, cupped the weight of her breasts in his palm. Her nipples, already

141

tight, tensed further in immediate, instinctive response. He pinched them meditatively between finger and thumb, then said, 'It is possible.'

'Really?' Her head was spinning.

'I'll prove it to you tonight.' He stood away from her, and as she turned to look at him he nodded. 'Not sure when and where yet. I'll find you in college this evening.' He turned to go, then had an afterthought and turned back. 'Make sure you have the right shoes. Four-inch heels at least. You have to be tall.'

And that was it. He turned his back and left. He wasn't going to stay, wasn't going to relieve her sexual tension, wasn't going to frig her or lick her or give her pleasure in any way. Just a vague 'tonight' and he was gone.

Catherine looked at the book, then slipped her hand up beneath her skirt. She needed an orgasm, and if Mike wasn't going to give it to her, she would have to do it for herself. There was still time before her three o'clock workshop.

The workshop passed off without much incident. One or two of the students had some interesting ideas, but none of them really struck her as major artists in the making. Not that she was, of course, but that didn't preclude her from recognising talent, if there was any.

Now it was time for a pair of killer heels. If Mike thought they would be necessary, it was certainly a good idea to buy them. Apart from anything else, really high heels felt very sexy to wear, and she hadn't possessed a pair for far too long. Her wardrobe was really getting too sensible, too late thirties. Time for something a bit mad.

She strolled along Henry's Parade, heading for the little street at the end where the more *outré* boutiques clustered. It was getting chilly in the brisk wind, and she wrapped her jacket closely around herself. She was looking forward to trying the shoes on. It was good to be wearing a skirt: it would allow her to enjoy the additional height she gained, the way her legs length-ened and her calf muscles tautened with the addition of those spikes.

There, on her right, was the bike shop. She had forgotten about her bike in the excitement of Mike's promise. But she had told Andy that she would be back in today, and here she was, passing by, so she turned in through the door.

Andy was standing at the cash desk reading a news-paper – the *Guardian*, she noticed – and sipping from a very large, very grubby mug: coffee, by the smell. He looked up as she came in and his heavy face brightened with a smile. He had a good smile, but it looked as if it didn't come that often.

'Thought you weren't going to bother to come in,' he said, folding up the newspaper. 'One of those fly-by-nights who come into the shop and get me to do something totally pointless like fetch a bike that nobody's going to buy, that's what I thought you were.'

'Well, here I am,' she said, opening her hands. 'Where's the bike?'

'Yeah, yeah, OK, slow down.' He went to the back of the shop, vanished, and presently appeared again, wheeling a bicycle. 'OK, here it is. What d'you think?'

'Well –'

'What do you know about it, anyway?'

She flung up her hands in mock anger. 'Do you want to know what I think of the bike, or not?'

'I want you to try it.' He kept a straight face the whole time. She was sure that he was teasing, but it was hard to tell. 'I need to make sure the saddle height and bar height are right for you. Hop on.'

She looked at him, then slid on to the saddle, one foot on the ground.

'Looks about right. I have a good memory for heights. Now take both your feet off the ground.'

A withering glance. 'You want to watch me fall over?'

'I'd love to, but you'd probably sue the shop. I'll hold the bike up. Put both your feet on the pedals.'

143

He was holding on to the frame below the saddle, but she didn't feel entirely safe. Did he know how much she weighed? 'I'm pretty heavy,' she ventured.

'You said it, I didn't. I'm pretty strong. Will you put your feet on the pedals, for God's sake?'

He looked pretty strong, too, standing behind her with one big arm holding the frame. He was wearing a shirt over a T-shirt, and it did not conceal the fact that the muscle of his arm bulged like a volleyball. She met his eyes for a moment, hoping that he would smile, because she felt tense. He didn't smile. She hesitated, then took her feet off the ground and put them on the pedals.

'At last. Now backpedal,' he said.

'Stop ordering me around!' she exclaimed. Why did every man think he could just give her instructions?

Andy looked startled, then grinned. 'Just trying to be quick and efficient, Modom. If it wouldn't be too much trouble, would Modom mind moving the pedals in the reverse direction?'

'I don't mind doing it,' she said. 'But I'd like to know why I'm doing it.'

He rolled his eyes. 'Everything's got to have rules, rules, rules. I want to see if the saddle height is right. If it is, there'll be a very slight bend in your knee when your leg is completely depressing the pedal, heel down. All right?'

'Thank you!' she said brightly, and obediently backpedalled.

For a moment Andy was silent, then he said, 'Okay. Just get to the bottom of the stroke and stop. Put your foot down.' She did so, and he let go of the bike and moved around to crouch beside her. 'Look,' he said, putting his hand on her ankle, 'You've got your toe pointed. You don't need to do that, the saddle's not too high, and it stops you from getting the full power that your legs can deliver. Keep your heel down.' He guided her foot into the right position.

She looked down at his hand on her ankle. It was a

big hand, with fingers like a bunch of small bananas, thick and strong. There were black hairs on the back of it, and thick hair on his wrists below the slightly-rolled cuffs of his shirt. His watch was huge, with a fat glowing face, but the size of his wrist dwarfed it. He was really big, considering that he wasn't much taller than her. The skin on his hand was hard, but he touched her gently.

He looked up, meeting her eyes. Someone so dark should have had brown eyes, but his eyes weren't brown, they were that odd bright hazel, starred with black lashes. They drooped slightly at the edges. They were nice eyes, smiling even though his heavy mouth did not.

'Take it round the block,' he suggested.

She glanced out of the window. 'Are you sure? I mean, I haven't paid for it yet.'

'Why do you keep on asking me if I'm sure? Do you think I don't know what I'm on about? Take the bloody thing round the block. Ride up to the UL and back, just try it out. I don't want to sell you a pup.'

So she cycled out of the Parade, turned right on to Silver Street, crossed the river, right again on to Queen's Road and along the Backs to the back of St Henry's and the passsageway for bikes and pedestrians that led to the UL. The bike felt good, and the hub gear shift was really easy. She enjoyed riding it, even though the blustery wind made it hard work. It was actually fun.

Back at the shop she dismounted, slightly out of breath, and Andy met her on the pavement. 'You like?'

'I like,' she confirmed.

'Put the colour in your cheeks,' he said, smiling now.

She grinned at him and touched her face. Her cheeks were cold and stinging from the wind. 'I need some practice,' she said. 'It's ages since I really rode a bike. My last one didn't even have gears.'

'You should have kept it, it would be an antique by now. Now, you need a helmet, bike pump, lock . . .'

By the time they were done he had sold her

£70-worth of accessories to go with the bike, and she didn't even mind. He was a very good salesman. When it was all done and he had written out a receipt, he looked up and said, 'And did you still want me to spray the frame metallic orange for you?'

She laughed, because she'd practically forgotten their last exchange. 'No,' she said, shaking her head. 'If black's good enough for you, it's good enough for me.'

Andy lifted his head and took a quick breath, then said with the same straight face, 'I can close the shop fairly soon. It's still light in the evenings. Do you want to come out on the bike with me and I'll show you a few of the off-road routes round here?'

Was he asking her out? His face was so straight it was hard to tell, but after a moment she decided that he was. It was a long time since anyone had done that, and it was with real regret that she said, 'I'm really sorry, Andy, I'm busy this evening.'

She half expected him to try for another time, but he just shrugged and continued swiping her credit card as if nothing had happened. Perhaps, then, he hadn't been asking her out at all. Or had she just missed her chance? He was friendly and cheerful as she left the shop, but she thought she detected something different about him.

Either way, it was a shame. She liked him. Not that she was likely to have much in common with a bloke in a bike shop, but she liked him all the same.

The killer heels didn't take long to buy. They were a pair of sandals, mock croc, black, of course, and as high as she could bear. She didn't think she would be able to walk far in them and hoped that it wouldn't be necessary. As she walked home the contrast of her purchases made her laugh. She was pushing her shiny new bike, with a bag carrying all its paraphernalia dangling from the handlebars, and in the other hand she held the little shoe bag containing this pair of delicate, designer sandals, as unsuitable for the outdoors as could be imagined, shoes for the boudoir. Perhaps she needed a boudoir bike, a little pink thing with fluffy wheels and a padded velvet saddle. It could have gilded handlebars and tyres made out of patent leather. Well, it wouldn't be any weirder than some of the other things in that book.

The crooked little house on Henry's Parade had another big advantage for Cambridge types: a safe little courtyard at the back with a rack that she could lock the bike to. She stood back from it, admiring it, and feeling a faint tinge of regret at passing on Andy's offer. What should she have done, accepted it and passed up on Mike? But if she had done that Mike might well have vanished without trace, and with the evening that she was expecting from him that would have been a real shame.

At the top of the stairs she heard music coming from behind Maggie's door and decided that she had to have her purchases approved by another woman, and Maggie would be perfect. She knocked and said, 'Maggie, it's me, are you busy?' just in case there was vigorous sex going on to an accompaniment of Catatonia.

'Oh, Catherine, thank God, come in,' said Maggie's voice, which wasn't the reaction she had expected. She opened the door and found Maggie standing in what looked like the aftermath of a small whirlwind. Practically every garment that she possessed was strewn around the room, and Maggie herself was standing naked in the middle of it, holding a skimpy halter-necked dress up against herself, wild-eyed.

She rather resembled the second picture which Catherine had found so arousing, and for a moment Catherine thought of going straight across to her and initiating sex, but if she did that she might be late for Mike, and that would never do. So she said, 'Bloody hell, Maggie, I only wanted you to see some stuff I bought. Perhaps I'll come back another time.'

'No, no, no,' Maggie wailed. 'You've got to help me.'

Catherine put her bags down carefully in a corner and sat on the edge of the armchair. 'What's up, then?'

'I don't know what to wear,' Maggie moaned. 'I'm going out, I'm going out with Ben, and I don't know what to wear.'

'Going out?' Catherine repeated. 'You mean going to bed?'

Maggie looked shamefaced and hung her head slightly. 'Well, no. Out for a meal.'

Catherine was really startled. 'I thought you didn't like that kind of thing, Maggie.'

'Well, I know, it's not something I usually go in for, but –' Maggie shook her head, surrounding herself with a cloud of golden curls, like a halo '– but this is Ben, Catherine! I've wanted him for, I don't know, ever since he arrived, and he's always just ignored me, and then today he sat with me at lunch and he actually asked me out, so I said yes.' She hesitated. 'I know I should have just insisted that he came to bed with me, but he didn't seem to want to do that, so I said yes. And now –' she gestured at the carnage around her '– I just don't know what to wear. I haven't got a clue.'

Shaking her head, Catherine prepared to give some practical advice. 'Where are you going?'

'To a new Thai restaurant he wants to try.'

'Very nice.' How civilised, to be asked out by a nice young man to a nice restaurant to have a nice evening. What a pleasant change it would make to have something like that happen to her! 'Is it posh, the restaurant?'

Maggie made an uncertain face. 'Search me.'

'Well, probably it's smart casual, that's the way most places seem to be these days, even here. Why not wear a pretty dress, or a skirt and top? You know you always look gorgeous, whatever you're wearing.'

'But I want to make him want to come to bed with me.' Maggie flaunted the dress she was holding, which was very scanty and made of flimsy fabric.

'You've already offered him that,' Catherine pointed out callously, 'and he didn't want it. Everyone in college knows you're a wild child. So why not show him that you can also be a nice, civilised girl? Wear something pretty.'

'Something pretty,' Maggie repeated, helplessly.

'Whatever has got into you, Maggie? Look, how about this?' Catherine ferreted in the heap and came up with a slip skirt, last season's but still pretty, a subtle shade of *eau de nil*. 'You could wear this with that little cardigan, the silver-grey one, and it would look just right; very proper, very attractive, quite grown-up, really.'

'Do you think so?' Galvanised, Maggie dived into a pile of tops and emerged a few moments later triumphant, clutching the appropriate cardigan. 'Oh, wait,' she said, and burrowed again. This time she came out with a similar top in a gorgeous shade of lagoon blue. 'What about this one?'

'Lovely,' Catherine said, because it was. That colour on Maggie looked like an advert for the Caribbean or a Greek island, sea next to blond rocks. 'Perfect, Maggie. And stockings, and nice shoes.'

'Stockings?'

'Well, it is October.'

Maggie nodded slowly, as if she felt calmer. 'Yes, all right, good idea. And I'll tie my hair off my face, what do you think?'

'Always looks good.'

'Great.' Still nodding, Maggie looked across as if she were seeing Catherine for the first time. 'Look, Catherine, I'm so sorry, I didn't mean to jump on you like that. But I was desperate.'

'So I see. I tell you what, Maggie, if you do end up in bed with him it'd better be at his place. If you bring him back here he'll think you're careless, to say the least.' Catherine smiled, indicating the abomination of desolation with a wave of her hand.

'I hope he does want to go to bed with me,' Maggie said, looking suddenly mournful. Then she pulled herself together. 'So what happened to you today? What have you got there?'

149

'Bike bits, and a pair of killer heels.'

'Interesting combination. Can I watch?'

'I already thought of that. Look.' Catherine unpacked the shoes and held them up to be admired.

'Mm, very nice. Something special in mind?'

'Mike promises it. I'll tell you tomorrow.' Catherine hesitated, then said, 'I got asked out today, as well.'

'Did you? Really? Who by?'

'Andy, the guy in the bike shop. He asked me to go out riding bikes with him.'

'Is he cute? Did you say yes?'

'No,' Catherine said, answering both questions together. 'No, he's not cute. But I like him. I sort of wish I had said yes, actually.'

Maggie shrugged, looking like her old self. 'Hey, there's always tomorrow.'

'And before tomorrow, there's tonight!' Catherine grinned. 'I'm going to have a shower. See you tomorrow, Maggie. Enjoy your evening.'

'You too,' Maggie said.

Catherine closed the door, bags in hand, thinking about that picture. Yes, she thought she probably would enjoy her evening. Oh, yes.

Chapter Nine

*P*repared, her feet clad in the killer heels, Catherine waited in her room.

It was dark, and getting late. Maggie had left for her date an hour ago, popping into Catherine's room in a fit of unaccustomed lack of self-confidence to be told that she looked beautiful. Catherine thought she ought to be irritated at being kept waiting, but somehow she didn't feel that it was important. It added to the anticipation, and anticipation added to the pleasure.

Perhaps Ben, Maggie's date, understood the importance of delaying gratification. There was a test which psychologists performed on children aged four or thereabouts. They were offered a sweet and told that if they did not eat the sweet while the tester was out of the room, they would be allowed another sweet as well when she returned. Children who had the self-control to wait ten or fifteen minutes, thereby earning a second sweet, were significantly more likely to be well-balanced and successful in later life. Maggie gave the impression of someone who had never waited for anything. It wasn't that she snatched, it was just that she wanted it now. Maybe it was Ben's plan to make her wait, so that she appreciated it more when she got it. It certainly seemed to be working, for now.

Did that mean that it was always good to wait, always good to deny yourself? No, that couldn't be right, either. Especially when it came to sex: too many people denied themselves not to increase later pleasure, but because they were scared, or ashamed, or afraid of what others would think of them. That wasn't self-denial, that was lack of self-confidence. God, it was complicated.

She mused over her day, and remembered how she had snapped at Andy because he seemed to be ordering her about. Why had she done that? Mike had done nothing but order her about since their first encounter, and she had always let him. Was her attitude with Andy betraying a certain impatience with Mike?

That also was too hard to think about, so she went and checked her earrings instead. She didn't remember whether the girl in the picture had been wearing earrings, but she didn't feel fully dressed without them, so they were on, just simple little gold stars the size of her little fingernail. She was also wearing clothes that were easy to remove, a blouse with buttons, a front-fastening bra, a button-through skirt. She didn't really want anything that she owned to be torn off her, so the line of least resistance was the obvious option. She sat down on the sofa and looked at the high-heeled sandals. They gave her legs a good line. When Mike saw them, he would want her. He would want to fuck her.

As if Mike had heard her thought, the door opened. He stood there, a shadow in the gloom. He was dressed in black: black jeans, black T-shirt, black leather jacket. It should have looked theatrical, but it didn't. It looked good. In one hand he was holding the green-covered book from the UL, loosely, as if it were philosophy.

'Come with me,' he said.

She wanted to ask where, but by now she knew better. She picked up her bag, a little clutch job containing a couple of banknotes and several condoms and not much else. Walking slowly, taking care not to teeter on those amazing heels, she stalked across the room to him and pulled the door shut.

He led her down the stairs and turned right, towards St Mary's and the Senate House. She said after a few yards, 'Is it far?'

'Don't worry about your feet. It's just off the market square.'

That was close enough that she could make it and still look elegant. Ridiculously, it felt as if a major worry had been removed from her. She relaxed, and with relaxation came a sense of expectation, of eagerness.

Mike walked ahead of her. He didn't turn round to see if she was following him. An image flashed across her mind of a veiled Muslim woman walking obediently three paces behind her husband, and with it came a flash of anger. She put it aside. After all, he was just showing her the way. She knew what she was going with him for, they both knew it. What need for small talk?

They walked down the passage by St Mary's church on to the market square. There was the new Thai restaurant, doubtless the one which Ben had invited Maggie to. And indeed, there were Ben and Maggie eating their meal at the table by the plate-glass window.

Catherine slowed down to look at them. No wonder they had been seated at that table. They made a handsome couple, both blonde and fit as if they had come straight out of a chewing-gum advertisement, eating their satays and smiling at each other. Maggie said something which made Ben laugh. He was a very good-looking young man, maybe four or five years older than Maggie, with a calm composure about him which Catherine thought very attractive. And Maggie looked lovely. Although, looking at her through the glass, Catherine saw for the first time how really young she was. It wasn't that she looked any younger, it was her demeanour that was different. Normally she behaved as if she had seen everything and all that was left for her to do was choose. Now she looked almost as if she were innocent. It suited her.

Mike was looking over his shoulder. He turned his

dark gaze on the couple in the window, then back to Catherine. 'Your friend?'

Catherine nodded. Of course Maggie was also her lover, but she didn't want to tell Mike about that. And besides, for both of them sex with each other was just a pastime, a pleasant diversion when there wasn't a man on the scene. They both knew that, they agreed on it. She felt no jealousy when she looked at Maggie's face, alight with pleasure and excitement as she talked to Ben. She was pleased for her.

Mike turned and began to walk again. With a last look at Maggie, Catherine followed him.

Across the market square she kept to the pavement. Flat stones were an absolute essential to walking in these shoes, cobbles would have been an instant disaster. They crossed the road into Rose Crescent, and after only a metre or two Mike turned into a little doorway and began to climb stairs. Following him, Catherine read the sign at the foot of the steps: DANCE AND AEROBICS STUDIO.

At the top of the stairs Mike drew a key from his pocket and opened the door, then walked quickly across the room and pressed the buttons to silence a bleeping alarm. Catherine entered, sensing a large space around her in the almost-dark of street lights filtering through closed blinds.

'How did you get the key?' she asked, wrapping her arms around herself and shivering slightly.

'Friends,' Mike said curtly. He came back to the door, walking confidently, as if he knew his way around very well, and reached up beside it. Brilliant spotlights lit, flooding the room with white light. Was he a dancer in his spare time? An odd idea, but then he was an odd man. Catherine blinked, then looked again.

A big room, surrounded on three sides with mirrors. The wall with windows in it had no mirrors, only a barre for dancers to balance against. In the corner by the door was a stainless-steel water fountain and a paper towel dispenser. The floor was boarded in pale wood.

About three-quarters of the way across the room was a pillar, plain plaster, with the marks of hands and shoes on it.

She swallowed hard, understanding at once why Mike had chosen this location. Not just the pillar, the perfect size for her to be tied to, but mirrors everywhere, so that what they were doing would be reflected back into her eyes whichever way she chose to look. She would have to be blindfolded to shut out the reflections.

Mike was watching her, a quiet, intense look. He closed the door and when she flinched at the slam said, 'You have a choice, you know.'

'That's a first, with you,' she said, trying to sound lighthearted. It came out sounding foolish, and she wished she hadn't said it. She shook her head and said, 'It's all right, Mike.'

'You want to do this.'

Was that a question or a statement? But whichever, the answer was the same. The book in his hand was drawing her. She wanted to be that fantasy girl. She said, 'Yes.'

He nodded slowly and flicked the snib on the lock. 'Good,' he said.

She took a couple of tentative strides across the room, then looked down at the floor. 'These heels are going to ruin the wood.'

'You won't be walking very far. But I'll get a mat for you to stand on.'

Her arms were still wrapped around herself, as if she needed to protect herself from what was about to happen to her. Mike brushed past her, walked across to the far side of the room and pressed the edge of one of the mirrors. It sprang open, revealing a cupboard full of equipment. He clearly knew the place well, because he reached into the cupboard and withdrew without hesitating a length of heavy chain.

'Position one,' he said, holding out the chain to her in both hands. It wasn't very long, and there was a big hook on one end. Guessing its purpose, she glanced up at the ceiling and saw a loop there. Mike nodded approvingly, and with the help of a small step-ladder he threaded the chain hook through the loop so that the chain dangled vertically, ending a few feet from the floor. Another trip to the cupboard yielded two long mens' skipping ropes, from which he detached the ropes with a couple of quick, deft movements.

He turned to face her, twisting the ropes between his fingers. 'Strip,' he said.

Catherine swallowed again, imagining those ropes around her wrists, around her ankles. She wouldn't be able to move. She wouldn't be able to stop him from doing what he wanted to her. If he wanted to push his cock into her mouth, he could. He could do what he liked.

She hoped very much that he would choose to push his cock into her mouth. She was acutely aware that she had never tasted him, never even seen him naked. She didn't imagine that he would be naked tonight, as she knew that in bondage scenarios being clothed was a sign of dominance, but she did hope to taste his cock. She wanted to suck him.

'Is there a problem?' he demanded. 'Get your clothes off.'

She felt cold all over, and at the same time hot and expectant. She began to unfasten the buttons on her blouse, feeling her cheeks stinging with a blush. As she pulled the blouse off and laid it on the floor behind her she glanced at the blinds, wondering. Would they stay closed? Or, when she was bound and unable to prevent him, would he open them so that anyone looking in from outside could see her being used?

He saw her eyes move and smiled slightly. 'I might,' he said, lifting the pierced eyebrow. 'Or then again, I might not. I might not want to share you with anyone else tonight.'

She hadn't told him that Dave had watched when he fucked her against her window, and she didn't intend to. Having a secret like that made her feel stronger. She unbuttoned and dropped her skirt, clicked open the bra and pushed it off, and stood before him in just her thong.

'The shoes are excellent,' he said. 'Take off your panties.'

She drew in a deep breath, watching her nipples lift, then put her hands to the thong and pushed it down her thighs. She removed it with exaggerated modesty, keeping her backside tucked in and her legs together. In the mirrors around the room her reflection posed like a pornographic Venus, naked except for the high sandals, one hand across her breasts, the other shielding her pudenda. The sandals did look good. She looked as sexy as she had hoped she would.

He nodded slowly. 'Good. Come here.'

She sucked in her belly as she walked towards him, acutely conscious of the fact that her breasts swayed with the movement. Her nipples were already erect, and she knew that the moment he felt between her legs he would encounter slippery wetness, proof of excitement.

His face showed no matching excitement, just quiet calm, but his eyes were very dark. When she was in front of the chain he said, 'Lift your hands above your head. Take hold of the chain. Put your weight on your hands.'

Obediently she reached up and grasped the chain over her head, tensing the muscles of her arms as if she meant to hang from them. He moved around to stand behind her, and as she met his eyes in the mirror she saw herself, breasts lifted by the tension in her arms, belly hollowed, pubic hair a dark flare, legs impossibly long on the delicate heels. He still did not smile, but he came close behind her. The leather of his jacket was cold on her skin. He reached around and put his hands on her breasts, cupping a whole breast in each hand, squeezing the soft flesh. She wanted to tilt her head back and gasp, but if she did that she would not be able to see herself, and it was wonderful to see herself. She looked so beautiful, naked, fondled and caressed by this black-clad figure.

'Good,' he whispered again, and suddenly he pinched her nipples hard, really hard, so that she gasped and jerked backwards against his restraining body. He did not move an inch. 'No need to ask if your cunt is wet for me,' his voice hissed in her ear.

There was no need, she knew it was. His fingers and thumbs were still tight on her nipples, and in the mirror she could see the swollen flesh darkening as he stimulated it. She caught her lower lip against her teeth, trying to keep silent.

'Don't let go. Don't say anything,' he hissed, and suddenly he let go of her breasts and knelt at her feet. The first rope was winding around her ankles, once, twice, three times, fastening her feet together. She could not move her legs. He knotted the rope with a knot that looked scarily secure.

'There,' he whispered, standing up. 'That feels good.'

How did he know? But it did feel good, it felt frightening and erotic. He returned to stand behind her again, showing her to herself in the bright mirror. She tried to move her feet although she knew she could not, and he gave a little laugh. Then he reached around with both hands, and this time he pushed his fingers between her tightly closed thighs, feeling for her sex. She moaned as the searching fingers spread her lips apart and pushed between them, dipping into the well of her juice, moving away.

He avoided her clitoris. He must have done it entirely on purpose. She groaned with frustration, and in response he pushed one finger right up into her. 'Squirm on that,' he whispered, and as her hips writhed in response he pulled the finger away, lifting it to his nose, smelling it luxuriously.

'Now,' he said into her ear, 'for the rest.'

His hands reached up for her wrists, held them, detached them gently from their grasp on the chain. Holding both wrists in one hand, with the other he pressed gently in the small of her back, bending her forward. She moved obediently, allowing him to arrange her as if she were a doll. Her wrists were resting now on her upthrust buttocks, and he was busy tying them together with the second rope. She turned her head to one side to watch in the mirror as he finished tying her hands then gradually began to lift them skyward. She had imagined that it would hurt, that it would stretch her in a way she didn't want to go, that it would be at the least uncomfortable. Much to her surprise, it was not. The weight of her upper body, resting from her hands, helped to counterbalance the tendency to fall forward off those heels. She felt surprisingly secure.

'There,' said Mike, removing his hands from the final knot. 'Very fine, I think.'

He was not inviting her agreement, but she did agree. It was amazing how like the picture she looked, even though she was not wraith-slender like the fantasy girl. Her pendent breasts were full and inviting, tipped with sharp, dark nipples, and when she looked back, towards her bottom, she could see her rear view reflected in the mirror behind her, a splendid expanse of white thigh and buttock, carved through by a dark, gleaming furrow in which the flushed lips of her vagina both proclaimed and concealed the heart of her.

'Now.' Mike walked around to stand in front of her and unbuttoned the fly of his black jeans. She lifted her head, eager for the sight and smell of his cock. Oh, to feel it in her mouth!

Reaching into the fly, Mike pulled out his cock and rubbed it meditatively. Catherine licked her lips. It was a splendid cock, not as big as Bill's but finely shaped and glistening with alertness. Mike pulled back the foreskin and she gasped, because the head of the penis was pierced with a little gold dumb-bell. A pierced penis! She had had no idea. How could she not have felt it inside her? But she hadn't. What would it be like to take it in her mouth? Would she have to be very gentle? She was thirsty for it, and she stretched out her neck in hope. 'Please, Mike,' she whispered, without thinking. 'Please let me.'

He took a step back, frowning. 'Quiet,' was all he said. His hand tightened on the shaft of his cock and rubbed up and down. She could smell it: a hot, tormenting smell. 'Please,' she whimpered again, though she knew it was useless. She tried to move, but the ropes on her arms and feet allowed her only to sway helplessly forward and back, like a dangling mobile.

'No,' Mike said. He took a condom packet out of his pocket and with one quick movement rubbered up. Teasingly, he offered the plastic sheath to her lips. 'Want to taste it now?' he mocked her, knowing that the smell of the spermicide was revolting, grinning as she turned her head away. He caught hold of her hair. 'I ought to make you eat it, rubber and all. I ought to make you suck it now.' For a moment she was afraid that he would, but then he laughed and let go of her. 'But not this time. I have something else in mind, this time.'

He walked around behind her, running his hand over her flank. She turned her head to follow his movement, taken aback again by how immobile she was held. He stood behind her, caressing the curves of her arse, meeting her eyes in the mirror. 'What a gorgeous behind you have,' he said. 'And you're so wet and ready for me. I bet you'd just love to have me shove my cock into you. I'm sure that's what you're waiting for.'

It was, of course, but she wasn't going to say so. She remained silent, sometimes meeting his eyes, sometimes watching his hands in the mirror as they moved over her skin, watching the fingers pressing, matching the sight and the sensation. She felt hungry and hollow for him.

'And of course,' he said softly, leaning forward a little, 'of course, I am going to shove my cock into you. I want to do that very much. But, my dear, I'm not going to shove it into your cunt.'

He waited a moment, waiting for the realisation and

shock to register in her eyes. Then he began to push his fingers into her, withdrawing them dripping with juice. He smeared the juice around her perineum, behind her lips, around her anus.

'Mike,' she whispered, 'don't.'

'Oh,' he said, 'what a shame: we didn't agree any sort of word that really means stop. So I don't know, when you say don't, whether you really mean don't, or whether you really mean do. So for the time being I'll assume you mean do. When I fucked you last, up against the window, you thought I might take you up the arse then, didn't you? And you didn't tell me not to. So I will make the assumption that you have a secret yearning to be fucked in the arse. That you want to find out what it feels like to have a cock there. I'll make that assumption.'

All the time he was speaking his hands were moving, spreading her juices, and then a finger pressed against her anus, pushing its way inside her.

'No,' she whispered, although she knew that he was right, that she did want to know what it felt like. And how better to learn? She could say, she could believe, that he had made her do it. After all, there was nothing she could do. She arched her back helplessly, and her dangling breasts swung with her movements as he pushed the finger further and further inside her.

'Feel that,' he whispered. 'Soon there'll be something much bigger there, my dear. Oh, much bigger.' He moved the finger to and fro.

Catherine moaned. She didn't know if what she was feeling was pleasure or revulsion. It was a strange sensation, all-consuming, there was no room for anything else in her mind while it was happening. Mike stood a little to one side and then with his other hand tugged her head around so that she could look in the mirror and see his finger sticking into her arse, moving in and out, gradually building up the pace until it felt as if he was fucking her there, fucking her with just that one finger and making her want it, making her want more.

She closed her eyes and moaned, and as if it were a signal Mike withdrew his finger. He moved up close behind her and his rubber-clad cock brushed against her buttocks. 'Now,' he whispered, 'must just get it nice and wet,' and without any preliminary he pushed his cock into her vagina, all the way in, and even as she cried out he withdrew it and thrust three fingers into her instead, drawing out juice that clung to his hand in glutinous strings, anointing her arse with it.

'Now,' he hissed, 'relax,' and he put the tip of his cock against her anus and began to push.

For a moment she watched in the mirror, wondering and horrified, but she couldn't watch, it was like watching a hypodermic syringe entering her skin. She closed her eyes and tried to relax even though every muscle in her arse was crying out to exclude the invader. At first she thought he would never manage it, but then he was there, just the tip lodged inside her, and she cried out with surprise and shock, and then he thrust hard and the whole head was in. 'Oh, oh God,' she moaned.

Then his hand was in her hair again, pulling her head round. 'Look,' he hissed. 'Look. Watch yourself getting fucked in the arse.'

So she turned her head, and there was the white curve of her flank, and the black pillar of his jeans, and in between them the cleft of her arse with the head of his cock stuck in it, stuck so tightly it seemed impossible that it should move. But he hissed, 'Watch,' and the shaft was moving, it was entering her, and the feeling of being crammed full was so immense that she thought she was about to burst, and she cried out, 'Oh, oh, oh,' and then with a lunge and a grunt he was right up her, his prick filling her arse to the brim, his thighs resting on her buttocks.

'Oh God,' she whimpered. If she could have moved, if she could have got away from him, she would have done. 'Oh please, Mike, please don't move, please don't fuck me, it's too much, I can't bear it.'

'You will bear it,' he whispered. Then he leant forward, so that his black-clad body arched over her, and he reached forward and took hold of her dangling breasts and began to squeeze them and pinch the nipples. He didn't move his cock, just stood there and fondled her breasts, and the sensation of fullness and discomfort gradually faded and was replaced by a terrible dark pleasure. He squeezed and stroked, and then he moved his right hand down to her crotch and pushed it through the thatch of her pubic hair and found her clitoris and began to tickle and tweak until she moaned.

'Now,' he hissed, 'now you're ready to bear it,' and his hips hollowed and thrust and the shaft of his cock slid out of her anus almost to the head and then back in, and his fingers were roiling her clit and her breast, and she twisted helplessly in the ropes that held her dangling, arching her back, arching her shoulders, not knowing if she was trying to escape or trying to pull him in further. She spasmed and he gasped, and then his finger on her clitoris touched her in a way that seemed magical and she was coming, unable to watch her own body shuddering in its bonds as he took hold of her hips and arse-fucked her hard and fast, just three quick deep strokes before he came too, his cock quivering and jumping, and then almost instantaneously he withdrew from her and her arse gave a tremendous clutch, almost as if it wanted to bite the intruder now it was too late, and it was over.

Leaving her dangling there he walked over to the water fountain, stripped the condom from his cock and began to wash it in the cold water. It deflated rapidly. She couldn't speak, just closed her eyes and gasped. Her orgasm had been as powerful as it was unexpected.

'Well,' he said, strolling back over to her with his flies buttoned, almost as if nothing had happened. 'Well, you seemed to enjoy that. A nice little appetiser.'

He unfastened her arms and she fell forward on to

both knees, gasping. 'Untie my feet,' she whispered, because she felt hardly able to do it for herself. 'Please.'

'Oh, no.' His voice told her that he was smiling. 'No, no. Not until after the main course.'

Maggie sat back, pushing her plate away from her. 'That was so good,' she said, 'but I couldn't eat another thing. Honestly.'

'Well worth waiting for,' was Ben's comment. 'That's the best Thai food I've had outside Thailand.' He mopped his lips with his napkin, then grinned at her. 'You've got mango juice on your chin,' he said, and before she could move he leant over and used his napkin to clean it off for her.

As he sat back she thought with a shock: *That's the first time he's touched me!* They had walked to the restaurant together, sat and eaten a meal together, conversed and laughed together, and in all those hours he hadn't set a finger to her flesh. Now he had wiped her chin with his napkin and her heart was racing as if he'd – as if he'd done something much, much more intimate.

What was the matter with her? She wasn't supposed to enjoy just going out with guys. She was supposed to enjoy them physically and not bother with all that emotional crap. But she wouldn't have liked to do without this evening.

'I fancy a coffee,' he said, 'but not here. Do you know the Bird, the jazz club up St Andrew's Street?'

'Er, I know of it, but I haven't actually been there.' She didn't like to tell him that in the past raves had been more of her scene than jazz.

'It's very good, and there's a woman singing there tonight I think you'll like. Very soulful, sensual music. I love it. And they do really good coffee. How about it, or are you one of those poor people who can't drink coffee after six p.m, without getting palpitations?'

She wanted to say *You give me palpitations*, but somehow it just didn't seem right. So she just said, 'So far I have been able to drink *caffè latte* any hour, day or night, without affecting any major physical functions.'

'Excellent. Let's go, then.' He caught a waiter's eye and made the universal sign of requiring the bill: a scribble on an invisible piece of paper.

When they left and turned down through Lion Yard he looked down at her – he was at least a foot taller than she was – and said, 'You know, Maggie, I'm really pleased that you agreed to come out tonight. I'm enjoying myself.'

'So am I,' she said, and although part of her still insisted that she would have enjoyed it more if they had stayed in together and fucked like minks, she felt less inclined to believe it now.

'Good,' he said. He reached down and found her hand and held it as they walked.

He was holding her hand! Nobody had held her hand since she was little, and when she saw couples walking along hand in hand she thought they looked ridiculous. And now Ben was holding her hand and all she could think about was how nice it felt, how comforting, and how big his hand was, soft and dry and warm.

At this rate, all she would get out of him this evening was a single kiss. On the lips, if she was lucky.

And thinking about that possible kiss, she suddenly felt uncomfortable, apprehensive, almost unaccountably anxious. What was the matter with her? Did she really think that in some recondite way she might not give satisfaction? How many men had kissed her before, and nobody ever complained?

But not this man. Not this man, whom she had wanted since her first year and waited for for three years. He had never kissed her. And now she realised how she felt about it.

She felt shy.

'Untie my feet,' Catherine repeated helplessly. 'Mike, please.'

He shook his head, smiling. 'Oh, no. Absolutely not. Why would I want to do that?'

'So I can walk to the pillar,' she suggested, half hopefully.

'Reasonable,' he agreed. 'But unnecessary.' And without another word he stood behind her, bent his knees, wrapped his arms around her hips and lifted her as if she was a mannequin in a shop window. She squeaked with protest and tried to push his hands away, but he was already almost at the pillar. Then they were there, and he put her down and spun her on her heels and grabbed her hands and pulled them around the pillar and began to fasten them securely behind it, wrapping the ropes around her wrists not tightly, but snugly, so that she knew there would be no escape.

'Hmm,' he said, when her hands were fastened. 'I could have you now, couldn't I? You do look delicious.' He gestured at the mirror, inviting her to look at herself.

As if she needed to be invited. Her breasts were heaving because she was breathing fast, and they were jutting out because her hands were tied behind her, and the dark fur between her legs was glistening with her own juice. Looking at herself was the perfect, narcissistic recipe for arousal.

'But,' Mike went on thoughtfully, 'you aren't properly trussed up yet, are you? You need to be tied so that you can't move. Otherwise, how can I prove to you that I can have you without your able assistance?' He looked at her for a moment, his head slightly on one side, and then pulled a fine white scarf out of his jacket pocket. He flourished it as he approached her. 'First,' he said, 'the gag.'

Catherine had never been gagged before, not even in play when she was a child. She found she did not like the sensation, the way the fabric pressed against her tongue and made it impossible to articulate, the way her saliva began to pool at the edges of her mouth. But it did look frightfully authentic, and the mewling noises which emerged from behind it stimulated her too, even though it was she who was making them. Was it possible, then, to be two people at once, one who wasn't enjoying herself a bit, the other relishing every mortification heaped upon her?

Mike admired his handiwork, then headed back to the cupboard for more ropes. He tied her bound ankles to the pillar, then wrapped another rope around her waist, pinning down her arms, making it almost impossible for her to move at all, other than her head. She moaned in protest and her hair swung heavily across her face, half blinding her. He had thoughtfully tied the gag beneath her hair, so as not to affect its movement. Now he reached up and swept the stray locks back from her face, revealing wide eyes. 'I wouldn't do that,' he suggested. 'It would be a pity if you couldn't see yourself.'

He stepped back and let her see herself, trussed like a prisoner, a hostage bound and awaiting her captor's ravishment. She breathed quickly, astonished and delighted by her own image, wanting nothing more at this moment than to be ravished. But she still didn't believe it would be possible. Her thighs were pressed closely together, she could not move her hips. How would he be able to penetrate her?

As if he had read her mind, he said, 'If I'm going to put my cock up you, you'll need to be good and wet.' If she had been able to speak she would have said that she already was, but no words could escape from the gag. 'Now, while I was shagging your lovely big arse, I couldn't help but notice that your cunt was as wet as a whore's.' He cocked an eye at her, wondering what effect this foul language would have. He must have seen that she actually found it arousing, because he did not desist. 'But I think it needs to be even wetter if I'm going to get myself up there now. It'll feel especially good and tight with you legs clamped together like this. You'll need to be really wet. I think I'd better make you come again, then I'll know you're ready for me.'

Suddenly Catherine was afraid. If she came like this,

167

tied like this and with a gag in her mouth, wouldn't she choke, wouldn't she suffocate? She squirmed and moaned, but Mike laughed at her. 'Playing chicken now, are we? Oh, I think not.'

He came close to her, stooped forward, and took one of her nipples into his mouth. Her moan of protest turned into a moan of delight as he bathed the stiff peak with his saliva, flickered his tongue against the cleft in the tip, wrapped it in his lips, sucked hard and harder until she was filled with pain and piercing delight. When the nipple was so turgid she thought it would burst he let it go, trapped it instead between two strong fingers, and turned his attention to her other breast. And he lifted his other hand and let it rest on the top of her thigh, the tips of his fingers just brushing against her fleece, promising delights. She moaned again, eagerly now, tying to encourage him to push his fingers between her legs. This was what she had imagined for this captive girl, a man stooped before her servicing her protuberant breasts with his tongue, sliding one deft finger between her closed thighs to flick and tease her clitoris. She wanted to feel him touch her.

But he did not touch her. He released her breasts and dropped to his knees, then pressed his face close to her thighs and drew in a deep luxurious breath. 'God, Catherine, you smell good. You smell potent. You smell good enough to eat.'

And now his face was pressing against her pubic hair and his tongue was working its way through the dark curls and now, unbelievably, his tongue was pressing against her clit, it was touching it, titillating it, and both of his big strong hands were reaching up to scratch against her nipples and she had never felt anything like it. She tried to move, tried to open her legs so that he would find it easier to lick her, but she was held immobile. She let her head roll back and cried out with ecstasy into the muffling gag, and now she knew that that was the posture of the girl in the picture, not protest, but the approach of orgasm.

'Ah,' Mike hissed between licks, 'you taste good, Catherine. Like a fine wine, you taste as good as you smell. Ah, that's nice.'

He could barely touch her with his tongue, it seemed almost impossible that he would ever actually bring her off with such delicate, such insubstantial stimulation. But the sensations were building, and the rough pinches and grasps of his strong hands on her breasts and nipples built her excitement up almost unbearably. She tried to cry out encouragement to him, tried to beg him not to stop, and all that came out from the gag were moans and whimpers. She sounded like an animal as he licked her slowly, slowly to orgasm, touching the naked stem of her clitoris so gently that it drove her mad. And then, just as she thought she would never make it and it would drive her mad, then he forced his face deep into her pubes and lashed her with his tongue, soaking her with his saliva, pinning down the engorged nub of her clit and worrying it until she screamed into the gag and shuddered convulsively as a massive orgasm racked her.

'Good,' he hissed, standing away from her and drawing his cock out from his jeans, fiercely erect again, the little gold dumb-bell gleaming. He unwrapped a condom and sheathed it, then advanced on her as she gasped. 'Ready?' he demanded. 'I'm going to fuck you now.'

She still didn't believe it would be possible. But he put his cock at the junction of her legs and thrust, and she was so wet and slippery that he slid between her thighs and between the lips of her sex as if they were part of her cunt, and unbelievably she felt the head of his cock lodge where it should be, where she felt so empty and hungry that she longed for him.

He stood straddled, legs wide, bringing his hips to a level slightly lower than hers. The fat tip of his cock wormed around, establishing its position. Then he thrust, gasping slightly as he did so, and she felt his cock begin to penetrate her, sliding up inside her, not quite as deep as it might in normal sex, but deep enough. The bottom of his shaft rubbed hard against her labia and clit, a delicious sensation.

'Damn, that's good,' he said, leaning back slightly as if to enjoy the view. 'Jesus, this is a great idea. You can't move, so I don't need to hold you to keep you still. I can just squeeze your tits and fuck. Excellent.'

Grinning fiendishly, he put one hand on each of her breasts and squeezed hard, almost painfully, and jerked his hips violently towards her. Because it was so hard for him to enter her every thrust brought the whole length of his cock into sparkling contact with her clit, almost as if he was just pushing his prick between her legs. She moaned and turned her head and saw herself in the mirror, rigid, bound against the pillar, and Mike with his hands grasping her breasts and his black-clad backside lunging at her, and suddenly her mind was full of a dirty magazine that she had found under her brother's bed when she was fourteen and a picture in it, a cartoon, a woman being fucked by two men at once, big black men fucking a white woman, the one behind her holding her wrists behind her back and with his hand clamped over her mouth, the one in front of her holding her breasts in his big hands, both of them thrusting into her so hard that little drops of juice and sweat flew from their loins. She had forgotten how she had masturbated looking at that picture, and now it was as if she was in it, and she relaxed against the cold hardness of the pillar and let her thighs soften to Mike's harsh vigorous thrusting, knowing that soon she would come again. He was fucking her hard and fast, grunting and gasping as he surged to and fro, her breasts clasped in his hands, and she closed her eyes and let the sensations take her, let the orgasm roll from her bound ankles up to her swollen clit and her stretched cunt, up past the ropes on her waist to her breasts and shoulders, and at last into her head, where it crashed and spun like an acrobat, so powerful that she could hardly even cry out. She was only vaguely aware of Mike lunging into her once, twice, and then letting out an anguished cry as he bent his head against her shoulder, shaking with the strength of his own climax.

A moment later he withdrew, tidied himself, and then removed the gag. He didn't ask her if she was all right. All he said was, 'I win, I think.'

'I don't remember betting,' Catherine retorted, sagging against her bonds.

They walked back across the market square together, still saying nothing. Catherine wondered vaguely how many words she had actually exchanged with Mike during the course of their relationship. If it was a relationship.

The Thai restaurant was still busy, but there was another couple sitting in the window now. Where were Ben and Maggie? Gone back to her room, for an evening of passionate sex? Somehow, on this occasion, it didn't seem likely.

Mike glanced across at her, a dark, unreadable glance. It was so difficult to know what he was thinking. He obviously didn't want emotional entanglement, and she could understand that and accept it. But right now she felt lonely, and she wanted someone to be with her, and he was there.

Of course, it was going to be risky, asking him if he would do something for her. But this one-sided state of affairs was not going to prove entirely satisfactory, if after a spell of such sexual excitement it left her feeling empty and unsatisfied.

They were nearly at the entrance to her room. Distances in Cambridge were so short they allowed no time for thought. She said quickly, 'Mike –' and when he looked at her, '– I'd really like it if you came up and stayed the night.'

For a moment he looked, not angry, but almost puzzled. Then he smiled a little and shook his head.

Catherine felt angry. 'I'm not asking you to marry me, for Christ's sake,' she said. 'Just come up to my room

171

and stay the night, in bed.' The request was so reason-able that when he went on shaking his head, not even deigning to answer her, she flared up. 'We could have sex again,' she said, not even caring if people overheard her. 'I could go down on you. I'd like to do that.' Still he didn't reply, and she almost shouted, 'Mike!'

There was a long silence. His eyes were shadowed, opaque. 'That's not what it's about,' he said at last.

'I see. What I want isn't what it's about. It's only what you want.'

'Don't tell me you didn't want what we have done,' he said calmly.

Infuriating, maddening man! 'Yes, I wanted it. That's not the point.' She waited, in case he might actually ask her what the point was, but he didn't. He never asked, did he? 'You never even ask me a question, Mike. You only make statements. All I want is something two-way. Is that so impossible?' He didn't look as if he even understood her, she might as well have been speaking Latin. 'Christ!' she exclaimed, suddenly amused by the absurdity of it. 'All I'm asking for is a chance to go to bed with you and go down on you. What kind of a weirdo are you, not to want that?'

His eyes were like pits. He didn't say anything, just looked at her and slowly shook his head. Then he turned and walked away.

Full of unresolved anger, ready for a fight, she stood and watched him go. His refusal to fight back made her even more furious. If she had been younger she would have run after him, grabbed him, demanded his involvement. But she knew that he wouldn't be drawn, and she wasn't going to make herself look a fool by tugging at his arm and importuning him. If he couldn't handle an argument, if he was so controlling that the idea of a woman's mouth on his cock made him walk away, then good riddance to him. She could do without him. She'd managed all these years without his kind of sex, and she didn't think she would miss it.

'Fuck off, then,' she said after him. He didn't turn,

and she clenched her fist and then swung into the doorway to the house and up the narrow stairs. The spike heels were hurting her feet now, she hated them. When she opened the door of her room she kicked them furiously off, sent them skidding across the carpet and under the bed, and yelled at them, 'Good riddance.'

Then she went and sat down at her computer and turned it on, trying to make herself believe that with that much angry energy in her she would be able to get a good bit of writing done. Of course she knew that she couldn't, and instead she flicked to her emails on the off-chance that there might be something there from a friend that would make her feel better.

There were emails from friends, but there was also one from James. So which one did she open, in her self-destructive mood?

Hi Cat, why haven't I heard from u? U coming to wedding? Cheap flights on Garuda right now but risk dropping out of sky. Recommend Singapore or Cathay. Try Trailfinders or Expedia for good prices. If hard up just ask me, Catherine, just ask, my air miles are at your disposal to have you there at my wedding. email v soon luv J xxxx

He'd pay for her ticket to have her at his wedding? It was as if he was determined to have her present when he was symbolically and finally detached from her.

God, what was wrong with her? She couldn't hold on to an old dear friend and she couldn't hold on to a new sexual partner, either. Not even dressed up to the nines, not even in four-inch heels. She couldn't start a novel or sort her life out. She was hopeless.

The only thing she felt able to do was shrug off her clothes and crawl into bed.

At the bottom of the stairs they stopped, still holding hands. Maggie looked up into Ben's face, wondering at the strange, warm, melting sensation in the pit of her

173

stomach. She knew that he'd say no, but all the same her pride made her say, 'Do you want to come up?'

He shook his head, very gently, smiling at her. 'Thank you,' he said, 'but no. Not tonight.'

Even though she wasn't surprised, she was disappointed. 'Why?' she asked, and then cursed inwardly because she was sure that she sounded petulant.

'I've really enjoyed the evening,' he said. 'More than I can say. But I'm training first thing tomorrow morning, and then I'm busy, and the first time I sleep with you I know I won't want to rush away in the morning. So for now,' he said, while she was still basking in the realisation that he was talking as if this was going to go on and on, 'for now, I'll say goodnight.'

He stooped his head and she lifted her lips eagerly to meet his kiss. It was warm, firm, but chaste; his lips were slightly parted, but there was not a touch of his tongue. Even so, it stirred her blood. She tried to reach up to catch him by the hair and hold him still so that she could kiss him properly, but he pulled free and stood up, smiling.

'Good night,' he said. 'See you at the boathouse in the morning.'

'Good night,' she said. He turned and walked away, and she stood quite still and watched him go. When he got to the porter's lodge he pulled open the little wicket-gate and stepped through it. She thought he was gone, but then he appeared again framed in the gateway and blew her a kiss.

She wished he had stayed. But then again, it was in a strange way rather nice that he hadn't.

Up in her room she slipped into bed and hugged the pillow, remembering the evening, the way he had smiled at her, the things they had said to make each other laugh, the warmth of his hand as they walked along the chilly street.

Perhaps they would go to bed together tomorrow. She hoped they would.

But if not, there was a lot to be said for his company.

Chapter Ten

*T*he morning wasn't any better than the previous evening.

There was nothing to eat in Catherine's room, and no milk for tea. This wasn't a problem, of course, with the college just across the road. So she went down to Hall for breakfast, but the sight of the boaties tucking into mountains of double egg, sausage, bacon, tomatoes, mushrooms, beans and black pudding was almost more than she could bear. She was going to go back to her room to be miserable in private, but if she didn't eat something she would get more depressed and then be unable even to work. So she poured herself a bowl of cereal and got some toast and retired to a quiet table in the corner, where she wouldn't have to watch aggressively healthy young men fill themselves with calories.

What would happen if Mike came into Hall? For a moment she tormented herself with the thought, and then she laughed and shook her head at her own foolishness. He would just ignore her, of course. Ignoring people was his speciality.

A manic laugh made her lift her head. Maggie! Perhaps she might be able to talk to her. Maggie would tell her that she was better off without Mike, or any man come to that and, even though she didn't believe it, it might be reassuring to hear it all over again.

Maggie was easy to spot, with her halo of vivid blonde ringlets. She was sitting at the boatie table, surrounded as usual by men. But although she was laughing, she didn't look quite her usual flirtatious self. In fact, all her attention was focused on the young man sitting in front of her. Of course, it was the same young man as last night: Ben. Catherine looked at him more carefully now, and found what she saw appealing. He was tall – Maggie liked them tall, of course – and well built, like most rowers, with broad shoulders and chest. He had a bony, intellectual face, a long, well-shaped nose, and a calm, stable air about him. She was quite surprised that Maggie fancied that calmness: clearly a case of opposites attracting. At rest his face was long and almost mournful. But when he smiled, it lit up. He would look good wreathed in cigarette smoke, like Gary Cooper.

In any case, Maggie obviously had eyes for no one but Ben. She was pushing her food around her plate, as if she were so absorbed in the contemplation of his face that she couldn't even remember to lift her fork. No help likely from that quarter, then.

Catherine finished her cereal, every spoonful a duty, and forced herself to eat a piece of toast as well. Then she returned to her room, turned on her laptop, and stared at a blank page.

The poetry translation was finished apart from the polishing, and now she was faced with the empty expanse that was her novel. She'd tried four different beginnings to the first chapter and scrapped them all. She hadn't even thought of a synopsis, and the technician in her knew that to start a novel with no idea of where it was going was a recipe for disaster.

She was a writer in residence, come to sort her life out and get cracking on a novel that was going to make her famous. And she was a writer in residence without a man, without even the man that she had been keeping by for a rainy day, and without a book, either.

It was too depressing to look at the empty page. She switched off her computer and got to her feet, stretching out both hands in front of her until her shoulders clicked.

Then she thought of her bike. Exercise! Yes, that was it. She would get some healthy exercise. No wonder she felt stale, cooped up all day between four walls. It was another glorious late-autumn day. Out on the roads with the wind in her hair she would feel better.

It was only when she got to the bike that she remembered that she didn't have a clue about where to go. Around Oxford at least she could have headed for a country village well known for a pleasant pub. Around Cambridge, she didn't even know which direction to point in, never mind where to stop.

Hadn't she seen maps and other stuff in the bike shop? She thought she had, and it was no distance, after all, so she scooted on the bike the hundred yards down Henry's Parade and pushed it through the door of the shop. As she went in she thought with pleasure of banter with Andy. She could almost hear him saying, 'Back already? Was it too hard for you?' Perhaps he might even repeat his offer of yesterday. That would cheer her up, for sure.

But he wasn't there. Another young man, much younger than Andy and tall, said, 'Can I help you?' in a South African accent. He was wearing shorts, revealing long, hard, tanned cycling legs.

'Is Andy around?' she asked hopefully.

'Nah, it's his day off,' said the young man. 'Do you want to leave a message?'

'No, no, he just sold me the bike,' she said, concealing the disappointment.

'No problem, is there? With the bike?'

'No, no problem, I just –' She jerked her head at the maps and books on the wall. 'I just wanted some idea on where to go around here.'

'Oh, right. Help yourself.'

She propped the bike against the counter and began to leaf through the books. Someone else came into the shop and engaged the young man in an earnest discussion about the merits and demerits of six- and eight-panelled shorts. Catherine sighed, because she could see that at least two of the books were just what she needed and she didn't really want to buy either of them, or even have to put herself to the effort of choosing between them. She must have been hoping all along, subconsciously, that Andy would be in the shop. Stupid, to set herself up to be even more disappointed.

'What are you doing back here?' said a familiar voice behind her. 'Haven't fucked it up already, have you?'

Her heart lifted and she turned and said, 'I thought it was your day off. Have you got nothing better to do but come in to work on your day off?'

'I was going to strip down my chainset in the workshop. My landlady goes apeshit when I do it on the floor of my room.' Andy gestured at the lean, low, black mountain bike he held. 'But you look as if you're looking for somewhere to go. Want to come out with me? I'll show you what's what.'

He was smiling, the biggest smile she had yet seen from him. It was a cartoon smile, curved like a crescent moon, turned up at the ends. She liked it.

'Sounds like an offer I can't refuse,' she said, returning the smile.

He nodded, his smile vanishing as if it had been switched off. For a moment she was disconcerted, but his eyes were still bright. Perhaps he was just someone who didn't smile very often with his mouth. 'What do you fancy?' he asked. 'Spinning along the flat? Hills? Fording rivers in spate?'

'Didn't think there were any hills around here,' she remarked.

'One or two, if you know where to look. You want to go off-road? I know a forest which is fun.'

'Don't get your hopes up,' she said, feeling suddenly

anxious. He was dressed in scruffy clothes, a battered rugby shirt and frayed chino shorts, and beneath the crumpled hems his legs were dark with hair and as sturdy and strong as tree trunks. 'I haven't done this before, remember.'

He shook his head. 'I'm the worst teacher in the world. I'm so impatient, it's ridiculous. Just try to keep up, yeah?'

Without another word he led the way out of the shop and mounted his bike. 'We'll go out along the Backs and past Churchill, all right? I'll take it easy. Any hint of effort and I start sweating like a Turk.'

She suspected that Andy's taking it easy would be hard enough to count as a workout for her, and she was right. He cycled fast and with extraordinary efficiency, the top part of his body completely still, tucked over the handlebars, his big legs pumping like machines. He looked really comfortable on his bike, and as she shifted about to try to find a soft spot on her saddle she envied him.

'You've done this before,' she said, when they stopped at the traffic lights behind St Henry's to let pedestrians cross.

'Once or twice,' he said, looking into the distance.

Once they were heading towards Churchill there was a cycle lane, and Andy slowed down enough to let her catch up with him. He took up station on her right, protecting her from traffic, and glanced at her with his dark eyebrows lifted. 'Doing all right?'

She nodded, then thought that if she didn't speak he might think she was out of puff. 'Fine,' she said. 'This is OK, I think I could do this all day.'

'Wait to see what your arse tells you tomorrow,' he said.

'You make it look really easy,' she commented, looking at the economical smoothness of his movement.

'Tell you a secret,' he said. 'I used to ride professionally, in road races and on the track. That was a long time ago, though.'

179

'Professionally? Here?' She'd never heard of a professional cyclist in England.

'Well, no, actually, in France.'

'What were you doing in France?'

Another glance. 'Living there. I'm French.'

She was really startled. He didn't have a trace of an accent: she would have sworn he was a native English speaker. 'You don't sound it.'

'We always moved around a lot. France, England, wherever. I learnt English really young. But I'm French. My name's André, not Andy. Don't use it here, though. You can imagine the sort of comments I'd get from the guys in the shop. Sounds like a hairdresser, they'd say.'

'I like it.' She did. It reminded her of Tolstoy.

'You can call me it, then.'

He seemed to feel that they had talked enough, because he put his head down and increased the pace slightly. She let him pull ahead and watched his movement, the strong muscles in his thighs and calves flexing and tugging. He might not be tall, but he was big, big all over, a big muscly backside pumping away under his shorts, heavy corded forearms tugging at the handlebars. Strong, capable-looking. A bit young, maybe, but he hadn't asked her how old she was so presumably he didn't care, and if he didn't why should she? He wouldn't have been the sort of man she would describe when asked what type she fancied, but now she was with him she could see that he had considerable appeal.

The next couple of miles were a range of slight hills, mostly up, and she found herself struggling for breath. She hoped he was the kind of man who found red cheeks and a sweaty back attractive. He looked as if he might be, and he had suggested going for a ride, after all.

When they were back on the flat he slowed down again, unclipped a water bottle from the frame of his bike and held it out to her. 'Want some?'

'Thanks.' It felt insecure taking one hand from the handlebars to take the bottle and drink, but she managed it. When she handed it back André took both hands off the bars to take his drink, flinging his head back and gulping without ever slowing his pace. Show-off! He was like a kid. Definitely slightly young.

'So,' she said, when the bottle was reclipped, 'what are you doing in Cambridge?'

'I could ask you the same question,' he said.

'Yes, you could. But I asked first.'

'Hoity, toity. I'm working in a bike shop. Just happened, really.'

'Long-term?'

'Hardly. The moment it gets colder I'm going to be off back to France. I fancy the *Pyrenées* this winter.' He pronounced the word unselfconsciously in French. 'Do some bar work, bit of building if I can get any, bit of skiing.'

A rolling stone, then. Not a long-term prospect, certainly. Just as well she hadn't got any hopes up.

'What about you?' he asked.

'I'm a writer,' she said. 'Books. I'm just in Cambridge for three months.'

Did he feel disappointed, too, that whatever became of this trip together was doomed to be short-term? If he did, he didn't show it. 'Writing's cool,' he said. 'I can't write a letter, never mind a book. You could do it anywhere, couldn't you?'

That was true, of course, and she wondered for a moment why she had always done it in safe, accustomed places like London and Cambridge. But all she said was, 'I wish it made more money.'

He laughed. 'Tell me about it.' Then he jerked his chin at the road ahead. 'See that lane on the right? The wood's down there. Ready for it?'

Twenty minutes later she was poised at the top of a switchback slope that curved between trees and down muddy banks to emerge at the edge of the wood into a sunny field of tall grass. André, beside her, pointed out the twists and finer points.

'Don't look down,' he advised her. 'And if you see an obstacle, don't focus on it. If you do, you'll ride into it. Keep it loose, keep it fluid.'

'Those are steep climbs,' she said apprehensively.

'Use a low gear, lean forward, and just relax. You'll be fine. Watch.'

He hoisted the bike into a wheelie and leapt down the first slope. Sliding, scrambling, and sprinting explosively with his strong legs, it was only about a minute before he was skidding to a halt in the grass. He turned the bike round and cycled back around the edge of the dell, panting a little as he climbed the last hill. His shirt was beginning to darken with sweat.

'See? Easy. Your turn.'

She was scared, but she didn't want to look like a wimp, so she gripped the handlebars tightly and tilted the nose of the bike over the first rim.

The suddenness of the speed astonished her. At the bottom she saw a tree root reaching out for her like fingers, and forgetting everything André had said she stared at it. A second later the front wheel hit the root and the bike lurched to one side and spilled her off. She landed on her hands in a patch of mud, gasping.

'Woah!' said Andy, sliding down the bank. 'You OK?'

Amazingly enough, it seemed that she was. She got up, shaking herself. 'I think so.' She didn't feel scared now, more excited, as if the worst had happened. 'Just glad I decided to wear old jeans, really.'

'Good girl,' Andy nodded approvingly.

'Good girl?' she repeated incredulously, staring at him. 'What am I, a dog?'

He opened his hands in an egregiously French shrug. 'Hey, I just mean that I like women who don't wince. You don't wince. That's good. You're a girl. Good girl.'

Perhaps he hadn't meant to be patronising. In fact, it sounded as if he had meant to praise her. He was definitely rather unreconstructed, but she decided to let it pass. 'Bugger,' she said, hauling up the bike, 'I have to push it up now.'

'Let me,' Andy said. He grabbed the bike and ran up the slope with it, and at the top he held it chivalrously for her to mount. 'Madam, your steed.'

He was sweet. Not subtle, but sweet. She got back on the bike and looked down the slope at her gouged skid-marks in the mud. 'Second time lucky,' she said, and pushed off.

Looking ahead, pedalling furiously up the hills, enjoy-ing the sense of almost zero-g as she crossed the peaks, suddenly she saw the grass ahead of her and then there was a yell behind her and André was overtaking her, pedalling like a fury, whizzing past as if she was standing still, and as she stopped in the grass he zoomed around her with his hands off the bars yelling, 'You did it! Great stuff!'

She punched her fists in the air, laughing, then dropped the bike, stepped out of it and fell over in the long grass. It was dry and cool among the green stalks, and the sun was warm on her face. She was panting and laughing and pleased with herself.

Andy stood over her, grinning. 'See? I told you you could do it.'

'Don't be smug,' she said.

The grin disappeared. He looked down at her for a moment in silence, then dropped to kneel astride her legs, still watching her face. She looked up at him, and she did not smile either. She could sense his tension, and it was catching. Her heart was pounding and she was acutely aware of the proximity of his body, of the sharp hot smell of his fresh sweat, of the dark hairs outlining the curve of muscle on his forearms. She felt as if she were sharing the field with an animal, some-thing tame – just – but not domesticated. She pushed herself up on her elbows and licked her lips. Her breasts rose and fell rapidly as she breathed.

For a long moment he stayed perfectly still, looking down at her. His hazel eyes seemed very dark. Then his nostrils flared as he took in a quick deep breath, as if he were getting up nerve. He said, 'Do you want to have sex with me?'

She didn't express her first thought, which was *Thank God, a man who asks me what I want*. She did express her second, which was, 'Yes.'

'Good,' he said, 'because I really want to have sex with you.'

Before he could move she suddenly realised that all she had with her was her college key and a ten-pound note. 'Oh God,' she said, 'I haven't got a condom.'

He smiled at that. 'I might have. And if not, we'll just have to manage.' He grabbed the hem of his shirt with both hands and in one fluid movement pulled it off over his head and dropped it in the grass. 'Hope you don't mind hairy blokes,' he said.

She looked up at him, assessing his torso. It was, as he said, hairy: a thatch of dark hair springing right across his broad chest, and finer, softer hairs clothing his flat belly. His skin was olive-dark and the muscles on his arms and shoulders were hard and thick. As he bent forward a little the muscle on his belly formed tiny ridges. She hadn't previously considered that hair was attractive, but Andy's body was so compact and taut and animal that it would have seemed wrong for him to be smooth.

He didn't seem to notice that she was giving him the once-over. His head was bent as he began on the buttons on his shorts. She was taken aback by how quickly this was all happening. Normally she wouldn't have said anything, but there was something very straightforward about André, something that made her able to comment. 'You don't hang about, do you?' she said.

He stopped in mid-button and looked serious. 'Problem?' he asked. 'I'm not in a rush, if that's what you mean. I just prefer to be stripped for action.'

There could hardly be more of a contrast with Mike. Catherine leant back into the grass and smiled, feeling suddenly very relaxed. 'No problem,' she said. 'As long as you don't mind me just enjoying the view.'

He grinned, totally unselfconscious. Then he got to his feet and pushed off shorts, socks and shoes all at the same time, and when he straightened he was naked.

Catherine sucked in a quick breath, admiring him. His whole body was broad and strong, perfectly in balance, and the cock that thrust its way forward from his crotch was sturdy and thick, noticeably fatter at the tip than at the base and ridged with heavy veins. He was circumcised, and the head of his cock was smooth and swollen and purple with lust. It was a stubborn, brutal-looking thing. Her mouth went dry at the sight of it.

He looked uncomfortable. 'Look,' he said suddenly, 'I was lying. I am in a hurry. I haven't had it for months.' His frankness surprised her: most men she had known would die rather than admit to a lacuna in their sexual activity. 'If we have sex straight away I'll come too quick,' he went on, looking very earnest. 'So, I wonder, I mean –'

He hesitated, and she smiled, understanding him. Not a controlling man, this one! She pushed herself up and licked her lips. 'I'd be delighted,' she whispered.

He stood still, and as she got to her knees and moved towards him he closed his eyes. She took her time about coming close, enjoying her slow examination of his body. She could see what Mike liked about being clothed while his partner was naked. If André hadn't been so quintessentially masculine he might even have seemed vulnerable, standing there with his eyes shut waiting for her to touch him. He was incredibly tense. As she drew closer her breathing stirred the dark hairs on his thighs and he shivered, the way a horse shivers when a fly lands on its skin.

She drew in a long breath, relishing the smell of him. He smelt of aroused male, of mud and sweat, and also, reassuringly, of soap. She brought her face very close to his crotch and closed her eyes, inhaling his scent and feeling her whole body react to it. She had wanted this so much with Mike, to breathe him in, to caress him with her mouth and lips, to taste him. Just smelling André was an erotic experience almost on a par with everything that Mike had done to her.

His cock twitched as she brushed against the hairs in his groin. She smiled at its eagerness and put both her hands on his thighs, bracing herself against him. He tensed, and the muscles beneath her hands felt as hard as wood. He wouldn't be a man to touch lightly, or to tickle. All those hairs would make it more of an irritation than a pleasure. He needed to be treated like a strong animal, simply, straightforwardly, with a strength to match his own.

Slowly, firmly, she ran her hands up his thighs to his crotch, then around to his buttocks. They were taut, solid slabs of muscle. She cupped them, holding him still, then ran her tongue around her lips, moistening them so that when she took the head of his cock into her mouth it would slide in smoothly and sweetly. She wanted him to remember this.

Now her lips were wet, and she stuck her tongue out further and just caught the tip of his cock with it, tasting the salty bead of fluid that hung there. Andy drew in a hissing breath and his arse clenched under her hands, making his cock jump and dance. She leant back a little, looking up at him, because she didn't see any need to rush. His face was tilted up to the sun, eyes tight shut, and his clenched hands hovered in front of his chest.

'Aah,' she whispered, and on the whisper she leant forward and opened her mouth to take him in.

Hot, hard, glossy, the head filled her mouth. The taste was different from the smell, clean and sharp, the taste of thoroughly-washed, soap and water man. She gasped with the pleasure of it, feeling the muscles of her cunt clench and tighten. André let out another breath, a sound almost of pain, as if it came from between clenched teeth. He was not noisy, it seemed. Catherine mouthed the head for a moment, letting it penetrate her lips again and again, not yet trying to take in the shaft. After a little while Andy moaned, 'Jesus,' and rested his hands on her hair, not hard, very gently, the tiniest pressure of his fingers on her scalp telling her that he was desperate to feel her take him fully into her mouth. She tightened her hands against his buttocks and sighed as she let his cock slide in deep, as far as she could, until the fat head touched the very back of her throat.

Now his urgency showed. His buttocks were tight under her hands and he gasped every time she swallowed him up. His hands in her hair were tightening as her movements grew faster, and after only a few strokes she felt his cock begin to twitch and shudder. She had teased him long enough, so now she gave it to him hard, sucking and swirling her tongue around him, pumping his stiff shaft until his hands in her hair became talons and he cried out as he came. She swallowed, gave another tiny suck to extract the last drops, and swallowed again.

'Oh, God,' he said, his hands shaking. 'So sensitive now, Jesus.'

She let him go, and he dropped to his knees beside her, his expression stunned. 'Bloody hell,' he said.

'Nice?' she asked archly.

'Amazing. Amazing. Where'd you learn to give head like that? You should do it for a living.'

That was deliciously flattering. She smiled and leant forward to kiss him. He swayed away from her, saying, 'Oh, really rude stuff, she's just swallowed my come and now she wants to kiss me.'

'Damn right I do,' she said, and then he grinned and took her shoulders in his big hands and put his mouth on hers.

He kissed her hesitantly at first, little kisses on each lip in turn, almost as if he didn't dare give her his tongue. When he did, it was breathtaking, strong and demanding, without any subtlety, but delicious all the same. She let herself soften into his arms, relishing the simplicity, the lack of sophistication that she felt in his touch. It was all so – so spontaneous, so unplanned. So unlike Mike.

His naked body pressed against her. His skin was hot, incredibly hot. She could feel the heat of him through her fleece and her T-shirt. His hands fumbled for the hem of her fleece, found it, pushed inside. He felt for her breasts through the T-shirt, nursed them gently, all the time dropping those soft pecking kisses on each lip in turn.

'Gorgeous breasts,' he whispered. 'Gorgeous. Beautiful. Show them to me.'

She didn't hesitate, didn't even think of trying to keep her clothes on. She pulled the fleece over her head, unzipped her muddy jeans and pushed them down, pulling off shoes and socks as she did so. Then the T-shirt followed the fleece, and she was dressed in just a cotton bra and knickers. The sun was warm on her shoulders, but a cool breeze touched her and made goose pimples spring up on her bare skin. She shivered and pressed closely to him. His skin was like a furnace, and the soft thick rod of his penis was beginning to harden again. It stirred against her like a serpent, and the feel of it made her quiver. Her insides churned and liquified.

'Mmm,' he said, nuzzling into her neck, 'you're soft.'

'Not enough exercise,' she excused herself.

'Don't take any exercise, then, I like women to be soft.' His big hands ran over her shoulders, settled on her waist, cupped her buttocks. They were gentle and very warm. She gave another little shiver and wrapped her arms around him, holding him close to keep her warm.

'You smell good,' he whispered, and his exploring hands slid down her buttocks and just touched the back of her thighs where the hair started, such an intimate touch that she couldn't restrain a little moan. She nuzzled into his neck, hiding her eyes. The rough stubble on his neck and cheek scratched deliciously against her face. His hands strayed back up her spine, found the catch of her bra and released it.

'My favourite moment,' he said, and pushed her away

from him a little to allow himself room to peel off the bra. He dropped it into the grass and gazed at her breasts, licking his lips. 'They're beautiful,' he murmured. 'Beautiful breasts.'

Catherine had often thought her breasts too big and soft to be aesthetically pleasing. She felt self-conscious now, and said uncomfortably, 'I wish they were a bit smaller, you know, and more self-supporting.'

He cupped her breasts in his hands, squeezing them gently. She closed her eyes. When she opened them again he was smiling at her. 'No, they suit you,' he said. 'And they're so soft, they're gorgeous. Those little pert ones aren't soft, you know. They're not so nice to squeeze.' And he squeezed again, less gently this time.

He stooped his head and caught one nipple in his mouth, suckling gently. Catherine let her head fall back, sighing as the sensations arrowed through her. He held her tightly enough for her to feel the strength in his hands, and moved from one breast to the other, caressing, sucking, nibbling. She relaxed completely against his support, her breathing harsh with pleasure.

André pulled back a little and smiled at her. 'Someone said,' he said, 'that if he was a woman he'd never get anything done, because he'd be playing with his breasts all day. I have to say I agree.'

'Women have gone a step better than that,' Catherine said. 'I read a book a little while ago called *What I Would Do If I Had A Dick For A Day*. It was written by lots of famous female writers.'

'Including you?'

'Not famous enough, alas,' she said, and then added accurately, 'not famous at all.'

'Good,' he said. 'Famous people can't be private.' He stooped his head to her breasts again, this time kneading the flesh with his hands as he sucked and licked. Catherine tried to relax, tried to let him take his time, but she wanted him very much now. After a moment she caught hold of his head and strained herself against his mouth, whispering, 'Please do it harder, please.'

He pulled back against her hands. His dark hair was surprisingly soft. 'Now who's in a hurry?'

'Please,' she whispered, sagging backwards hopelessly.

He didn't say anything, just caught hold of her knickers and pulled them down, then took hold of her legs by the ankles and pushed them apart. Before she had a chance to feel shy he slipped down between her legs and pressed his lips to her belly, then ducked his head and gave her a great slicing lick, all the way from her arsehole to her pubic hair in one salacious movement. It was so unexpected that she cried out. Then he pressed his face to her thighs and drove his tongue into her, all the way into her, exploring her depths with ferocious greed. She cried out again, aroused beyond bearing.

She had to have him. Grabbing hold of his hair, she pulled his head away from her and hissed, 'Where's that bloody condom?'

'Calm down,' he said, and reached out for his shorts. She watched with anxiety, then sighed with relief as he withdrew the little packet from a side pocket.

With a single fluid motion he pushed the condom down over his cock. It was fully hard now, and it looked even bigger than it had before. It looked like a club. She was terrified of it, she lusted after it, she wanted to feel it penetrate her. She lay back, her thighs parted. The long stems of the grass beneath her were cool and scratchy. She smiled and reached out to him.

Instead of lying on her, letting her feel his weight, he nudged his way on his knees up between her thighs, spreading them wide. With one hand he pushed her knee away from him and with the other he held his cock, rubbing it over her vulva, teasing her as it slid into her entrance and away again, edging over her clit, slithering down almost to her anus. She squirmed, enjoying it, but desperate to feel him inside her. After a moment she hissed, 'André, please, please.'

'Just playing,' he said, 'just playing with you.' He let the head of his cock lodge where it should be, at the entrance to her sex, and spread his knees wider. He pushed her thighs apart with his hands so that she was spread wide open to him, everything exposed. 'God,' he said, 'that looks rude. Jesus, you look good.' His eyes were dark with lust. 'I really want to fuck you.'

'Fuck me then.' She wanted to reach down and pull him in, but because he was kneeling upright she couldn't reach far enough, and she didn't think she would be strong enough to make him do anything he didn't want to do. All she could do was beg, 'Fuck me, then.'

'Yes,' he hissed, and the big slabs of muscle in his buttocks tensed and his flanks hollowed and he was entering her.

She could really feel the shape of his penis, the way the huge head stretched her, the narrower shaft behind it sliding in easily. The sense of ravishment as the big knob eased into her was incredibly erotic. Either he sensed her excitement or he enjoyed that first moment of penetration too, because he withdrew almost at once and entered her again, again, again, just the first couple of inches of his thick cock sliding into her and out until she was almost mad to feel him all the way inside her, really fucking her. She arched and writhed, trying to draw him in, and when at last he pushed his cock right the way up her cunt she almost screamed, because he penetrated her so deeply. He kept his hands on the insides of her thighs, pushing them apart as far as they would go, so that she was almost at the threshhold of pain, and with his strong arse he fucked her so hard and deep that she could almost believe that he would kill her.

'Oh God,' she moaned, twisting her shoulders from side to side with the potent mix of pleasure and pain. She wanted to heave up her hips to meet his thrusts, but his strong hands were holding her still and she couldn't move her lower body at all. 'Oh, Andy, that's so good, don't stop, please don't stop.'

'I want – you – to – come,' he gasped, the words

coming in rhythm with his thrusts. 'I want you to come while I fuck you. I want you to come.'

She wanted to come, too, but the sensation was so intense, so all-enveloping, that she didn't know whether she would be able to. She slid one hand down her belly and touched her clit, and it was as if fireworks went off in her head. She hardly needed to move her finger, just rest it there, and the tiny pressure on her clit turned the savage sensation of his fierce movement into the most intense pleasure. She closed her eyes and with her other hand began to fondle her breast, squeezing her swollen nipple, and it was amazing, incredible.

'Don't stop,' she moaned, feeling every stroke of his cock inside her bringing her closer. 'Don't stop, don't stop, oh please, do it harder, harder.' She felt the orgasm begin to brim up inside her and she gasped urgently, 'I'm coming, Andy, I'm coming, oh do it now, now –' And as her climax filled her and burst he let go of her thighs and fell forward on to his hands, poised over her and gasping as he pounded into her once, twice, three times, then a sudden flurry of short deep thrusts followed by a final desperate surge. He didn't cry out, just flung back his head, face contorted, then sagged down on to her.

He wasn't as heavy as she had expected. His head was buried in her shoulder. His hair was soft against her neck, and the stubble on his chin grazed the top of her arm. She fondled his hair, smiling. When she opened her eyes, she could see blue sky behind him, white clouds sailing past, glowing with the bright sunlight. It felt like the morning of the world, and suddenly she remembered that unbidden fantasy of sex with sinful Adam in Paradise. It hadn't included bikes or mud, or condoms, come to that, but this had felt remarkably close.

With a sigh, André pushed himself up from her. Very gently, wincing a little, he withdrew from her and peeled off the condom. Then he looked at her, a little apprehensively, she thought. 'Nice?' he asked.

She liked it that he wanted to know. 'Very nice,' she said. She stretched out her hand to him. 'Come back here and keep me warm.'

'OK.' He settled down beside her and she crept into his arm. He really was like a nuclear reactor, glowing with heat. 'But not for long, though. I don't want to fall asleep, we'll freeze and get all uncomfortable.'

She nuzzled against the hair on his chest. Like the hair on his head, it was surprisingly soft. 'All this fur must keep you warm,' she suggested.

He laughed. 'Makes me sweat, more like.'

She pushed a little back from him. 'D'you want to come to a pub, have a bite to eat?'

He grinned and shook his head. 'I can always eat, but I really do need to strip down that chainset. I ought to get back to the shop.'

She was rather taken aback that he would prefer to work on his bike than spend time with her, but he had already described himself as a rolling stone. She shouldn't be surprised, really. Besides which, she too had work to do. Perhaps it might go better after this pleasant little interlude.

'I could handle a pizza tonight, though,' he went on, looking hopeful, like a dog which brings its lead to ask for a walk.

She hesitated, then smiled. 'Why not? That would be nice. When?'

'I could come along to the Lodge at about six-thirty,' he suggested.

'Fine.'

Now it was his turn to hesitate. 'But, you know, I can't really ask you back to my place. I just rent a room, and it's pretty grotty, and the landlady doesn't like people having sex under her roof, miserable fat cow.'

Catherine tutted. 'I don't know. You can't strip down your chainset and you can't have sex. Not sure I'd stay there, myself.'

'Ah, but it's cheap.' He kissed her. 'Do you mind? About my place, I mean?'

She shook her head. 'Mine is nice. Double bed included.'

His eyes lit up. 'Perfect.' He kissed her again, then sat up. 'Come on, get your clothes on. I'll take you back by the alternative scenic route. Includes a ford. Sound OK?'

'Jesus,' she said, and reached for her knickers.

Chapter Eleven

Catherine parked her bike behind the house and stood for a moment looking at it. It had started the day shiny and new. Now it was covered in mud, and there were long stems of grass caught in the mud-guards and around the edges of the chain. Her jeans were in much the same state, and she wouldn't be surprised to discover that she had grass stains on her arse, either.

Altogether, it had been a very satisfying morning. It was sad, in a way, that it was over. As she set off up the stairs she thought with pleasure of meeting Andy in the evening, having a meal with him, bringing him back to here and going to bed with him. And she realised that she wasn't interested in the day that came between. With each step that brought her closer to her computer and her work a black mood was descending, a defeatist mood, as if she were beginning to accept that she couldn't write this novel, that she was just a hack without an original bone in her body, after all.

This was not a good state in which to start writing, and without much hesitation she knocked on Maggie's door, instead. She didn't need sex, not today, but she did feel that she needed some company. And besides, she was curious about Maggie and the wonderful Ben.

195

'It's open,' came Maggie's voice from within.

Catherine pushed through the door and closed it behind her, saying at once, 'Well, what happened?'

Maggie was sitting cross-legged on the floor by the window looking out, nursing a mug of coffee. She smiled crookedly at Catherine and said, 'We-ell . . .'

Without asking Catherine found her way to the kettle and began making a mug of coffee for herself. 'So,' she demanded, quite conscious of the fact that she was just wasting time and that she ought to be writing, 'Did you get to bed with him?'

Maggie looked almost ashamed. 'Well, no, actually.'

'Oral sex in a punt? Shagging under the stars?' After all, with Maggie, nothing would be a shock.

'No . . .' Maggie shook her head. 'He kissed me goodnight.'

Now that was a shock. Catherine took the coffee and went and sat down opposite Maggie. 'You didn't have sex with him? Not at all? Nothing, *nada*, *niente*?'

'He said he thought it was too soon,' Maggie said, looking down into her coffee cup.

'And you were sitting with him at breakfast? Maggie, this isn't like you.'

'I know!' Maggie sounded genuinely worried. 'I wouldn't give a stuff normally, would I? If I wanted to shag him and he wasn't interested I'd just wave bye-bye, plenty more fish in the sea. But this is Ben. I fancied him for so long, and it just seemed that he wasn't even interested, and now . . .' Her voice tailed off and she slumped a little forward, as if the very thought of him left her weak.

Catherine smiled. At the beginning of term Maggie had told her that she had never been in love. It looked as if she was about to remedy that. She was showing every sign of being as smitten as a sixteen-year-old. And what had done the trick? The good old treat 'em mean, keep 'em keen. The biter bit, hoist by her own petard! 'Well,' was all she said, 'there's always tonight.'

'Oh, he does want to have sex with me,' Maggie said

196

suddenly. She obviously hadn't been listening. 'It's not that he doesn't fancy me. He just said he wanted it to be special, that he didn't want us to have to rush or hurry or worry about being tired.'

'So,' Catherine said patiently, feeling old, 'there's always tonight.'

Maggie nodded. 'There's no outings tomorrow for the boats . . .' She took a sip of her coffee and seemed to sink into a reverie. Then she jumped and said, 'Oh, lord, Catherine, I didn't even ask you how your evening went. I am sorry. Did the shoes work?'

Yesterday evening seemed a long time ago, somehow. Maggie was so distracted she hadn't even noticed Catherine's state of mud and sweat. Catherine shrugged. 'I suppose they did. I mean, Mike seemed to approve, and he got quite, well, quite inventive.' She thought that Maggie would demand the salacious details, but surprisingly she didn't. So Catherine went on evenly, 'I think you were right about him, though, Maggie. He is a total control freak. At the end of the evening I asked him to come home with me. I wanted to go down on him, if you can believe it, that's all I wanted, and maybe to have some company in the bed. And he wouldn't.'

Maggie shook her head sadly, as if she wasn't surprised. 'So?'

'So I gave him the bum's rush.'

That startled Maggie. Her big eyes opened wide. 'You dumped him?'

'I told him to fuck off.'

'I say, jolly good show,' Maggie said in her *Bunty* voice. 'Well done, that girl. Catherine, honestly, you're better off without blokes like that.'

Catherine sighed. 'I went out this morning with the guy from the bike shop, and he's really nice.' Maggie still hadn't asked about the mud, and Catherine decided not to bother to volunteer the information. 'But I don't think we have an awful lot in common, and he comes across as a real rolling stone. Honestly, Maggie, I think perhaps I'm better off without a man at all.'

Maggie laughed. 'I would have agreed with you before today. But right now I feel a bit different. I know, call me a hypocrite.'

Catherine shook her head. 'No, Maggie, I don't think that at all. But I'm old compared to you. Perhaps what I need is to have some time really on my own, without any man, not even James in the background.' She listened to her own words and frowned. 'Perhaps,' she said again. 'That sounds right, somehow. Perhaps I've hit it.'

'Do you want to go out shopping?' Maggie said. Her attention span seemed to be limited today. 'I want to get something new to wear tonight.'

'No, I can't. I have to get some writing done. And I'm meeting Andy again this evening, so I don't have much time.'

'Andy is that bike man?'

Bike man. Catherine laughed. 'That's him.' She finished her coffee and put down the mug. In her own room she would have tidied it away, but the debris in Maggie's room made one more coffee mug irrelevant. 'Perhaps I'll see you again before the evening, Maggie. Otherwise, have a good time.'

'You too,' Maggie said. She didn't get up or show any signs of being about to go shopping, just went back to staring out of the window. Catherine shook her head, then returned to her own room.

Some time entirely alone, without any man to depend on. It sounded good. A woman who could do that sounded like the sort of woman who would be able to start a book and finish it.

She stripped, put her filthy clothes in the laundry bag, and headed for the shower. Her hair was a mare's nest and there really were grass stains on her bum and shoulders. She washed herself from top to toe, drifting as she did so into pleasant reminiscences of sex with André that morning.

How refreshing it had been. Nothing complicated, nothing sophisticated, no props at all. Just a blue sky

198

and grass and a strong man with a big fat cock who was desperate to have sex with her. It would be easy to want a lot more sex like that.

But André had already said that he would be leaving soon. No need to get herself into a state of mind where she might have to rely on him, no need at all. He could be just a passing amusement, that delightful sex with no strings which she had been hoping for when she came up to Cambridge.

She dressed comfortably and made herself a cup of tea. She had time for about four hours' work before she needed to meet Andy for their pizza. She sat down at the desk, turned on her computer and fired up word processing. Time for that first chapter which would grip the reader by the throat. What reader? A reader who had an interest in ancient Rome and had bought it because of the attractive and well crafted jacket. A liker of historical novels, more likely to be female than male. A literate reader, who was interested in Roman poetry.

Rather a wide-ranging audience. But never mind. Soldier on, think of that first scene. Stick with that earlier idea, make it the scene of the final row between Catullus and Lesbia. Make it their bedroom. Drag the reader straight into their turbulent, furious affair. Show them the bedsheets, tangled and wet with sweat. A Roman summer, hotter than a furnace, smelling of food and wine and too many people living too close together.

He thinks he is in for a lazy afternoon of wine and sex with his mistress, the maddening, desirable, unfaithful aristocrat, brother of a public enemy, epitome of the debauch of ancient Rome. But he isn't. This is the day he is going to find out just how many other men this woman has been with. The shock will drive him away, and he'll live just long enough to write some of his bitterest and greatest poems and then he'll die, short-lived like so many poets.

The scene was there, she could see it. But she didn't want to write about it. The obvious way to frame it was in the first person, but she didn't want to talk with the voice of Gaius Lucius Catullus. A poet who dies of a broken heart? Please.

All the same, she tried, and it was like rolling a stone uphill. She kept her nose to the grindstone for three whole hours, without even another cup of tea, until she had finished the scene. Then she read it back. It read all right: after all, writing decent prose had never been a problem for her. But she didn't think that anyone reading it would be inspired to go on and read the rest of the book. It made Catullus sound like a wingeing bore.

She put her head in her hands. Perhaps she ought to give up the idea altogether, forget it and write some other sort of book. Just because she had translated his poems, why did that mean she had to write a novel about him?

But she did want to write the novel. She knew all about the subject, and she knew that there was a book about Rome inside her, and she thought it would be saleable. If only she could just get it started, it would develop its own momentum.

Sabotaging herself yet again, she turned instead to her email system. It told her that there were two new messages. One of them was spam. The other was from James.

Typical! When she wanted to hear from him there was nothing but silence. Now he couldn't wait to talk to her and pester her to approve of what he had done. She closed her eyes and sighed, trying to push away the ache in her heart, and opened the message.

> Cat, where u at? Worried not to have heard. Absence of reaction makes me wonder if I'm doing the right thing. Tell me u happy for me. Cat? U there?

She stared for a moment, then hit the DELETE key.

How dare he? Was he trying to suggest that something she might say would affect his decision to get married to this woman she had never met? Was he trying to get her to take responsibility for his decisions?

She could hardly believe that he would do that to her. She knew he was self-centred. He had to be, in his job. But first to pull the rug from under her and then to ask her to tell him that he was 'doing the right thing'! That was too much.

Was all this business about being alone just so much flannel, a smokescreen that she was putting up so that she didn't notice how much James's defection had hurt her? Did she simply want him back?

She thought of eating out with him, of their easy conversations about everything from politics to cartoons, everything from history to the future. She thought of sex with him, of his long, slender body, his sensitive hands with their long fingers, his slow, languid loving, his absorption in sensuality, the way he would kiss her from top to toe. She had even got impatient with him sometimes, tried to get him to hurry up and actually penetrate her. He always took his time. Making love to him had been memorable. And when he wasn't in touch, she missed him.

Perhaps that email suggested that all wasn't well with him. Perhaps if she didn't respond it might push him to changing his mind about this wedding. She didn't expect him to come rushing home on her account; but it would be nice to know that he was there, in the background, the way he always had been.

Time to get ready. She got to her feet, trying to set aside thoughts of James as if they were a garment that she didn't want to wear that evening, and changed into chinos and a sweater. Andy wasn't the dressiest man she had ever met.

As she walked down towards the Lodge she knew that James was still lurking in the back of her mind. But when she saw Andy waiting for her, smoking a roll-up cigarette, she forgot about him for the moment.

He put the roll-up out when he saw her coming. 'Sorry,' he said, looking guilty. 'You probably loathe and detest smokers. You probably don't want to eat with me now.'

He had gone home and changed, he was wearing black jeans and a shirt with a check like a French café table and a battered suede jacket. They suited him, and what she really wanted to do was go to bed with him. She said, 'Don't smoke in my room, and don't blow the smoke in my face, and apart from that, no problem.'

'Really?' His face lit up.

'Several of my friends still smoke. My landlord down in London smokes. I'm used to it.'

He nodded, clearly pleased. 'Let's go to Pizza Express,' he said. 'I'm ravenous.'

Catherine was ravenous too, ravenous for a re-run of the morning's entertainment, but she acknowledged that big muscly men need lots of calories and that the way to Andy's dick would probably start off by being through his stomach. So she said, 'Great.'

They set off, and he said, 'How's your work going?'

She made a face. 'Terrible. I can't seem to get started. I'm writing about –' She hesitated, making a quick assessment of his likely interest. 'About a man in ancient Rome who has an affair with an amazing woman but she's unfaithful to him. He's a poet. I just don't seem to be able to get the right mood.' She shook her head, not really wanting to think about it. 'How about your chainset?'

'Yeah, piece of piss.'

It wasn't far to Pizza Express, but getting there and getting a table and ordering took some time. Then, while they waited for the pizzas, Andy drank his beer and told her something about his life. It was an interesting life, compared to hers. His father had been a boxer and had travelled a lot between France, England and Italy, and little André had grown up speaking English and French with equal ease. He had left school as soon as he could and got a job as a cyclist in a French racing team. But being a *domestique*, a slave of the star cyclist, had not suited his independent nature. He had stuck it for a while, then given up and taken a series of cycling-bum jobs in France, England and Spain.

'How old are you?' Catherine asked.

'Thirty-four.'

Not that much younger than her, then. But that was quite an old age still to be a bum. Something must have shown in her face, because he said, 'You're thinking that I'm a loser.'

She shook her head. 'Not a loser. It's just a really different sort of life from mine.'

'Differences are interesting,' he said.

The pizzas came. Initially Catherine felt hungry, but soon she ran out of steam. Her mind wasn't on her stomach, but on Andy's cock. From the way he was looking at her in between bites she rather thought that he felt the same.

Sure enough, when only half of his pizza had gone he said, 'I can't concentrate on this.'

'Why is that?' she asked, for the sheer pleasure of hearing his reply.

He leant forward, glancing left and right as if to ensure that nobody would hear him. 'Because all I want to do is go to bed with you.'

She grinned. 'Same here. Shall we get the bill?'

As always, when you really wanted to get out of a restaurant it seemed to take forever to get the bill. But at last it came, it was paid, and they were out of the door and heading for home. They walked apart for a while, and then Andy reached out and took hold of Catherine's hand and held it. Like his body, his hand was very warm, hard and strong. Catherine's hand was not small, but she felt it vanished into André's hairy paw. This was very pleasant. It made her feel feminine.

It was dark, and as they cut through a quiet side-road Andy turned to her and wrapped his arms round her, pulling her close. They kissed hungrily and his hands pushed inside her sweater, seeking her breasts. 'God, I hate towns,' he hissed. 'I want you right now. And we've got to walk all that way back.'

He obviously liked his privacy, so Catherine wound him up a little. 'You could always just push me up

203

against the wall here. We're about the right height for it.' She thought of that fantasy she had told James, about the Roman noblewoman picking herself a bravo off the street and fucking him against a wall. She dressed André's body in Roman costume. Not aristocratic costume, oh no, just a commoner's tunic. Or maybe the leather and steel of a gladiator. Yes, she could see him as a gladiator, naked except for a leather tunic and leather wristguards and a heavy sword.

'You cannot be serious,' he hissed, hesitating a little. She grinned at him and pulled his mouth back to hers and they snogged like teenagers, gasping and fumbling. She moaned when his fingers found her nipples and pushed her body against him, delighted at the feel of his rigid cock pressing against her through his jeans. She put her hand on his crotch, rubbing, but he pulled away. 'Don't, not here, or I'll get you to take it out and suck me off.'

She looked both ways. There was nobody coming. 'I'm game.'

He frowned, then said, 'No, come on, I want to have you in a bed, come on.'

He grabbed her hand and pulled her towards the college at a run. She followed, laughing helplessly, and when they got on to Henry's Parade she tugged him away from the gatehouse and into the door of her house. It was dark and quiet, everybody out for the evening. There wasn't any sound from Maggie's room; she must be still working on the delectable Ben. She fumbled for the key with Andy panting beside her, and as the door swung open he pounced on her.

He caught her under her arms and her knees and swung her off the floor. She wasn't light, and he lifted her with an ease that made her gasp. Street light came through the windows and in its glow he kicked the door shut, strode to the bed and threw her down on it, then flung off his jacket and began on the buttons of his shirt.

Catherine was still breathing quickly with the shock of having been carried across the room. Nobody had

204

ever done that to her, and nobody had ever lifted her with such ease, as if she were weightless. Her heart was pounding.

'What's the problem?' André demanded as he shook his shirt to the floor. 'I thought you were in a hurry too. Get naked.'

She said, 'But,' and then she pulled herself up and took off her sweater and unbuttoned her trousers. Underwear today was nice, the same set that she had worn for the orgy, and she didn't take it off at once. She wanted Andy to notice it.

He pushed off his jeans, stood up naked, with his thick cock sticking straight out in front of him, and saw her. He whistled. 'Hey, nice gear.' He jumped on to the bed beside her and touched her bra strap, then ran his fingers down the curve of her breast. 'Very nice. Very pretty.'

She lifted her haunches, showing him that the bottom half was a thong. He stretched his eyes. 'Very nice. Very rude.' He caught hold of her hips and pulled her around so that she was facing away from him, and for a moment he was silent. She glanced over her shoulder and saw him admiring her arse, and then his hands began to move over her buttocks, touching and stroking. One finger slid beneath the string of the thong, lifting it away from her crack, then returning it to its place.

Catherine let her front half settle on the bed, her head resting on her folded arms, eyes closed, enjoying his exploration of her backside. His fingers were firm but gentle. He ran them right over each buttock, down on to the tops of her thighs, between her legs. She gave a little moan as his thumbs brushed against her *mons*. Then he shifted position and in a moment she felt his lips on her backside, kissing each cheek in turn. One hand caught the string and pulled the thong aside, and then she felt his tongue right in her crack, bathing her anus with saliva. For a moment she thought that he was going to prepare her to be fucked in the arse, and she felt a momentary twinge of disappointment. But then his tongue moved down, easing beneath the pouch of the thong, finding her vagina, delving a little way into it, then moving forward.

'Oh,' she said, as his tongue found her clitoris. 'Oh, that's nice.'

He licked her clit very, very gently to begin with, and she gasped in rhythm with his movements. She was already wet, and the caressing of his tongue just made her wetter. She longed to feel his cock in her, but she also didn't want the pleasure of his tongue to stop, and she squirmed and sighed in delicious indecision.

For a moment he stopped and reached forward to push down the cups of her bra and expose her nipples. They were already tight and hard. For a moment he nursed her breasts in his hands, nipples trapped between his strong fingers. Then he let them go and returned to licking her. Her breasts were sensitised now, and she began to touch them herself, pinching her taut nipples, sending little ripples of fire through her with every touch.

Andy was licking harder now, pushing his face up against her as if he wanted to consume every morsel of her juice. It felt incredibly lewd to have him do this to her while he knelt behind her, his tongue on her clit, his nose pressed against her slit. It felt dirty and sexy and gorgeous. She moaned louder and thrust her hips backwards and his big fleshy nose slid a little way into her cunt as he licked harder and harder.

She was desperately excited, arching her back, tugging at her breasts. She cried out and pushed back again and the sensation of his nose poking into her as his tongue lashed her clit was so weird and erotic that she came all of a sudden, spasming fiercely and then falling forward, away from his working mouth, collapsed in a sticky heap on the duvet.

'Jesus,' André's voice hissed. He moved, and she heard the rustle of a condom. Then he was back behind her, grabbing her hips in his strong hands and hauling them up. Again he pulled aside the string of her thong, and this time it was the fat head of his cock which she felt between her cunt lips.

'God, you're so wet,' he said. 'You look so rude, it's amazing, I'm going to fuck you so hard.' And then he lunged into her, right up her in one fierce thrust, so hard that she screamed.

He gave no quarter now, but shafted her with all his strength. Every stroke went into her so deeply that she whimpered, at the point of pain but also wanting even more. The sensations were so violent that she felt as if her orgasm were going on and on, as if every thrust sent her back to a high plateau of pleasure. She shoved her hand down to her clit, and then cried out over and over again, and again and again he lunged into her, his loins slapping against her arse. He showed no sign of tiring and after long minutes she knew that she could hardly bear any more, it was too much, too intense. She moaned, 'André, God, you're killing me.'

He shuddered when she spoke and his hands gripped her hips so tightly that she cried out in pain. He did not speak, but he gave three guttural shouts and on the third one pushed himself into her so deeply, so strongly, that she really thought that he would go right into her womb. She felt him quiver and pulse inside her, and gradually she let herself subside down to the bed, like a pricked balloon, encouraging him to settle gradually until he was lying on top of her, his belly to her back, his softening cock still buried inside her.

'Blimey,' he said, after a moment.

He was heavy, and it was hard for her to breathe, but somehow it felt wonderful. She stretched her hands out along the duvet and he reached for them and held them and they lay still for a moment, their breathing synchronised, bodies rising and falling as one.

Then he said, 'I'll squash you,' and he rolled off her. She drew in a deep breath, then lay on her side, watching him removing the spent condom.

He set it aside, then met her eyes. 'You're amazing,' he said, and when she raised her eyebrows explained,

'Your body is gorgeous, it's a proper woman's body. And you smell great. You're amazing to fuck.'

'So are you,' she said, wanting to return the compliment. 'Your body is really compact and strong, and I like it that you're hairy.' To prove it she rested her head on his shoulder and let her cheek nestle against the thick, dark pelt of his chest. 'Your cock is beautiful.'

'Hmm,' he said in a long purr. 'More.'

Catherine laughed. 'That's enough, or you'll get complacent.'

He smiled at her. 'I need a wash,' he said. 'I'll be wanting a blow-job next, and I wouldn't like you to get a gob full of insecticide.'

'Spermicide,' she corrected without thinking.

'Whatever. You got a toilet here?'

'Just through there,' she said, pointing. He got up from the bed and vanished into the bathroom. She watched him go, then lay back and folded her arms behind her head, listening to the water running.

After a few minutes he reappeared. 'Nice room, this,' he commented.

'It is,' she agreed.

He lay down beside her and put his arms around her. His body was warmer than a cat's, it was wonderful to hold. 'Nobody can see in, can they?'

She shrugged. 'Someone looking out of the porters' lodge upper window might, but it's dark in here. They wouldn't see past the glass.' She thought of Mike screwing her against those windows, of Dave's astonished eyes below her. Not Andy's scene, that was for sure.

He jerked his head towards her desk. 'Is that where you write?'

'Sometimes.'

He hesitated. 'Do you want to talk about it? It sounded as though you didn't, earlier.'

She shook her head. 'I don't mind. It's just that it's such a struggle. You see –' She outlined briefly the life of Catullus and how she had translated his poems and now wanted to put him into a book.

208

André frowned. 'The woman, what's she called again?'

'He calls her Lesbia, but that's just a *nom de plume*.' Catherine felt self-conscious about her French pronunciation. 'People think her real name was Clodia. She was an aristocrat, from one of the oldest and most powerful families in Rome, and a real bitch, by all accounts. Though all the accounts are by men! I think she must have been a remarkable woman, the sort of woman that nobody ever forgets.'

Andy rubbed his hands down her back as if she were a pet. It felt nice, and she stretched and arched against the pressure. After a moment he said, 'To be honest, it sounds as if you're more interested in her than in him. Couldn't you just write the book about her?'

She opened her mouth to explain why the book was about Catullus rather than Lesbia, and then she closed it again.

Why shouldn't it be about Lesbia? Why not write it from her perspective? Fill it with all the interesting men in Rome, dissect their foibles the way only a woman could, and show Catullus up for the limp fop he might have been? It was certainly a different idea.

It was an interesting idea. She said, 'André, that's inspired.'

'Just an idea,' he said, looking a bit shocked by the strength of her reaction.

Just an idea! She practically wanted to get up and start writing it now. If she hadn't been held in his strong arms, she might have done just that. What time she had wasted struggling to try to get to grips with Gaius Lucius!

'Thank you,' she said. Then she heard Maggie's laugh on the stairs, and a moment later she heard the door open and shut.

'Friend of yours?' Andy asked, cocking his head at the sound.

'My friend Maggie,' Catherine said. 'If I'm not very

much mistaken, we might be hearing something very interesting soon.'

Andy looked anxious. 'Does that mean that they could hear us?'

'They could.' She smiled. 'But somehow I don't think that they'll be listening.'

Chapter Twelve

Maggie closed the door and shut the inner door too. She stood with her face to the door for a moment, taking deep breaths, steadying her nerve. He was here, in her room. He had made it clear that he was prepared to have sex with her this time. Now she had to perform. He would be bound to have high expectations of a girl with her reputation. She thought briefly through her repertoire. Surely it wouldn't be hard to impress him? He struck her as fairly inexperienced, maybe even naïve. She didn't know a single girl at college who had slept with him.

Smiling, she turned to face him. 'That's it,' she said. 'Shut out the world.'

Ben was standing by the sofa. He glanced around the room and said, 'Nice place. You must have come high up the room ballot.'

How could he talk about room ballots at a time like this? But she didn't feel that she could push him. If she said, 'Shut up and come and fuck me', he might just walk out of the door, and she didn't want that. Instead she replied, conversationally enough, 'It wasn't a ballotted room, actually. It was a scam.' She flickered her eyebrows at him and walked across to the mantelpiece above the gas fire to light the candles.

'Very entrepreneurial,' he said approvingly.

Maggie lit the candles, then went back to the door to turn off the light. The room was plunged into a gentle, golden gloom. Much more atmospheric, much more suitable.

'Do you want some music?' she suggested. What a weird situation! A nice meal, candlelight, soft music: classic seduction stuff. But she did want him so much, and somehow she knew that her usual techniques would not be appropriate.

'Good idea,' he said.

And now what! She had to choose something from her discs that she thought he would like, and something that would be good to have sex to. The pressure of deciding made her quiver, but finally she chose Des'ree and programmed the CD to play 'I'm Kissing You'.

'Very nice,' Ben said, as the music began. 'She's got a great voice, hasn't she?'

Why wasn't he taking the hint? Maggie said, 'Yes, she has,' and her voice quavered slightly with the anxiety that she might get something wrong.

Ben leant back against the sofa, long legs extended, and smiled at her. It was a warm, gentle, knowing smile, and seeing it she felt her heart wrench and lurch in a way that was completely unfamiliar to her. He said softly, 'Come here, Maggie.'

She crossed the room and stood in front of him, not daring to reach out. He took her hands and looked deep into her eyes, so deep that she could hardly stop herself from looking down. He said, 'I've been keeping you waiting.'

'Too bloody right,' she retorted, with a flash of her old self.

'I did it on purpose,' he said. 'I wanted to see if you would wait.' She frowned, and he said, 'I'm not the flirty type, Maggie. I've waited a long time to ask you out. I don't want it to go wrong.'

What did he mean, he'd waited a long time? 'You've ignored me for two years,' Maggie said.

He shook his head. 'I waited. I could see you had a lot of wild oats to sow. If I'd tried last year or the year before I'd just have been another of your conquests, wouldn't I? And I didn't want that.'

Almost afraid, she said tentatively, 'So what do you want?'

'Time,' he said. 'Fidelity.'

Fidelity! The word echoed from side to side in her brain like a shout in a tunnel. He wanted a relationship, that was what he wanted. He wanted commitment. He wanted everything she had said she never meant to give a man.

Why didn't she tell him where to get off? Why was she standing there staring at him like a rabbit in the headlights? She wanted to speak, but the words wouldn't come. And then he got up and pulled her close to him and lifted her chin with his hand and kissed her.

Oh, he was a good kisser, better than good, he kissed better than anyone else Maggie had ever met. His lips were warm and soft and his tongue was firm and probing and gentle and when he touched the insides of her lips she felt herself shiver and soften with wanting him. She knew that she ought to do something, that she ought to take the initiative and show him what she was made of, but she couldn't. She couldn't even move. She simply stood there, head tilted back, body limp, sighing as he kissed her and kissed her.

'You're so lovely,' he whispered. 'I wish I could kiss you all night.'

Did that mean he couldn't? He wouldn't? He had to go, he didn't want to stay? The possibilities made her mind spin with wild surmise. But all he went on to say was, 'But I can't deny myself.'

She was pleased about that. She didn't want him to deny himself, not at all. He kissed her again, and then his lips travelled from her mouth to her chin, her cheek, her ear, her neck, and she lifted her arms and draped them over his shoulders and moaned as he sucked gently at her throat. She loved it that he had to stoop to kiss her there, had to bend his tall supple body to caress her. She slipped her hands into his hair and held his head against her throat, arching her back to offer him her breasts. She was tongue-tied, unable to say how much she wanted him.

He slipped gently down to his knees. Kneeling, his head was on a level with her chest. He smiled up at her for a moment, then lifted one hand to stroke back her wild hair and with the other began to unbutton her little blouse. She tensed. She wasn't wearing a bra, so when the blouse was open he would be able to see her breasts. They were so small, she looked like a boy, perhaps they wouldn't please him. As the last button came undone she closed her eyes and leant her head back, not wanting to see his reaction.

'Aah.' It was a sigh of the deepest contentment. 'Maggie, you're perfect.' His smooth hands pushed the blouse from her shoulders. Reassured, she looked down and he smiled at her again and then cupped her tiny breasts in his hands, shielding them, allowing her small pert nipples to slip between his fingers. Then he squeezed, fingers tightening on her nipples, palms pressing and lifting the taut flesh of her breasts, and she moaned and gasped. For a few moments he did nothing else but squeeze and knead that tender flesh. Then he removed one hand and put his lips to the exposed nipple, first licking it, then suckling gently, and then setting his teeth to the hard peak of flesh, nibbling at it so that she cried out with pleasure.

'That's good,' he whispered. 'I like to hear you moan, Maggie. I'm going to make you moan again, so soon.' He stood up and caught her face in his hands, kissing her again. One hand buried itself in her hair, keeping her still to receive his tongue in her mouth, and the other slid down her naked torso, fingernails scratching at her rosy nipples, down to the fabric of her skirt. He caught hold of it and bunched it up, lifting, creasing, until his hand could move down on to the naked flesh of her flank.

'Are you wet for me?' he whispered.

She knew that she was as wet as a river, but she could hardly respond. He placed the palm of his hand flat on her flat belly and she managed at last to sigh, 'Yes.'

'Let's find out,' he murmured, and his fingers slid beneath her panties, down through her pubic hair, down to her clitoris. He touched her, and her legs were weak and she staggered. He laughed and held her up, letting his finger squeeze into the cracks of her sex, exploring her labia, sliding a little way inside her. She was wet and slippery, his touch inflamed her, when his finger touched her clit again she cried out sharply as if he had hit her. She wanted to feel him inside her, but she couldn't speak, let alone make demands.

'Sweet,' he whispered. 'Soft.'

Maggie hadn't been much of a virgin. She had masturbated every day from an early age and found things to push inside herself almost as soon as her periods had started. When she had begun to have sex with boys it had never hurt and it had never seemed new or special, just natural, just something that she wanted to do as much as possible. Now, limp in Ben's arms, with his tongue in her mouth and his fingers frigging her, she felt as if she knew what it would be like to be a real beginner. The sensations coursing through her seemed new and strange, as if nobody had ever touched her before. When his finger slid across her clit and pushed a little way into her vagina she shuddered and whimpered as if the feelings were a surprise, and when he took his hand from her hair and wrapped it around her so that he could fondle her breasts while he fondled her sex she moaned helplessly and opened her mouth wider for his kisses.

'You like that,' he whispered. 'You like it.'

'Oh yes,' she moaned, 'yes, Ben.'

'I won't stop, then.' He stroked her again and again, so gently that she thought she would die, and his fingers

215

on her breasts were soft and demanding. She shuddered and clutched at him and her body began to heave with its own rhythm, pulsing as he drew her closer and closer to climax with his delicate touch. At last she was at the point of orgasm and she began to cry out, little quick cries almost as if she was about to sneeze, and he held her more tightly and touched her clit hard and kissed her as if he wanted to taste her excitement, and she came like that, hanging in his arms, his tongue deep in her mouth, his fingers touching her everywhere.

After a moment he pulled her a little closer to him, her head against his shirt. She opened her eyes very wide, hardly able to believe what she had felt and was still feeling. He dug his hands into her hair and pushed her head back so that he could look into her eyes, and once again she felt that strange melting sensation in the pit of her stomach, as though his pupils were little lasers.

His eyes sought something in her face. She didn't know what it was, but she hoped that he could find it. At last he said, 'Was that different?'

How had he known? She didn't reply, just nodded. He smiled and kissed her again, and it seemed that his mood lightened a little. 'Here,' he said, putting her hands on his front, 'help me get this shirt off.'

So she unbuttoned his shirt and laid it on the sofa. His body was not strange to her, she had seen him in the summer sculling in nothing but a Speedo, and she knew that his tall frame was broad-shouldered and well-clothed with slender muscles and that he had the strong back and arms and legs of a rower and a lean narrow waist. She knew that he was tanned and that his skin was soft, his legs and arms downed with blond hairs, his torso with hardly a hair on it. His nipples were small and neat, brown rather than pink, satisfying on his golden skin.

But she had never seen him naked. When she removed his shirt he smiled and unfastened the button of his jeans, then put her hand on his fly. 'Feel,' he said softly.

She hoped to God he had a nice one. She wanted him so much, she didn't want to be disappointed by a squib instead of a Roman candle. She knew she would put up with anything, but she really wanted it to be nice. Slowly she let her fingers dig into the fabric, feeling, and her breath left her in a long sigh as she realised that his cock matched the rest of him. It was long and firm and it twitched as she touched it. Her insides wrenched with wanting him and now she felt brave enough to whisper, dry-mouthed, 'Please, Ben, can I suck you?'

He pressed himself against her hand like a big cat consenting to be stroked, and smiled. 'Let's get comfortable,' he said. 'It's not every day you see a double bed in a college room.'

She nodded, aware that he hadn't exactly answered her question, and pushed his jeans from his slender hips. He was wearing boxers, and they came off at the same time. His cock sprang forward, hard and eager, and she drew breath at the sight of it. It was gorgeous. She could smell him already, she couldn't wait to taste him.

'Let me,' he said, pushing her back a little so that he could take off his shoes and socks. As he did so he smiled up at her, 'Are you going to keep that skirt on all night?'

She had forgotten that she was still half-dressed, still in skirt and panties and shoes. She unbuttoned the skirt and let it slip down, and his eyes darkened as he saw her just in her skimpy panties and high heels. It was good to know that he was susceptible to her, just like other men. She eased the panties down her thighs to her knees, feeling them leaving damp trails as they descended. They slipped off and she stepped out of them.

Ben straightened, gazing at her naked in the candle-light. 'You are so gorgeous,' he said. 'So small, so

217

perfect. It's as if somebody sculpted you. God, you're lovely.'

He stepped forward and dropped to his knees in front of her and this time he pressed his face to the join of her thighs, burying himself in her golden fleece, drawing in a long, luxurious breath. This wasn't what she wanted. She wanted to worship, not be worshipped. She wanted to show him how much she had wanted him, how much she was prepared to do for him. But she couldn't make herself stop him.

Suddenly he stood up and caught her hand. He towed her to the bed, flung himself down, pulled her after him. She closed her eyes as he wrapped his arms around her and strained her against him. His body was warm and hard and everything that she had imagined it would be, and his hands were running up and down her back and he was whispering in her ear how much he wanted her and she could do nothing but lie there sighing with delight and waiting for the next instant of bliss.

'Now,' he whispered, 'come here.'

He caught hold of her and swung her body over his so that she was straddling his face. She tried to hide her eyes in the flat muscle of his belly, suddenly embarrassed at showing herself to him in so intimate a way. But his cock was there, proud and erect, and without even opening her eyes she found it by touch and smell and drew it into her mouth and moaned with pleasure as she sucked it.

Then she felt his lips and tongue between her legs, stroking and caressing, probing and teasing, and her moans became smothered cries. He was responding too to what she was doing to him, deep breaths turning to sighs, sighs to groans, and as another climax loomed over her she began to suck him harder and harder because she wanted to feel him come just a moment before she did, she wanted to taste his come in her mouth before her lips slackened as she came. She called up some of her old skills and twisted her mouth on his glans, pushed the tip of her tongue into the tiny weeping eye at the tip of his cock, massaged his balls with her hand, and she felt him reacting, his body tensing and arching. He licked her harder and it was as if they were driving each other on, hurrying up the slopes towards the peak, and she gobbled him greedily and arched her back to thrust her pelvis into his face. He responded eagerly, swirling his tongue over her clitoris and thrusting it deep into her cunt, and she felt his cock throb and surge and her mouth was full of his salty, delicious come, and as she swallowed and sucked again her own climax grabbed her and she shuddered and slumped down on to him, still sucking ever so gently at his dwindling, softening cock.

He pushed her hips away from his face for long enough to whisper, 'Don't stop,' and then burrowed back between her legs, suckling so gently that her oversensitised clit did not protest, and now beginning to touch her there too, stroking his fingers along the insides of her thighs, fondling her anus and perineum. She gasped and nursed his balls with her hand, her cheeks hollowing as she sucked him.

Sure enough, after only a few moments he began to get hard again. This time, without the urgency of an approaching orgasm, she could really enjoy sucking him, really admire the long, clean lines of his cock. It was gorgeous, thick enough really to mean business, but not so thick that it was unaesthetic. She released it and began to lick the sides of the shaft as if it were an ice-cream, teasing him until the glans twitched and seemed to be trying to push itself back into her mouth. Then she put her hand around him, testing his hardness. Perfect, firm as a piece of wood, ready.

He released her and she turned over him and kissed his face. He was slippery with her juice, musky and delicious. For a moment she licked him, like a cat, and then he caught her and pushed her on to her back. She caught her breath and gazed up at him, hardly able to wait for the moment.

219

'No need to ask if you've got any condoms,' he murmured.

'In the jar,' she said, indicating the bedside table with her eyes.

She would have liked to put the condom on for him, but she didn't seem able to move. So she just lay there and watched him ease the smooth rubber down over his penis and give the shaft an experimental pump with his hand as if he was checking its readiness. She felt nervous again. What would he want from her? Would he expect her to be able to do all sorts of sexy stunts, like milking him with her vaginal muscles? She could do that sometimes, but her body wasn't being very obedient this evening. What if she let him down?

He pushed her thighs apart with his knee and came between them, resting his weight on his arms. His long body was suspended above her, the head of his cock nudging up between her thighs. She caught hold of his shoulders, looking up into his eyes, biting her lip in anxious anticipation.

'Are you ready, Maggie?' he whispered. 'Do you want me to put myself inside you now?'

Such gentle words, as if they were newlyweds and she was young and innocent, not the brazen hussy she was. Maggie closed her eyes, overwhelmed with shyness.

'Do you?' he insisted.

'Yes,' she said, her voice soft as a breath.

He lowered himself on to his elbows and ran his hands through her hair, and the hot head of his cock slid over her wet flesh, hunting for the spot. He found it, gave a little thrust, and the head was wedged home. She moaned, because it was as if this were the first time.

'Ready?' he hissed again, looking down into her face. 'Are you ready?'

'Yes,' she replied.

She tried to tilt up her hips to let him enter her more easily. He pushed himself in another inch, another, and all the time he held her eyes as if she would lose her nerve and pull away the moment she stopped looking at him. 'There's more,' he whispered. 'More of me to go inside you, Maggie. I'm going to push it inside you now.'

'Oh, God,' she moaned, and then she felt him sliding into her until his body was right against hers, his cock buried in her to the hilt, and almost before she realised that he was fully in her he pulled out and thrust again, harder this time, driving himself back into her with a smooth steady stroke, and she thought of him on the river, body flexing and tugging in that smooth steady time, all his bones and muscles focused on achieving what he wanted, a fast five hundred metres or the fuck of a lifetime. She cried out and arched her body up against him and he gasped and smiled and suddenly her inhibitions were gone. She clutched at his buttocks to pull him into her harder, writhed her body to rub her clit against him, and shouted out encouragement. 'Yes,' she cried, 'yes, yes, Ben, please, do it now. More, more, deeper, oh God, that's so good.' Like a good oarsman listening to the cox he responded, and she screamed with delight as the man she had wanted for two years finally fucked her, hard and fast, his naked body banging against hers, his face contorted with the effort of ensuring her pleasure.

Next door Andy pushed himself up in the bed, his face revealing amazement. 'Blimey,' he said, 'she really is a goer, isn't she.'

'She is,' Catherine agreed. She smiled, because she was very pleased to hear that Maggie had got what she wanted at last.

Andy shook his head. 'Jesus,' he said, 'she sounds like a bloody wank flick. Hasn't she got any shame? Doesn't she know that people can hear her?'

Catherine smiled up at him. 'You're awfully prudish about noise, aren't you.'

He frowned. 'I'm not prudish. I just like my privacy. And I like other people to have their privacy, too.'

Next door Maggie shouted, 'Yes! Yes! Now! Oh –' and her cries degenerated into the inarticulate howls of a woman in the throes of a really strong orgasm.

Andy was silent for a moment. Then he said, 'Kind of rude noises, though, aren't they.'

Catherine glanced down at his body. He had been lying stretched out, totally relaxed, every muscle limp. He was still lying in a relaxed posture, but now his cock was reviving, twitching and thickening and lifting as she watched.

She felt mischievous. 'Mmm,' she said. 'Fancy that blow-job now?'

'Do I!' he said approvingly, settling back.

She got to her knees and leant over him, drawing in an appreciative breath. Despite having washed after sex he smelt of his own quintessential masculinity, and also of her. She took hold of his cock and rubbed it a few times, enjoying the feel of it filling out and hardening at her touch. Then she put her hands on the insides of his thighs and pushed. To begin with he resisted her, and it felt like trying to push two tree trunks apart. Then he realised that she wanted him to spread his legs, and he shifted and settled in the new position, putting his hands behind his head and closing his eyes.

He found it very easy to lie back and enjoy himself. He obviously wasn't a man who worried too much about his partner's pleasure if she was prepared to worry about him! That was all right, though, because he seemed to be well equipped for giving pleasure. And besides, on this occasion Catherine had designs on him.

She knelt between his open legs and kissed his belly. It was soft when she first touched it. Then her kiss must have tickled him, because his skin twitched and the muscle of his stomach became hard and rigid. She rubbed her cheek against it and then moved down, touching her lips to the points in the hollow of his flanks where there was no hair and his bare skin was white and soft and delicate as a child's. He shivered and his penis jerked towards her mouth.

She ignored it and instead let her lips slide further down, down to the soft taut sac that cradled his heavy balls. She mouthed it, pushed her tongue between the two eggs of his testicles, trickled the tip of her tongue behind it. He moved his legs a little further apart, inviting her to go further.

Good. He liked her to explore him, and she wanted to. She had a feeling that she would be able to make him forget his inhibitions about noise. In fact, she was making a bet with herself that she could make him shout.

She slid to a lying position on the bed and buried her face between his legs, ignoring his erect penis, concentrating on licking and nibbling the delicate, smooth flesh of his perineum. He arched his back and after a moment said in a voice of surprise, 'God, that's nice.'

Everything was going according to plan. She pushed at his buttocks and he responded as she had hoped, by rolling his hips up slightly to expose more of his arse. She licked a little further down, teasing him, her tongue slipping into the crack and finding the tightly-puckered entrance to his anus, then moving away, then returning.

Although he was hairy he was very clean, and it was actually pleasant to lick him there. It reminded her of sex with Maggie, teasing and titillating the delicate flesh with her tongue, probing just inside and then running her tongue right around the rim. The skin there was improbably soft and sensitive, and when she penetrated him with her tongue he moaned out loud.

That was an excellent start. She drew back, guiding his hips back to the bed, smiling to herself when he let out a little noise of disappointment. She cradled his balls in her hand, then returned her mouth to his cock. Ignoring the staring glans, she licked the sides, then mouthed him crossways, her lips wrapping around the shaft alone, sliding up and down to moisten it without ever taking him right into her mouth. He wriggled with frustration, and to punish him she took her mouth away completely, just rubbing him with her hand until he settled down and was still again. Then she lifted his throbbing cock and let her mouth descend on it, taking him in as deeply as she could, until the head touched the back of her throat. He put his hands in her hair again, as if he wanted to hold her still and shaft her mouth, but she pulled back, refusing to allow it. He huffed in protest, but let his hands fall.

Taking his cock back into her mouth she began to swivel her head from side to side, twisting her lips around his glans with a circular motion. He let out a long breath and she knew that what she was doing was arousing him. She let the hand which was cradling his balls move back, stroking her finger across his perineum as her mouth swung on his cock, and then she found his anus with her fingertip and began to probe and press.

Would he flinch now and pull away? Some men didn't like to be penetrated, they felt it impugned their masculinity, but she had the impression of André as someone who would go along with pretty much anything as long as it felt good. She wasn't wrong. To minimise the shock of what she was doing she began to take him deeply into her mouth again, sucking hard, and as she did so she pushed her finger into his arse and he didn't resist, just moaned with pleasure.

Still only a moan. That wasn't good enough. She had promised herself that before she was done with him he would be shouting. She settled to a slow, steady rhythm with her mouth, taking his penis right in, then letting it slide out to the very tip. The tip of his cock was sensitive, the way he had played with her showed it, so each time she released it she flickered out her tongue like a snake to catch him just below the tip of his penis, where the little triangle of flesh seemed to connect the head to the shaft. He moaned again and responded with an involuntary thrust of his hips every time she took him in.

And every time she took him in she worked her finger a little further into his anus. She wasn't moving it yet, wasn't trying to fuck him with it, just pushing it a little more each time. It was his prostate she was aiming for. James had taught her how to find it and what to do, and it had never failed to have a startling effect on him. She was almost certain that Andy would never have been with anyone who knew that he had a prostate gland, let alone managed to find it and use it to make him scream.

He was enjoying himself now, squeezing her buried finger a little with each thrust, relaxing into the caress of her mouth. He didn't know what she was planning. She let the speed build up until he was panting in time with her movements, and then she reached with her finger.

And found what she sought, the little buried mass. She touched it, stroked it, and André jerked as if she had sent an electric shock through him. She didn't release him, didn't let up the speed or the pressure, and now with every stroke, with every suck, she teased her finger against the infinitely sensitive nut of his prostate. He whimpered and wriggled almost as if he wanted to pull away, and suddenly burst out, 'Jesus, God, that's so –'

He couldn't finish, and she could feel the effect of what she was doing to him in the helpless spasmodic jerks of his cock in her mouth. He wanted her to speed up, to finish him quickly, but she wouldn't. She let each stroke draw out, the rhythm smooth and strong and slow, and now with each touch he began to moan. Her lips closed tighter on his trembling cock, her finger in his arse edged a little deeper, and she prepared him for the come of his life.

Now she increased the pace, just a little, letting him know that the build up was coming. He said again, 'Oh, God,' helplessly, as if he didn't know what to do. Then he cried out, and that single cry told her that he was ready for everything she could give him.

Sucking furiously, she pumped his cock with her mouth as hard as she could, and her buried finger rested

225

against the soft mass of his prostate and stroked, stroked. His body gave a sudden jerk and she felt the clenching pulses of climax begin in the base of his belly, tightening his sphincter around her finger, and instead of slackening her speed she sucked harder, faster.

'Jesus,' he shouted, as loudly as she could have hoped for, 'Jesus Christ,' and then he was coming, his cock surging in her mouth, his arse clenching frantically around her buried finger, his mouth open in a roar of astonished pleasure.

She hung in there until it was all over, then very gently released his penis and withdrew her finger from his anus. He had his arm over his face, his chest heaving as he panted. She watched him for a moment, smiling, and then caught hold of his arm and pulled it down. He let her move it, but turned his face away.

'What was that you said,' she asked politely, 'about privacy? Your privacy and other people's?'

He scowled at her. 'Witch.' Then, without warning, he rolled over and grabbed her and she was underneath him, pinned down. She tried to move, but it was like trying to shift Stonehenge. 'You're a witch,' he said into her face. 'What are you?'

'A witch,' she agreed.

'Damn right,' he said, and rolled off her as if that one demonstration had taken all his remaining strength. She turned on to her stomach and ran her hand through his hair, the soft dark upright mass of his hair. He looked sulky, but she didn't think he was really unhappy.

After a moment he turned his head and looked at her. His eyes were bright. 'You've robbed me of my strength,' he said. 'I've got the strength of an ant. Nothing left.'

'Perhaps we've discovered what Delilah did to Samson,' she suggested. 'Perhaps cutting his hair was just a front.'

'Great movie, that. Victor Mature and Hedy Lamarr,' Andy said, unexpectedly. Then he lifted his hand and touched her face, and his eyes softened. 'That was amazing,' he said. 'Incredible. Nobody ever did that to me before.'

'I guessed as much,' she said. 'What do you think?'

He grinned. 'I'll be ready for you next time. You won't get the same reaction again.'

She raised her eyebrows. 'I'll just have to think of something else to surprise you, then.'

Chapter Thirteen

When a strange trilling sound woke her Catherine didn't have a clue what was going on. After a second she realised that Andy had struggled from the bed and was now throwing his clothes from side to side, hissing, 'Fuck, fuck, fuck.' At last he unearthed a mobile phone and gasped into it, 'Hello?'

Then he began to speak in French. He sounded tired, but pleased. It was odd to hear him talking in another language as easily as he talked English. Catherine rolled over to look at her clock.

8 a.m. No wonder she felt so terrible. They had stayed awake late into the night, until the small hours, having sex and resting and listening to the sound of Maggie and Ben making love next door and then starting again. It must have been after five when they finally succumbed to exhaustion.

'*Oui, bon, d'ac,*' André was saying, '*oui, certainement, je viens. Bravo.*'

Catherine rolled on to her back and stretched. She ached everywhere. There were bruises on her knees from coming off the bike the day before, and she didn't remember ever having been so sore between her legs in all her life. Andy wielded his prick like the club it resembled.

'*Comment?*' Andy asked the phone. '*Que dis-tu?*'

After a night like that she would normally feel disinclined to knuckle down to anything except sleep and repeated cups of tea. But this morning, despite her exhaustion, her computer was calling to her. Her mind was already spinning with ideas for the book that was to be about Lesbia. What a range of styles she could choose! An aristocratic woman given to sleeping around and political intrigue. It could be a Roman version of Jackie Collins, or Jilly Cooper, or even a political memoir. She ought to get hold of a copy of the book by that Frenchwoman who had been a president's mistress, *La Putain de la Republique*, The Republic's Whore. Good groundwork.

All the same, a cup of tea would be a good start. She staggered up and went through to the bathroom to fill the kettle.

When she returned Andy had finished his call. 'Sorry about that,' he said apologetically. 'Patrice always forgets that it's earlier here. Just as well he rang, though, I still have to go to work today.'

She switched on the kettle. 'I ought to work, too.'

He came over and put his arms around her. 'You walk around naked,' he said. 'I like that. I walk around naked too, when there's nobody to see.' His warm, furry body pressed against her, and his penis began to stir against her pubic hair.

'Oh Lord,' she said, half laughing, 'André, I don't think I can, my insides are all mush.'

'I'll be very gentle,' he said, looking innocent.

She laughed again and tried to push him away. It was like trying to move a mountain. 'You don't know the meaning of the word. All you know is how to turn grown women into purée.'

His expression became hurt. 'What do you mean? I do.' He pulled her closer, and despite herself her body began to respond to the closeness of his embrace, the warmth of his skin, the smell of sex that saturated them both. 'Let me show you,' he said softly, and dipped his head to suckle on her breast.

She couldn't prevent her body's instinctive response, the arch of her back, the slow release of breath. But she was so aware of how sore she was that she resisted him, turning the arch into a struggle, pushing against his biceps with her hands.

'Let me,' he insisted, moving closer to her as if she had not even tried to keep him away. 'Just relax. Let me.'

She didn't have the strength to go on fighting, and besides, she knew it was pointless. Physically she didn't stand a chance against him. So she gave up and let him push her back on to the sofa, slumped into it, her thighs slack and parted. She closed her eyes, listening to the pad of his feet as he found a condom, the rustle and little liquid sound as he rolled it on. Then he was back, the heat of his body preceding him, kneeling between her legs and cupping her breasts in his hands.

'Relax,' he murmured, and the head of his cock was between her legs, nudging its way into her.

She couldn't keep in a cry that was half of pain and half of incredulity. How could she still be so sensitive, after such a night? How could she still feel tight, as if her body was squeezing him as he entered her? She ought to be as limp and sodden as an old glove, and yet the muscles of her vagina were twitching and contracting around him as if she hadn't had sex for months.

He sighed with pleasure as he slid into her up to the hilt, then wrapped his arms around her and pulled her up from the sofa, holding her close against him. 'I'll be gentle,' he whispered into her ear. His hips flexed, just stirring his buried cock. 'See how gentle I can be?'

'Oh,' she whimpered. She felt so sensitive, bruised and pulpy, and yet the faint movements of his cock inside her made her tingle with pleasure. 'Andy, that's lovely.'

His arms held her securely, she needed to do nothing but lean her head on his shoulder and sigh as he moved

230

within her, so slow and soft that it was hardly movement at all. Every now and again her pussy tightened involuntarily around him, and then he let out his breath between clenched teeth and stopped moving for a moment until she released him again.

'Baby,' he said softly, 'my baby,' and he cradled her as if she really were a child, helpless in his arms. The endearment sounded strange coming from him, and yet it made her heart soften. She lifted her hands so that she could bury them in his hair and stroke him as his cheek brushed her forehead.

'Squeeze me again,' he said, his hands tightening on her back. 'Squeeze me, sweetheart.'

She gasped and tried to tense her inner muscles to grip him. It was difficult, because with his thick shaft buried in her all her body wanted to do was open to him, but she concentrated and managed to squeeze, once, twice. He gasped and his body stiffened and jerked against her and his strong fingers dug into her shoulders as he pulsed quickly to orgasm.

She sighed and rubbed her cheek against him. She didn't mind a bit that he had come so quickly, or that she hadn't climaxed. It felt flattering, that after a night of constant sex he still wanted her, that she still aroused him so much that he came in only a few minutes. She wanted him to stay inside her, and whimpered in protest when he said, 'Oops, condom coming loose,' and pulled out.

He held her for a moment, then drew back. 'Need a shower,' he said. 'Shower and then I have to get to work.' He got to his feet and staggered through into the bathroom. 'Jesus,' he said, looking at himself in the mirror, 'the guys are going to know what I've been up to. I look shagged.'

'And I don't suppose you usually go to work in a jacket,' Catherine said, returning to the kettle, which had boiled. 'Tea or coffee?'

'Coffee. Tea is pigswill fit only for English people. One sugar.'

She made him Nescafé, hoping that he wouldn't turn up his nose at it. He spent a long time in the shower. She glanced through the door and saw him absolutely covered in foam, scrubbing at himself and lathering frantically. No wonder he smelt so clean.

'Coffee's ready,' she said, when the sound of water ceased.

He came out, still damp, rubbing his wet hair with a towel until it stood up in spikes like a porcupine. 'That call,' he said, 'that was my cousin Patrice. He's found me some work down towards Andorra, just beyond Foix.'

There was no point in feeling disappointed, was there? He had made it perfectly clear from the start that he was just passing through. It was just as well that she had made the most of him. 'Good work?' she asked curiously, sipping her tea.

'Yeah, just what I want. Doing a spot of work on the buildings until the snow starts. Sheepfolds and that kind of shit. I like labouring,' he said, drinking half the coffee in one gulp. 'And then when it snows we'll do some painting stuff in the towns. He's a signwriter, Patrice, but he does other stuff too. Signwriting's no job these days, everyone gets stuff done by laser and in plastic and whatever. I like proper old signs, like the ones they used to have when I was little.'

'Where I stayed in Paris,' Catherine said, 'there was a *boulangerie* with the most beautiful sign, dark green with gold writing. It was a pleasure just to look at it.'

'Yeah, that's the sort of thing.'

She said after a moment, 'So when will you be going?'

He shrugged. 'Couple of weeks, I suppose.' He put down his mug and began to pull his clothes on. 'Jesus, look at the time. I have to go. Look, do you want my mobile number? Give me a call.' He pulled on his shirt, then wrote down the number on a scrap of paper on her desk.

If he was going to be gone in a couple of weeks, she

232

ought to get as much mileage out of him as possible. 'What are you doing tonight?'

'Don't know,' he said. 'Depends on what comes up.'

'You could come here,' she suggested.

'I could.' He grinned.

They heard the slam of the door in the corridor. 'Sounds as if Ben's decided to get to work as well,' Catherine said.

André actually blushed. 'Jesus, they'll have heard everything we did.'

She smiled at him. 'Oh, go to work.'

He kissed her and squeezed her breasts. 'See you later.'

She drank her tea, then had a long, leisurely shower, marvelling at the elasticity and resilience of her body. It was nothing short of miraculous. She was dressing when someone knocked gently on the door and Maggie's voice said, 'Catherine, are you there?'

'Come in,' Catherine called, and flicked the switch on the kettle for more tea.

Maggie appeared, dressed in sweatpants and a fleece, her hair tousled, dark streaks under her eyes. She looked at Catherine and started to laugh, and Catherine laughed too. 'No need to ask if you had a good night!'

Maggie folded her hands before her breasts like a Renaissance virgin and swooned her way over to the sofa. 'Oh,' she announced, falling into it, 'I love him.'

Catherine raised her eyebrows. 'That's a bit quick, isn't it, Maggie?'

'No. Not at all. I love him and I want to have his babies.'

Frowning, Catherine looked into Maggie's face for evidence of a wind-up. 'Are you joking?'

'Not at all.' The big eyes were wide and apparently sincere. 'We were talking about it last night. He'll have finished his PhD in a few months and then he's got a job to go to in Chester. Once I've finished my course, in June, I could go and be with him. We could live up

233

there in the country, it's lovely. And I could have babies.'

She sounded absolutely serious, which was ridiculous, but Catherine knew that if she treated it seriously it would just make it more real. 'Well, it makes a change from working on the rigs.'

'He's wonderful,' Maggie breathed, gazing at the ceiling in wonderment. 'He's wanted me for ever so long, did you guess, Catherine? And he waited and waited to ask me until he thought I was ready. And then, just when I thought I was getting a bit bored with everything, then he asks me! It's like magic.' She shook herself and sat up. 'How about you? How was Andy?'

'He was – great.' He had been great, and good company, too. 'He gave me a really good idea for the book. I'm going to work on it today. I can't wait.' And then he said that he was going to be gone in two weeks. But I can handle it, she told herself firmly. I'm an independent woman, like Lesbia. I can handle it.

Maggie hadn't really been listening. 'I'm going to go to that nice deli and get some Italian stuff,' she said, 'and tonight I'm going to cook him dinner. He makes me want to do things like that for him, Catherine. I want to be – I want to be feminine for him.' Her eyes were starry. 'I really love him, you know. Incredible, but true.'

That had been nice about André, too; that he made her feel feminine, without preventing her from feeling strong. It was as if he actually liked her to be strong. That was new to her. But there was no point in mulling over his good features, because he wasn't going to be around in the future.

'I'm seeing Andy tonight as well,' she said, and went on, 'but I think I'll call it a day after that.' Then she frowned, surprised at herself.

'Call it a day? You mean chuck him?' Maggie looked horrified. Like all new converts, she seemed to want everybody to share her experience.

'Yes.' As she spoke Catherine understood why. 'I'm

234

not going to wait until he trots off somewhere else and waves me goodbye. I'll finish it. I can, you know.'

'Oh, sure. I understand.' Maggie grinned, suddenly her old self. 'This is a bit of a turn up for the books, isn't it? Would you have expected this when you arrived?'

'No,' Catherine admitted. 'I wouldn't. Absolutely not.'

'You think Ben and me won't last,' Maggie said, her head on one side. 'Admit it.'

Catherine couldn't help laughing. 'Well, call me an old cynic, but I do think it's a change that's rather extreme to be maintained.'

Maggie was smiling too. 'I know. I know, Catherine. I'll probably be back to my old self in a few weeks.' She shook her hair. 'But give me a chance to enjoy it, yeah? This lurve thang is new to me. I want to be able to look back on my life at some stage and say, Well, there was a man I wanted to have babies with.'

'That's something that's never happened to me,' Catherine said, a little sadly.

She spent a couple of pleasant hours committing to paper all the possible permutations of the Lesbia novel. It was wonderful to be sitting on this excellent idea and know that she had any number of choices. It was tempting, in the rarefied air of a Cambridge college, to aim for something worthy and literary. But at present she was inclining to the choice which might make her the most money. Why the hell not go for a book that was simple and fast to read, full of action and sex and interesting characters? Something which might make a good movie, now that ancient epics seemed to be coming back into fashion?

She sketched out a possible opening chapter, launching straight into the sex and the politics with a party at Lesbia/Clodia's magnificent mansion, all the famous men of the day either invited or talked about, her brother Clodius hatching his latest plot, she herself tormenting half a dozen suitors and finally having sex with – who? No need to decide at the moment, not till she was clear on the plot. She felt like hugging herself with glee.

Then she felt hungry, and thought that as things were going so well she would allow herself an hour off to go and enjoy a sandwich and a cup of coffee at one of the trendy little places on Rose Crescent. She put on a thick jacket, because it looked cold outside, and looked searchingly at herself in the mirror before pushing a brush through her thick hair until it shone. She looked good, despite the lack of sleep. Inspiration obviously agreed with her.

Outside she wrapped the fleece around her closely, because it was as cold as it had looked, and glanced down the street towards the bike shop. She felt like going in and embarrassing André in front of his colleagues. But there again, it hardly seemed fair to do something like that when she only meant to be with him for one more night. And besides, she would see him this evening.

As she looked the other way, towards the Gonville and Caius end of the Parade, something caught her eye and made her turn her head back towards the gatehouse. For a moment she didn't know what it was that had attracted her attention. She rubbed her eyes, and then slowly lowered her hand as she saw him.

James. It was James, standing in the archway of the gatehouse, turning his head from side to side, looking for something. He was looking for her, for the place where he could find her.

He hadn't seen her. As he looked down at the piece of paper in his hand, then set off across the Parade, she moved back into the doorway of the clothes shop behind her to hide herself. She wasn't ready to meet him, not quite yet.

He looked tired, but perhaps he'd just flown in from Malaysia. Anyone would look tired, carrying twelve hours'-worth of jet lag. His pale skin was dark with tan, weatherbeaten. There were streaks under his blue eyes and his hair was rumpled and it needed cutting. He looked dishevelled and beautiful.

Heading for the entrance to her house, he walked right past her. He didn't see her. She half-expected him to sense her presence, to stop in mid-stride and turn towards her. When he didn't she felt ridiculously abandoned. She had sensed him, hadn't she? She had known him, even though she had caught only the tiniest glimpse of him out of the corner of her eye.

He disappeared into the passageway leading to the staircase to her room. She realised that she was breathing quickly and that her heart was racing.

Why had he come? Had he come to persuade her to get on a plane and come to his wedding? If he had, she didn't want to talk to him.

Perhaps she didn't want to talk to him at all. She had meant what she said yesterday, about needing time alone, time without any relationships to confuse her. And especially now, when she had a new exciting project to work on, something that could make her name. She didn't want a man around to upset things: not André, not even James.

But even as she thought it she knew that she had to find out why he had come all that way to see her. If she let him go without speaking to him, she would always wonder.

She waited, and after a few minutes he appeared from the doorway, frowning. He looked very disappointed. Good; and yet the sight of his face made her pulse race again.

He turned towards the gatehouse, and she stepped out from the shop doorway and said, 'James.'

Her voice sounded steadier than she expected, but when he swung round and his eyes met hers she took a step back. It was easy to plan to dismiss him. But the reality was different. He strode towards her and wrapped his arms around her and said, 'Cat, God, it's good to see you,' and her resolve wavered and she found herself hugging him back. Her eyes were full of tears, her face was hidden in his hair, the familiar smell of him enveloped her. She had missed him so much more than she had known.

He pulled back, gazing into her face. 'You look wonderful. Honestly, Cat, you look great.' That soft Scottish accent, melting her resolution. 'Are you going out or coming in? I'm so glad I caught you. I can't stay long.'

'You never can,' she said, laughing and blinking hard to clear her eyes. 'I was just going out for a sandwich. I've got work to do.'

'Have a coffee with me,' he said. 'Look, here's a place, right here. Come in and have a coffee.'

She didn't stop him when he pulled her into the coffee shop and sat her down. He ordered two *lattes* and then took her hands across the table and gazed at her. 'I bet you're wondering what I'm doing here,' he said.

'No shit, Sherlock.' Oh, she was full of bravado today. What would she do if he asked her to the bloody wedding again? Would she have the bottle just to walk out?

'I had to come over for an editorial meeting. And I have about half a day to spare. So I had to come and see you. Flying over I was thinking about not having heard from you, I emailed you again and said how strange it made me feel.' Why didn't he think about how long he had kept her waiting for replies in the past? One law for her, another for him. 'It made me wonder if I had made a mistake. I –' He stopped, hesitated, swallowed hard, and his hands tightened on her fingers. 'Cat, I was wondering if I had asked the wrong woman to marry me.'

Outside the window the cars stopped passing, people froze in mid-stride, a pigeon hung suspended in the air, feathers spread for landing. Catherine's throat was icy. 'You were wondering – what?'

'If –' He drew in a deep breath and looked down at

the table. 'Cat, I made a mistake. I realise it now. I've spent the last twenty-four hours realising it. I came here to put it right.' He looked up at her, and she had never seen his eyes so bright.

Well, there it was. There was the offer she had been expecting for the last ten years. He had recognised everything she had always believed, and now he wanted to spend the rest of his life with her.

'You're hesitating,' he said. 'I can see why. I mean, it's not long since I was flooding you with emails singing the praises of Elaine. I just – It was an aberration, Cat, that's all it was. Just an aberration.'

The coffee came. The waitress looked at them both with frank curiosity, then left them alone. Catherine detached her hands from James's and reached for a straw of sugar. She concentrated on opening it, on pouring a single teaspoon of demerara carefully into her coffee cup.

An aberration. She wanted to believe it, desperately. But when she looked up at him somehow she could imagine that in a year or two he would be saying the same thing to another woman, about her.

They had spent ten years as friends and lovers, ten years in which he had roamed the world, reporting on his love affairs, encouraging her to have affairs too, returning to her when it suited him, leaving when he had had enough. Why had she convinced herself that when she finally wanted it he would miraculously change, become ready to settle down? Leopards don't change their spots. He was as much of a rolling stone as André, and it had taken a proposal from him to make her realise.

'Look,' he was saying, that gentle voice reasonable and calm. 'I realise this must be a hell of a shock, I mean it's only a couple of days since I was pestering you to come to KL to see me get married. But I do mean it, Catherine. Really, I do.'

It was amazing how much of her desperately wanted to believe him. That was the part that cried at soppy

239

movies, that believed in happy endings, that thought it was wonderful how her mum and dad had managed to be happily married for forty years. The part that could forgive him for her pain and disappointment without even blinking. But she managed to keep that part quiet and let the other part talk. It said, 'I'll need to think about it, Jamie.'

He nodded. 'I understand. I really understand. Take your time, Cat. You know how to get hold of me. Just let me know.'

It was strange, knowing that she already knew what her answer would be, looking up at his eager, expectant face. He didn't have a clue how she was feeling. He thought she was just startled; unable to come to terms with her good fortune, perhaps. He didn't realise that she had already decided to tell him No.

She looked at him with new eyes, eyes that didn't have the filters of hope and expectation. He was a very good-looking man, that was for sure. Long, lean, and growing old more gracefully than anyone had a right to expect. The sun and wind and outdoor life had weathered him like a piece of leather that just grows more supple and silky and rich in gloss as it is used. He pushed back his hair with one hand, and for the first time she noticed how self-conscious his movements were, as if he planned them for maximum effect. Why hadn't she seen it before?

It would be a shame, though, to let him go without one last experience of his body. He knew her so well, understood her. To lose him without reminding herself of it would be a waste. She said, 'How long is it before you have to go?'

He caught the overtones in her voice as she had known he would. His face tilted into a sexy, lopsided smile. 'An hour or so,' he said. 'If there was something specific you had in mind?'

'You know my room's just upstairs,' she said, poker-faced.

He fumbled in his pocket and put a £5 note on the

table, then got up. 'Come on,' he said, holding out his hand.

He didn't spare a look for the room, just crossed it fast to draw the curtains. Then he turned back and smiled at her and she felt a strange sense of power as she returned the smile. How many times had they made love in the past? And now she was the one who knew that this time would be the last.

As he came closer to her she knew that he would take her face between his hands, and he did. 'I've missed you,' he said, before he kissed her.

His kiss was so familiar, so sweet. She let herself sink into it, responding as she had always responded, with delight and immediate arousal. The feel of his long arms wrapped around her was like sleeping in a bed she had known for years. She didn't reply, because she didn't want to say anything that he could hold against her later on. She just kissed him back, letting her mouth open and soften under his, pierced with the knowledge of never again.

He didn't rush. He never rushed. Even though he knew they only had an hour, he lingered, kissing her lips, her cheeks, her eyelids. His hands stroked through her hair, again and again, reducing her to a jelly of expectation. Her eyelids quivered as he sucked at her throat. She returned his caresses, stroking his black hair back from his high brow, kissing his forehead and his eyebrows. She did not feel ill will against him. In fact, she felt grateful to him for all the friendship and pleasure she had had from him in the past. She wanted to show him that gratitude, before she told him No.

At last he put his hands to her shirt and began to unfasten it. She did the same, knowing that echoing of what he did to her would please him. He smiled as she mirrored his movements, unfastening button for button, pushing back the shirt from his shoulders at the same moment that he removed hers.

241

His lean body was dark with sun. She kissed his shoulder and said, 'You look good, James.'

'So do you,' he said, kissing her mouth again.

'You still running?'

'Whenever I can. With the Hash House Harriers, sometimes. That's fun, haring through the jungle.'

'It works for you.' She set her lips to the hollow of his collar bone and buried her tongue in the smooth depression in his flesh. Then as he reached around behind her to unfasten her bra she matched his movement and began to stroke her fingers down the groove of his spine. He was very sensitive there. Touching his back had always aroused him.

It aroused him now. As her fingers trickled downwards he shuddered and pulled her close to him, his head tilted back in ecstasy. 'God, Cat, you know how to turn me on.'

'I should do, by now.' She slipped her fingers below the waistband of his trousers and rested them gently on the little dimples above his backside. He gasped and kissed her hard, his tongue driving into her mouth, his hands reaching for her naked breasts. He stroked them softly, teasing the delicate skin until her nipples were hard aching points, then caught the tight peaks between finger and thumb and squeezed, harder and harder, until she cried out and writhed to try to get away from him.

He let her go then, and she realised that in fact he couldn't hold her if she didn't want to be held. He was lean and fit, but not strong in the way that André was, and for the first time she saw that as a shortcoming. But it didn't matter now. So she pushed off her trousers and then came back to him, dressed only in her panties now, and embraced him.

'Where's the bed?' he whispered, unzipping his trousers.

'Behind you!' she chanted, in the best pantomime tradition.

He laughed and took her hand and drew her over to the bed with him. Then he solemnly pulled off her panties before lying down and holding out his hand to her. 'Come, my lady,' he intoned.

Naked she lay beside him, and their skin clung together all down the length of their bodies as they kissed. After a moment he raised himself a little above her and began to kiss her shoulders, her breasts, her belly, her thighs. All the way to her feet he kissed her, little feathery kisses which made her shiver with anticipation. Then he swung his feet towards the head of the bed and lay down, catching her hips and pulling them towards his face.

She smiled and reached out for him. Sixty-nine with him had always been delicious. She knew before she touched it exactly how his cock would taste, the sweet salt smell of him. They liked to do it lying on their sides, faces pressed closely into the other's loins, gently, slowly licking and sucking.

The first touch of his tongue on her clitoris made her sigh. He knew exactly how she liked to be touched, knew that the more gently he licked her, the stronger her response would be. They knew each other so well that they did not need to send messages, just concentrate on giving the other pleasure. Catherine took his hot stiff cock deeply into her mouth and sucked the shaft with long, slow, gliding movements, moaning as he caressed her clit more and more firmly with his searching tongue. Before long she was on the point of orgasm and she held it off, moving her body fractionally away from him so that she could delay the climax until he was ready too. She began to suck him with hard, regular strokes and soon she heard him cry out. His hips jerked and she knew that he was coming, and she pushed herself against his face and slipped effortlessly into her own orgasm as his sperm jetted into her mouth.

They lay for a few moments suckling like babies,

enjoying the afterglow, and then he turned and lay beside her. She said gently, 'Roll over,' because she knew what would make him ready for another round. He smiled at her and rolled on to his stomach and she began to knead his back and shoulders, pressing her fingertips into his spine, caressing the edges of his shoulderblades. He sighed and shifted and she leant forward, using her tongue and lips now as well as her hands, moving her caresses downwards to concentrate on his lower back and buttocks. She committed each curve of his flank, each ridge of his vertebrae to memory. Never again, never again.

He moaned, and her searching hands slipped between his legs, finding the tautening pouch of his balls, fondling. He was almost ready, and so was she. She was trembling with the need to feel him inside her. She kissed his flank, licked his hipbone, and as he turned towards her tongue she rolled him over so that he was lying on his back. He smiled at her, arms flung wide, cock hard and erect against his flat lean belly.

There was a condom in the bedside table, and she unwrapped it and rolled it on. James reached out for her, supporting her as she straddled him. She held his penis up towards her and slowly, slowly lowered herself, gasping as she felt him slide up inside her.

Never again, never again, and every stroke, every movement was invested with such deepness that it made her shudder and cry out. He reached up and began to caress her breasts, and she looked down into his face and saw that he believed that she was all his and she felt so powerful that she almost came then and there. It was stronger even than the wild sex that comes after an argument, the strangest and most satisfying sensation that she could imagine.

She fucked him hard, rising and falling on his stiff cock until they were both gasping. But she didn't want to come that way, she wanted to come with him on top of her. When they were both almost at the peak she stopped moving, slipped down on him, taking him right into her, and then slowly rolled to one side. He held her and rolled with her and as he came on top of her he began to move, driving himself into her with hard thrusts of his hips. She lay back, slipped her hand between them so that she could stroke her clit, and gave herself up to the feelings, shuddering as he powered into her, revelling in her strength.

'Oh, Cat,' he husked, 'Cat, I'm coming.' She was coming too, the ripples and stars of orgasm sparkling through her, and as he clutched her and jerked as he came she cried out with her climax and then held him close, feeling suddenly as if she wanted to laugh.

He held her for a little while his breathing slowed. She found herself comparing him to André. Was it just André's novelty that made him exciting? Or was there something else?

After a moment James slipped out of her. He lifted his head to look at the clock on her bedside table and said, 'Oh, God, I have to go.'

He jumped up from the bed and began to find his clothes, and she lay on her side and watched him. It was time to tell him now, and yet she felt suddenly tongue-tied. What should she say? How should she phrase it? She wanted to be clear and unequivocal, but she didn't want to hurt him unnecessarily. She tried this phrase and that in her mind, tasting them, unwilling to speak quite yet.

When he was dressed he began to say something, then seemed to register the expression on her face. He said cautiously, 'Cat?'

She sat up. 'James,' she said, 'the answer is no.'

He didn't look particularly concerned. 'Cat, I know it was a shock. You –'

'It's not the shock.' She should have realised that he would be dense. He could be both dense and stubborn, when something didn't suit him. 'James, I don't just mean that I don't want to marry you. I mean it's over. We aren't going to be lovers any more. Friends, sure, but not lovers.' It wasn't as hard to say this as she had feared it might be.

'Look.' He seemed puzzled. 'What is it? Is it Elaine? I told you, she's nothing, she doesn't matter. I'll sort it out.'

His casual callousness about a woman who presumably thought that he still meant to marry her made Catherine even more certain that she was doing the right thing. 'It's nothing to do with Elaine. It's to do with you.'

But it didn't seem to be working. He frowned, then his face cleared. He came to the bed, stooped to kiss her, and stood up, shaking his head. 'Look, I'll email you. It'll be OK, Cat, believe me. Honestly.'

She said, 'James,' but he wasn't listening. He headed for the door almost at a run. 'I'll email, I'll call. I'll see you again soon, I'll come back as soon as I can. I promise, Cat.'

And he was gone.

He hadn't wanted to hear what she had to say to him. But she had done what she had to do, and she had done the hardest part, the part to his face. Now she would have to hammer the message home, again and again, on the phone and by email, until he understood what she was telling him.

She felt curiously light, as if she had shed a burden. As if something that had been hanging over her had gone. She believed, cautiously, that this was a good thing.

And also, she was hungry. Hadn't she been going to get something to eat, before James popped back into her life? She would have another shower, and then head out to her original destination.

And then she would come back and wheedle some clean sheets from the housekeeper to get the bed ready for André. This evening should be a doddle. If she could make love to a man who had been her lover for ten years and then dump him, it would be easy to do the same thing to a man she had known for a week. And then there she would be, a free woman, with no encumbrances and a best seller to write.

But she didn't want to do it straight away. She wanted to have sex with him first. Maggie would be proud of her.

Chapter Fourteen

*A*fter eating her sandwich she decided that it would be positively rude to invite André to her room just to fuck him and chuck him. She really ought to feed him as well. She knew better than to cook something complicated when the food had to fit around their other entertainment. Much better to have some good bread, some ripe cheese, perhaps a few slices of Parma ham and a couple of ripe figs or peaches or whatever. It sounded as if a trip to the deli was in order.

Returning, carrier bags in hand, she met Maggie on the stairs. 'Thought I would see you in the deli,' she said. 'I am also planning to feed a man tonight.' She thought of telling Maggie about James, but decided that she might not obtain the sort of supportive reaction that she was hoping for.

Maggie smiled. 'You know,' she said, 'I've been thinking about him all day. Part of me thinks I'm a complete idiot, but it's just so lovely, Catherine. I'm in love, aren't I?'

'You've certainly got all the symptoms,' Catherine agreed. She leant forward and hugged Maggie. 'Why not just enjoy it? There's a first time for everything, Maggie.'

'No wonder all those poets say it's a madness,' Maggie said, rolling her eyes. 'I would go anywhere for him, honestly, Catherine. Anywhere.'

She had felt that way about James once. Now she just felt glad to be rid of him. She said, 'You know, Maggie, I owe you something. I feel a lot freer since I came here, and I know that part of that has been knowing you.'

Maggie looked startled, then touched. She kissed Catherine on the cheek. 'I hope we stay in touch after you finish at the end of term. I'd like to.'

'If you want to, we will. And if you do marry Ben and have babies, I want to be godmother.'

'Oh Lord,' Maggie said. 'Weddings! Christenings! Churches! Hats!' She didn't look as though the prospect appalled her, and she swanned off down the stairs singing.

Catherine stuck the food in the fridge and then sat down at her computer. She read over what she had done in the morning and liked it. But she didn't seem able to find the will to add to it. It was as if there was unfinished business. So she hung around in the room, tidying things, smoothing the bedsheets, making sure there was no evidence remaining of the afternoon's activity with James.

She didn't understand why she felt so calm about finishing with James. When she had found out about Elaine she had been so distressed, and now it was as if he didn't matter to her, as if he had never mattered. Perhaps it was all true, and that as long as he treated her mean he kept her keen, and vice versa. Why should it work that way?

Perhaps she was just in shock, and would feel it later. But somehow it didn't seem that she would. It felt good to be free.

She had forgotten the time, and when Andy knocked on the door she jumped in surprise. He walked in without waiting for her to respond, tossed a bottle of wine on to the sofa, strode over to her and wrapped his arms round her. He kissed her lips, little pecking kisses, squeezed her so tightly that she gasped, and said, 'Now, now, now.'

She couldn't help but laugh at him. 'Didn't anyone ever teach you that anticipation is part of the pleasure?'

'What they taught me was to get it while you can. Gimme, gimme.'

He kissed her again, hard this time, and she felt the thick rod of his cock quivering inside his jeans. For a moment she tried to resist him, putting her hands against his arms and pushing hard. He tensed in response and the muscles of his biceps felt as hard as footballs, and suddenly her whole body was alive with desire. She wanted him, now.

She said his name and pulled his mouth to hers and returned his kiss, arching herself against him to offer him her breasts. He laughed and pulled up her blouse and thrust his hand inside her bra, finding the nipple, pinching it, and his other hand rucked up her skirt and felt between her legs, stroking over the fabric of her panties. Her legs were weak with the suddenness of her need and she moaned and he pushed her across to the sofa and lowered her on to it, then flung himself down beside her. She grabbed for his fly and he fought with the buttons on her blouse, got them undone, pushed the blouse off her shoulders and bared her breasts so that he could lick and suck her erect nipples. She moaned and managed to get his fly open and pushed her hand inside. He wasn't wearing anything under the jeans, and the hot shaft of his cock sprang at her touch. She pulled it out and began to rub him hard with her hand and with her other hand she grabbed his wrist and pushed it between her legs because she wanted him to finger her.

He grunted as she masturbated him and pulled her into the crook of his arm so that he could fondle her breasts with one hand and kiss her mouth and finger her cunt all at the same time. She slumped against him, moaning as his tongue slipped between her lips and his fingers eased their way into her. She was already wet, and as he pinched her nipple and penetrated her mouth with his tongue she thought of her fantasy, of the girl on the sofa dishevelled and frigged and fucked, and the thought of herself in that state was so arousing that she began to whimper and moan.

'Jesus, you're so horny,' he hissed. His big hand cupped her breast, nursing the nipple between his fingers. 'You sound as if you're going to come already.'

'André,' she moaned, thrusting her hips up towards his hand, 'please put your fingers up me, please.'

Thick fingers, strong fingers, sliding into her wet vagina, first one, then two, and then when he knew that she was ready three, sliding in and out with great force. His tongue was in her mouth as she cried out, intent on her own pleasure. She took her hand from his cock so that she could touch her other breast, roll the taut flesh between finger and thumb, letting out rhythmic cries as she humped herself against his hand. He followed her rhythm, fucking her with his fingers, fucking her mouth with his tongue, and in moments she was climbing up the spiral of climax and then letting out a helpless shout of delight as she reached the peak and shuddered to stillness.

He didn't give her a chance to recover. Pushing his jeans down and off he knelt by her head and thrust his staring cock to her lips. 'Suck me,' he demanded.

She opened her mouth and without hesitation he thrust himself between her lips, pushing in deep. He didn't want her to suck him, he wanted to fuck her mouth, and she let herself go limp and looked up at him, foreshortened above her like a Michaelangelo, all working muscles and gleaming sweat, flanks hollowing as he drove himself into her willing mouth. It was so erotic to be used like this, she couldn't stop herself from touching herself, rubbing one finger delicately against her still-throbbing clit, bringing herself back up to the plateau and then holding herself there, ready to come again whenever she wanted.

Suddenly he pulled away from her, leaving her gasping.

'No,' he hissed. 'I want to come inside you.' He dug around inside his jeans and finally pulled out a condom, rolled it on, then grabbed her by her thighs and dragged her towards the edge of the sofa.

'Over the arm,' she suggested breathlessly.

He looked puzzled, then understood what she wanted and nodded. She swung her hips so that they were resting on the arm and she could look down the length of her own body to her spread thighs, to the dark fur between them. She would be able to watch him moving in and out of her. 'Come on,' she said, reaching for him.

'Calm down,' he said, and then he was between her legs, the swollen scarlet head of his cock tilted downwards towards her wet ready tunnel, and with a single thrust he slid into her to the hilt and she screamed.

'Hssh,' he gasped, 'someone will hear you.'

'I don't care,' she insisted. 'Harder, Jesus, André, do it hard.'

He did do it hard. He put every iota of his strength into it, withdrawing his thick hard cock to the very tip, then ramming it back into her to the hilt, every thrust as deep as the last, every thrust making her cry out and heave her hips towards him as if she wanted to pull him right inside her, as if she couldn't get enough of him, as if she wanted to consume him utterly. Between her legs she could see his cock moving, sliding out gleaming with the juice of her desire, hammering back into her until his balls brushed her arse. She felt herself coming again and she reached up to stroke her clit with one hand, the other catching hold of his shoulder, her fingers digging into his flesh. 'André, I'm coming, I'm coming, come with me, please, please.'

'Yes –' he responded, and speeded up until the shaft of his cock was a blur of motion between her spread thighs and she wailed as she climaxed, dragged over the top and held there by his furious movement deep inside her. Her belly quaked and he cried out and thrust himself deep and hung there, eyes closed, head flung back, expression contorted as if he were in pain, his cock buried and twitching.

Then he pulled out and staggered around to sit beside her on the sofa, holding her in his arms. 'That's better,' he said. 'I was thinking about that all day.'

She smiled at him, because it wasn't entirely true for her but she did know what he meant.

'Why don't you go and have a wash,' he suggested practically. 'That stuff tastes awful. I wouldn't like to be put off later on.'

That seemed sensible enough, so she said, 'Okay.' As she got up she said, 'I got some food.'

'Oo,' he said, approvingly.

'Cheese, and bread, and Parma ham and stuff, is that OK?'

'A woman after my own heart,' he said.

So she unpacked the food and spread it about on the table and left him to it while she went to clean herself up. She took her clothes off and left them on the bathroom floor, and as she washed she thought about what she was going to say to him. *André, I really don't want to be in a relationship now.* Or *André, you're going to be gone in a few weeks and there doesn't really seem to be a lot of point in going on with this.*

What was she talking about? He was going to be gone in a couple of weeks, so there wasn't really any point in breaking it up now. Wouldn't it make more sense to carry on, enjoy this fine enthusiastic sex for a couple of short weeks, then wave him goodbye and no harm done?

It wasn't what she had intended, but she could feel herself beginning to be convinced. She wandered back into the room, naked, and helped herself to some Brie.

'Top scoff,' Andy said, his mouth full of ham.

'Tell me,' she said curiously, 'have you ever had sex with food?'

He swallowed quickly, half-choking. 'What?'

Why did he look so startled? In some ways he seemed very naïf. 'You know,' she explained. 'Making banana splits out of your willy and such like. Frozen Mars Bars in unexpected places.'

He frowned. 'Not sure about that.'

Perhaps it really would be a waste, to bin him just when she had the chance to take his education in hand. She applied herself to the Brie, thinking.

He seemed to have finished his food for now. 'Don't move,' he said. He came and knelt behind her and she felt his mouth on her buttocks, biting softly at the plump fullness of flesh there.

'Gorgeous arse,' he said between nibbles. 'I've never understood blokes who like these skinny bony-arse bitches. They look as if they would break if you did anything to them. Give me something you can get hold of.'

He made her laugh. Then he pushed his tongue between her buttocks and that made her gasp. 'Nice,' he whispered, pulling back for a moment. 'Clean. Bend over.'

She obliged, holding on to the table, and kneeling behind her he began to lick her, all the way from clit to anus, long, lubricious licks which made her moan. For a moment she thought of offering him her arse to fuck, but if he was as innocent as he appeared he might be shocked. She didn't want to spoil this evening.

'God, you taste of woman,' he said, burrowing his tongue deep inside her. 'Mmm.'

'Let me do you,' she suggested.

'Both together? Nice.' He went to the bed and lay down, inviting her to straddle his face.

For a moment she felt shy, because that position was so exposed. But he was so matter of fact, there seemed to be no reason to be shy. She knelt beside him, then put one leg across his face. He caught hold of her hips and pulled her down so that he could lick her.

He was as unlike James as could be imagined. James was all cool control and gentle eroticism. André was greedy, in a hurry, gobbling everything within reach like a child at a birthday party. It was a less certain method of achieving orgasm. But he could learn to take things more slowly, after all. She didn't think James would ever recapture the delicious urgency that filled Andy's every movement.

She reached for his cock, tilted it up to her lips, then savoured its smell. He smelt of earth and man, like Adam in her fantasy. She buried her head between his legs, sucking on the soft globes of his testicles, then returned to the head of his cock. It was weeping with need, and she took it into her mouth to comfort it. In reaction he sucked on her clitoris so hard that she cried out, almost unable to bear it.

This was lovely, but she wanted to feel him inside her. She pulled away from him and reached for a condom, rolled it on to his cock and straddled him. He smiled at her and folded his hands behind his head, obviously ready to be pleasured.

His cock stretched her as it entered her. She leant forward a little, bracing herself with her hand against his belly, and began to ride him. He closed his eyes and sighed with pleasure, and she began to grind her clit against him at the end of every stroke, clutch at him with her inner muscles, twist a little as she rose, everything she could do to increase the sensation for both of them. He began to rock a little, encouraging her to move faster and faster. She tried, but the muscles of her thighs were beginning to tire.

After a second he opened his eyes and reached out for her. His strong hands took hold of her hips and began to lift and lower her on his cock, sliding her up and down as if she were weightless. She was startled, and stopped moving. He grinned at her and said, 'Bit of work needed in the gym there,' then held her above him and arched his hips up from the bed, pounding into her fast and hard, bringing himself to a quick, violent orgasm.

He lifted her off his cock and she lay down on him, running her fingers through the hair on his chest and listening to his heart beat in the slow, deep pulse that followed orgasm.

'You didn't come,' he said. 'Sorry.'

She shook her head. 'No, it's OK.' It was, too. There was more to sex than orgasms, and just to be used sexually by a man so strong and simple was itself powerful and satisfying.

How long should she leave it before she told him? She nestled her head more closely against his shoulder, feeling like a traitor.

'What's the matter?' he said, lifting his head.

'What do you mean?' She was shocked by his perception, and didn't know how to respond.

'Something's bothering you. What is it?'

'Oh –' She improvised hastily, 'I, er, I saw an ex-boyfriend today. It got to me a bit, I suppose.'

'If he's ex, why worry?' Andy lay back and put his arms around her, holding her on his chest. He seemed to be about to say something, but then he frowned and didn't speak.

'Now something's bothering you,' she said.

He hesitated, still frowning. Then he said, 'I was speaking to Patrice today. About the job in France.'

What now? She made a non-committal, enquiring noise.

'He says he's looking after an old house there, a nice old *mas* in a little village in the foothills. Beautiful, he says, and he's got it all winter. That's where I'm going to stay. It's huge, great big kitchen, open fireplaces, lots of bedrooms, you know the sort of thing? So I thought perhaps you might like to come and stay there too. You could get some writing done,' he finished lamely, with transparent hopefulness.

His heart had speeded up, but it felt as if hers was slowing down. He had taken her completely by surprise. All by itself her mind dashed off to investigate the possibilities. Quiet, beautiful surroundings, a big house, books borrowed by post from Cambridge University Library, lots of time, good French food, a man around in the evenings to talk to and sleep with. Why had she never tried going somewhere else to write? With a new sort of book to be written, wouldn't a new sort of writing life be a good idea?

'Patrice is getting the house for free,' André added temptingly.

And no rent to pay!

But what about her resolution to free herself of the shackles of relationships? What about being a strong single woman, with nothing to concentrate on except her work?

She looked down into André's face. His eyes were wide and anxious, like a dog's.

'Let's have sex again,' she said, 'while I think about it.'

BLACK LACE NEW BOOKS

Published in December

EARTHY DELIGHTS
Tesni Morgan
£5.99

Rosemary Maddox is TV's most popular gardening presenter. Her career and business are going brilliantly but her sex life is unpredictable. Someone is making dirty phonecalls and sending her strange objects in the post, including a doll that resembles her dressed in kinky clothes. And when she's sent on an assignment to a bizarre English country house, things get even stranger.

ISBN 0 352 33548 3

WILD KINGDOM
Deanna Ashford
£5.99

War is raging in the mythical kingdom of Kabra. Prince Tarn is struggling to drive out the invading army while the beautiful Rianna has fled the fighting with a mysterious baroness. The baroness is a fearsome and depraved woman, and once they're out of the danger zone she takes Rianna prisoner. Her plan is to present her as a plaything to her warlord half-brother, Ragnor. In order to rescue his sweetheart, Prince Tarn needs to join forces with his old enemy, Sarin. A rollicking adventure of sword 'n' sorcery with lashings of kinky sex from the author of *Savage Surrender*.

ISBN 0 352 33549 1

THE NINETY DAYS OF GENEVIEVE
Lucinda Carrington
£5.99

A ninety-day sex contract isn't exactly what Genevieve Loften has in mind when she begins business negotiations with James Sinclair. She finds herself being transformed into the star performer in his increasingly kinky fantasies. Thrown into a game of sexual challenges, Genevieve learns how to dress for sex, and balance her high-pressure career with the twilight world of fetishism and debauchery.

This is a Black Lace special reprint.

ISBN 0 352 33070 8

Published in January

MAN HUNT
Cathleen Ross
£6.99

Angie's a driven woman when it comes to her career in hotel management, but also when it comes to the men she chooses to pursue – for Angie's on a man hunt. For sexy, challenging men. For men like devilishly attractive but manipulative James Steele, who runs the hotel training course. When she turns her attention to one of her fellow students, Steele's determined to assume the dominant position and get her interest back. This time it's Steele who's the predator and Angie the prey.

ISBN 0 352 33583 1

DREAMING SPIRES
Juliet Hastings
£6.99

Catherine de la Tour has been awarded an assignment as writer-in-residence at a Cambridge college but her lover James is a thousand miles away and she misses him badly. Although her position promises peace and quiet, she becomes immersed in a sea of sexual hedonism, as the rarefied hothouse of academia proves to be a fertile environment for passion and raunchy lust.

ISBN 0 352 33584 X

MÉNAGE
Emma Holly
£6.99

Bookstore owner Kate comes home from work one day to find her two flatmates in bed together. Joe – a sensitive composer – is mortified. Sean – an irrepressible bad boy – asks her to join in. As they embark on a polysexual ménage à trois, Kate wants nothing more than to keep both her admirers happy. However, things become complicated. Kate has told everyone that Sean is gay, but now he and Kate are acting like lovers. Can the three of them live happily ever after – together?

This is a Black Lace special reprint.

ISBN 0 352 33231 X

To be published in February

STELLA DOES HOLLYWOOD
Stella Black
£6.99

Stella Black has a 1969 Pontiac Firebird, a leopardskin bra and a lot of attitude. Partying her way around Hollywood she is discovered by a billionaire entertainment mogul who wastes no time in turning Stella into America's most famous porn star. But the dark forces of American fundamentalism are growing. The moral right-wing are outraged and they're out to destroy Stella any which way they can.

How will she escape their punishing clutches?

A sexy saga of guns, girls and grit!

ISBN 0 352 33588 2

UP TO NO GOOD
Karen S. Smith
£6.99

Emma is resigned to the fact that her cousin's wedding will be a dull affair, But when she meets leather-clad biker, Kit, it's lust at first sight and Emma ends up behaving even more scandalously than usual. They don't get the chance to say goodbye, though, and she thinks she'll never see her mystery lover again. Fate intervenes, however, and they are reunited at yet another wedding. And so begins a year of outrageous sex, wild behaviour and lots of getting up to no good!

Like *Four Weddings and a Funeral* with explicit sex and without the funeral!

ISBN 0 352 33589 0

DARKER THAN LOVE
Kristina Lloyd
£6.99

It's 1875 and the morals of Queen Victoria have no hold over London's debauched elite. Young and naïve Clarissa is eager to meet Lord Marldon, the man to whom she is promised. She knows he is handsome, dark and sophisticated. He is, in fact, louche, depraved and consumed by a passion for cruel sexual excesses!

This tale of dark, Gothic debauchery is a Black Lace special reprint

ISBN 0 352 33279 4

If you would like a complete list of plot summaries of Black Lace titles, or would like to receive information on other publications available, please send a stamped addressed envelope to:

Black Lace, Thames Wharf Studios,
Rainville Road, London W6 9HA

BLACK LACE BOOKLIST

Information is correct at time of printing. To check availability go to www.blacklace-books.co.uk

All books are priced £5.99 unless another price is given.

Black Lace books with a contemporary setting

DARK OBSESSION £7.99	Fredrica Alleyn ISBN 0 352 33281 6	☐
THE TOP OF HER GAME	Emma Holly ISBN 0 352 33337 5	☐
LIKE MOTHER, LIKE DAUGHTER	Georgina Brown ISBN 0 352 33422 3	☐
THE TIES THAT BIND	Tesni Morgan ISBN 0 352 33438 X	☐
VELVET GLOVE	Emma Holly ISBN 0 352 33448 7	☐
THE FLESH	Emma Holly ISBN 0 352 33498 3	☐
SHAMELESS	Stella Black ISBN 0 352 33485 1	☐
TONGUE IN CHEEK	Tabitha Flyte ISBN 0 352 33484 3	☐
FIRE AND ICE	Laura Hamilton ISBN 0 352 33486 X	☐
SAUCE FOR THE GOOSE	Mary Rose Maxwell ISBN 0 352 33492 4	☐
HARD CORPS	Claire Thompson ISBN 0 352 33491 6	☐
INTENSE BLUE	Lyn Wood ISBN 0 352 33496 7	☐
THE NAKED TRUTH	Natasha Rostova ISBN 0 352 33497 5	☐
A SPORTING CHANCE	Susie Raymond ISBN 0 352 33501 7	☐
A SCANDALOUS AFFAIR	Holly Graham ISBN 0 352 33523 8	☐
THE NAKED FLAME	Crystalle Valentino ISBN 0 352 33528 9	☐

- - - - - - -✂- - - - - - - - - - - - - - -

Please send me the books I have ticked above.

Name   ....

Address   ....

          ....

          ....

          .... Post Code ....

Send to: Cash Sales, Black Lace Books, Thames Wharf Studios, Rainville Road, London W6 9HA.

US customers: for prices and details of how to order books for delivery by mail, call 1-800-805-1083.

Please enclose a cheque or postal order, made payable to **Virgin Publishing Ltd**, to the value of the books you have ordered plus postage and packing costs as follows:
 UK and BFPO – £1.00 for the first book, 50p for each subsequent book.
 Overseas (including Republic of Ireland) – £2.00 for the first book, £1.00 for each subsequent book.

If you would prefer to pay by VISA, ACCESS/MASTER-CARD, DINERS CLUB, AMEX or SWITCH, please write your card number and expiry date here:

....

Please allow up to 28 days for delivery.

Signature ....

- - - - - - ✂- - - - - - - - - - - - - - - - -